RISING SUN

NEW MOON SERIES BOOK THREE

BELLE HARPER

For my best friend, Rebecca.
You encourage me every step of the way, you are always there for me when I need you.
Love you xx

CHAPTER ONE

LEXI

Rain... I glanced up to the dark clouds above and felt another raindrop hit my cheek. It rolled down...like a silent tear. Even the heavens knew I was holding them in. My mother was not a vampire. No, she was as human as I was... well, at least I'd thought I was human a few months ago. Pack Bardoul said she was human, so she wasn't a vampire, she couldn't be. I clutched my stomach. None of this made sense.

Tobias' hand was still on my shoulder, and I could feel the energy running through him to me, like we were connected. Our energy knew each other, like long-lost friends. I felt a strength with him beside me. He was my father... My dad was an angel, and so youthful that he looked like my older brother more than my father. This was so...weird.

I felt a chill over my skin, and my chest became tight. I took in a shaky breath. My knees weren't working, feeling like jelly, but my mates still had me. They were holding me just as Tobias was.

But the pain in my chest... I'd just hurt them, yet they still had me. Maybe they were worried I was going to fall, or held me just to reassure themselves that I was still here. That I was alive. I let out a shuddering breath and swallowed down the lump in my throat. I didn't want to think about what could have happened.

"We should return to the main house. I've rounded up all the shifters that came for Lexi. They're waiting for you to punish as you wish. The night vamps, those who were not fighting with you, they are all...disposed of." I looked up at Tobias' face, and this close, I could see his short stubbled facial hair. It wasn't something I normally noticed much on guys. It made him look older. Wiser? *How old was he?*

He wasn't glowing as he was before. It was as if someone had put out the light that was surrounding him. He really did look a lot like me, or I looked like him. My amber eyes were dull compared to his almost gold ones. They glowed a little when he glanced down to me, and I almost stumbled back at the intensity of them. My eyes traveled over to see who Tobias was speaking to.

"Thank you for your help, Tobias. Everyone, back to the house at once." *Alaric*. He was standing close to the tree line, his face drawn... tired. He looked older than he was a week ago. This had taken a huge toll on him, on them all. My eyes dashed to the left to see Nash, but his face didn't give away anything. He just watched me with those same green eyes all the Lovells had. His were most like his father. I didn't look away, I just watched him as his eyes crinkled a little in the corners and he cocked his head to the side. Was he smiling at me? Shit, I didn't think he smiled. It wasn't much of a smile, but still. It was enough to get me to look away first.

Jett and Lyell stood a few feet away from him. Jett gave me a smile that didn't reach his eyes, and Lyell watched everyone like he was studying us. When he caught me watching him, he took a stumbling step backwards. He looked so out of his element right now. The Lovell family were all here...and I only just noticed they were all naked, covered in mud and blood.

When no one moved, Alaric growled, then shouted in that alpha tone, "Everyone. Now."

Tobias let his hand drop from my shoulder as my feet started to move with the others in the direction of the house...home. *My home.* I had a home to go to. Whether I was still welcomed there... No. They would understand why I did what I did.

There was a cold breeze, and Tobias was no longer standing there. I stopped as everyone else did and glanced up to see he was flying. His wings were magnificent, with a huge span, and even though the sky was dark and grey, the feathers glowed a deep gold from within. Words couldn't describe the beauty and elegance of this angel. We all watched in awe as he flew over the trees and towards home like it was normal to see a man flying in the sky. Home. *Home.*

"The others." My chest tightened as I stumbled forward. I needed to get back. What if my blood hadn't worked, hadn't healed them? What if they were all dying while I was here, watching the sunrise with my mates? I could never forgive myself for forgetting about them all. Oh god, Ada was there. She was human. Josh... Oh god. *Joshy.*

The pain in my chest tightened, and I felt like I was going to be sick. I tried to suck in deep breaths, but it was like someone was strangling me from within.

"Lexi." Galen stood in front of me, his hands on my cheeks. I couldn't look at him. I didn't want him to see me like this. God, I was so weak, so pitiful. He wrapped his arms around my back and pulled me into his chest, helping to keep me steady. "What *others*? Let me carry you, my love."

The lump in my throat returned as too much emotion ran through me. He'd called me his love. I'd jumped off a cliff, and still, Galen called me his love. What did I do to deserve him? *All of them.* He was too good. I leaned into him, taking what strength I could, and breathed him in. *Sunshine.* If sunshine had a smell, that was Galen, my light. Where everyone else would think he was dark, he was my light. I just couldn't stop this guilt over everything I had done from eating me up.

"The...the injured ones." I choked on my words, trying to hold back tears.

"They're okay, I can hear them. They're fine." He pulled me back, his hands on my face again, his eyes searching mine. "Don't beat yourself up. They're healing. Trust me?"

My shoulders dropped, and I let out a huge exhale. He could read me like a book. I nodded. I trusted him, and I always would.

"Please let Galen carry you." This time, it was Maverick asking me. I shook my head. I didn't want to be carried back like some precious flower.

"I want to walk." I knew I didn't have the energy. But I didn't care. I just didn't want to see all the looks on everyone's faces when I got back. *I ran.* I ran from them all when they needed me to stay safe. *Oh god, Ada.* I'd said goodbye to her, and I didn't give her a chance to respond. I just ran out on her. *Fuck.*

I fucked everything up, just like I always do.

CHAPTER TWO

LEXI

My feet were numb... I'd run out of the Lovell house barefoot, not that that was important right now, but with every step, the twigs and small rocks were cutting into my feet. I didn't care. It wasn't like they wouldn't heal, and it was keeping me focused. I was alive. I felt pain, so I was still here. I got to live, but how many had to die for that?

Too much had happened.

If Tobias hadn't been there, if he'd been a second too late... My heart dropped just at the thought. But he wasn't. He'd caught me.

When I was a little girl and in one of the many foster homes, I would dream that someone would come for me. They would tell me they had been searching for me and now that they'd found me, they would take care of me. They would catch me if I fall and kiss my boo-boos better. This wasn't the same dream, and I was older now. Did I still want those things?

I didn't know where Tobias would fit in my life. Would he want to stay? Would he leave? Did he have a family somewhere waiting for him? So many questions needed to be answered. The most pressing being about my mother and what he knew of her.

Warm hands touched my bare skin, and the contact almost burned me. *My mates.* I couldn't talk to them right now. I had apologized, but it wasn't enough. It would *never* be enough. God, how could they still want me after what... I...

I let out a deep breath, my throat tight. I was worked up and emotional.

The rain got heavier, and I was cold and shaking. My wet clothes clung to my body, but I didn't care. I felt like this was the way it was supposed to be. I stopped and held my hands up to the sky. The clouds were so dark, so angry, and I watched as the raindrops hit the tree canopy above and rolled down the leaves. I could hear the guys talking around me, worried I was losing it. I shut it out. I just concentrated on breathing.

"Lexi, please. Please let me help you. I can help you." I couldn't shut out Galen, and he knew it. I tried to ignore him, but his voice was laced with worry and pain. He knew I'd heard what he had said but didn't push me.

The blood and death from the night before was being washed away from the earth, but it would never erase this night from my memory, or from that of anyone who was here. It felt freeing, though, letting the rain wash me, clean me. I was alive to feel the rain. We all were alive. I crouched down and felt the damp, cool earth. I squeezed the wet dirt through my fingers as I stood.

Moving forward again, I felt as if I wasn't in my body as my legs carried me home. But then I snapped out of it when another sharp rock I didn't see stabbed the sole of my foot. I couldn't see much in front of me. My eyes were glassy, and I was cold. *So fucking cold.* I wiped my face with my palm and felt a strange grit. I glanced down, my eyes focused again, to see my hand was still covered in the dirt.

Someone grasped my shoulder. Galen? Another took my hand and squeezed. My heart felt lighter. I shouldn't be acting like this, I needed to snap out of this fog I was under. I needed to be strong for everyone, in control. So I put one foot in front of the other.

. . .

I jerked to a stop when I saw two naked asses in front of me, and not just anyone's bare ass. *Oh god.* I adverted my eyes again. Was it wrong that I saw Nash and Jett's asses? And well, to be honest, I saw much more than that just earlier. I let out a snort as I rolled my eyes at myself. I needed to get used to all the nudity, and I had a feeling they had been holding that back here for me. But to be honest, Jett did have a nice ass...and so did Nash. He was just so...ugh. Alpha.

"Lex? I can carry you, sweetheart." Ranger's voice was soft, and I let him pull my face close to his. His eyes darted back and forth, a worried look in his eyes. I shook my head.

"Not used to seeing your family so naked in the morning." Ranger's brows lifted at my words, and I gave my best smile to reassure him that I was fine. I felt my body being lifted from the ground, the air leaving my lungs in a whoosh. My body felt tingly all over at the sudden change. I turned into the chest I was now cradled against to protest, but the look in Maverick's eyes told me he wasn't going to let me argue this. Which brought me back to why I wanted to walk. I just...

How did I process this? All of it, what had happened in the last two days. Was no one going to mention the fact I'd just jumped off a cliff...without wings?

Oh god. I looked back and saw the blank expression on Raff's face. He wouldn't even meet my eyes. I'd fucked up so badly and broken his trust again. How could I even start repairing this? It was a long walk back to the house, but I needed it to gather my thoughts before I got there. I didn't want to have a full breakdown in front of everyone. I was always so together...well, I used to be. I'd thought I was, at least. But now I was gathering too many thoughts. My body was shaking hard from the cold, at least I thought it was from the cold, and my chest felt tight. *Shock?* Could I be in shock? Made more sense than anything else.

I needed to get down, but as I twisted, Maverick just held me tighter and made a "shh" sound, as if I was a baby. But with my head pressed tightly to his chest, I could feel the rumble in his chest as he spoke to the others about the fighting... I was too exhausted to listen or fight him about being carried, so I just relaxed into his warmth and breathed in his scent. *Pine.*

It was quiet for a while. The rain had stopped, and all I heard were our footsteps as we all moved through the forest. Jett and Nash had gone now, and I assumed they had shifted after I talked about their nakedness. I glanced around at all my mates. Huh... I guessed I was starting to become immune to the nudity everywhere around me, because I didn't even notice they were all naked too. Well, except for Galen, but his clothes were pretty much gone. His arms... Oh god, his chest was scarred also. I wanted him to open up and tell me about his past. I quickly looked away before I made him uncomfortable, my eyes wandering to a very sexy bare chest ...then my gaze drifted lower to some seriously amazing abs. This was a good distraction. I needed that, to think about anything but—

"You like what you see?" Ranger teased with a wink, running his hand down his chest. I smiled—a real smile this time—at being caught out. The swaying was lulling me, but I needed to stay awake. I needed to help when we got back. I knew for sure we had lost some pack members, since there was no way we'd gone through this without some death. Only I couldn't stop thinking about one thing, no matter how hard I tried.

My mother was a vampire?

CHAPTER THREE

GALEN

As soon as Lexi passed out in Mav's arms, I reached for her. Mav didn't have to say a word as he handed her over. He knew, like me, that it would be faster for us if I ran back with her and they shifted and followed. I looked down into her face as she slept, not affected at all by the movement to my arms as she snuggled into my chest, like she knew it was me and that she was safe.

I was glad she had stopped fighting sleep. I could not only smell the fear and hurt rolling off her, but I could feel it too. I felt how tired she was, how hard she was being on herself. Her blood connected me in so many ways, yet I couldn't hear her thoughts. I wished to know what she was thinking so I could help her, but she wouldn't tell me, she wouldn't talk to us. Lexi could try and hide her pain, but she forgot she could never fully hide it from us. It hurt me to see her like this, but now she was asleep, all the pain and hurt were gone, replaced with something lighter. Dreaming of something happier, I hoped.

Her father was an angel, and he hadn't known about her until now. And he'd just dropped that huge bomb that not only was her mother a vampire, but he was actually half wolf shifter, half angel. I knew the guys didn't miss that bit of information. That was huge.

I couldn't stop thinking about it. Was that why Lexi's scent called to the wolf shifters? Was that why I was so drawn to her, because of her being an angel?

She was so beautiful, angelic, almost as if she wasn't real. She was perfect, right down to the little bits of dirt still on her face. Her lips parted on a deep exhale, and I froze, worried she would wake. But when she pressed her head in closer and sighed, I felt this warmth flood through my body. Was that her feelings or mine?

My chest was tight with emotion. Before Lexi, I didn't know these feelings existed. I had thought I'd known love, but now I knew that wasn't true. This was what true love felt like. And when she... when she'd jumped, I knew I would have followed her right off that cliff. I knew then in that moment I wouldn't want to live in a world without her. I had known since the first day I saw her in the office at school. Those big amber eyes... She'd had my heart, and there was no way I could've gotten it back. I didn't want it back.

My senses were so heightened now, more so than I would have believed possible. I could sense everything, from hearing a honey bee to smelling pine mixed with the scent of blood. My fangs itched...but not in the way one might think. The blood was that of shifters, my instincts telling me to be prepared for a fight. Being around the guys and breathing in their scents were not helping matters either, even though I was getting better, learning their scents. I quickly cleared my head of all thoughts to stop my fangs from dropping.

"Raff?" Maverick's voice was lined with concern.

I looked back to see a wolf where Ranger was. But Rafferty? He stood there, his long pale hair plastered around his face. He was covered in dirt and blood, his tattoos almost hidden. The rain had washed some of it away, but it wasn't enough to clean him. It was his face that had my attention, though. It was pale, and not his usual paler complexion compared to the twins. You could see the color had drained from his face. I was concerned about him too.

"Raff?" I hissed out. His blue eyes flicked up to mine. You could see he was lost in thought, like we all were, but I needed him to snap out of it, just for now. He wasn't a big talker, and I knew it would take time before he opened up to one of us about what all had happened here tonight. But with Lexi trying to... When she jumped, in her mind, it would save us all, but it wouldn't have solved the problem. It only meant that we would've had to live in a world without her, and that would've been a dark place without our Lexi, our angel.

I really needed to speak with Rafferty when we got back, as I knew he was hurting. She had left him once, twice...but this was different. His old pack, his own blood, had betrayed him over and over, tried to take the one good thing he had away from him. He was broken, but now wasn't the time to figure this out. We needed to get back, to end this all, and tomorrow, we would take care of all the emotional damage.

I took off for the house before the other two shifted, hoping that Rafferty would follow. I cradled Lexi to my chest, and when I arrived at the lawn, I could see the three packs—Kiba, Rawlins and Kenneally—together in a large circle. They surrounded a beaten down group of wolves that was seated on the lawn... When I saw the scum from Pack Russet, my fangs descended and I stalked forward, Lexi still sleeping and unaware of what was going on.

I got to the edge of the circle and hissed low at the sight in front of me. So many... There were at least a hundred or so shifters and a couple day vampires in front of me. They weren't moving, they just stared at us, fear rolling off them. Some of their eyes gave me mixed emotions, but I didn't know what was going to happen to them. The alphas hadn't spoken with me about this, and I wasn't invited to those meetings, only the ones where they needed vampire input. I could envision what I wanted to happen to them all. They were all threats to Lexi as long as they were alive.

I saw a flash of gold out of the corner of my eye, and knew that Tobias must be controlling all our attackers. Up on the cliff, I had felt the power oozing from him, but now I could really see the effects of it. There would be no way I could ever go up against Tobias and come out alive. I just hoped that he wouldn't take Lexi from me, *from us*, now that he was here. Would she go with him? Fuck. I never thought she might want to.

"How is she?" a female voice asked from my left. I turned, baring my fangs at the sudden move towards me, but the face I saw before me wasn't scared and didn't even flinch away. She just gave me a sad smile as she looked down at Lexi.

"Zara, I—" She held up her hand and shook her head.

"No need. If you didn't react like that, I would have been worried." She reached down and stroked the hair from Lexi's face. She held Lexi's hand in hers as she looked back up at me. Her face held many expressions, happiness, sadness. You could see her heart was breaking, and not just for Lexi, for everything that had happened this night. But also for Callum. Him being Ranger's packmate would have meant Lexi would have become her daughter-in-law. Not only did she lose a son when he was sent away, she lost the chance at having a daughter. *Grandchildren*. She had two other sons, but none as close as Callum was at having a mate when Lexi chose Ranger.

"She is safe. We all are." When I looked up around me, so many members from Kiba surrounded us. Everyone was grouped in their packs.

Ranger pushed his way through the group, Rafferty and Mav right behind him. When Ranger saw that Zara held Lexi, he froze. I knew he felt guilt for the way everything went down with Callum, but Zara was such a strong woman. I knew she didn't have any bad feelings towards Ranger, as she had told me herself. She wiped a stray tear away and turned to Ranger. He hesitated at first before she nodded her head at him. He went to her, wrapping his big arms around her small frame.

"It's okay, Ranger my boy. I know. I know…"

CHAPTER FOUR

RANGER

When I saw Zara holding Lexi's hand, I lost it. Not only did I lose my best friend, Callum, when he was banished, I'd lost her as my second mother. That was what she had been since my mother died.

I'd needed her when I lost Callum. I needed her forgiveness, because it was my fault he was gone. I had ignored it for as long as I could, but now, here... I shouldn't be doing this, now wasn't the time, but her face, the way she was looking at me and nodding, I couldn't hold back. My arms engulfed her small frame, but she held me tight. I tried to speak, but my throat felt thick.

"It's okay, Ranger my boy. I know. I know..."

My body shook with sobs at her words. *My boy.* She had been calling me her boy for as long as I could remember, because even when I was a child, I was one of hers. Callum and I had grown up together, best friends since the day we were born. We would talk endlessly about how we were going to be mate bonded to the same female, and when we were thirteen, we made the packmate bond. We were going to be together forever, but I ruined it all by not talking to him, for picking Lexi over him without explaining. I should have known it would set him off like that. I'd just needed time...time with Lexi to explain better what it meant to break the bond, what Callum meant to me and could mean to her.

But in all honesty, Callum and I had been drifting apart for a while. We'd made the packmate deal when we were too young to really know what it meant. I knew that now, and even though I didn't want to acknowledge it, I could see it clearly.

He had become angry and more aggressive over the last few years, and I'd spent most of the school year trying to get him to calm down. He was fighting all the time with the other packs at school... and yeah, I was too. It was hard not to when he was always starting fights. I had jumped in with him to finish them, backing him up, but this was different. His wolf, his anger, they were controlling him, much like mine was.

It wasn't always my anger that had my wolf coming out all the time. It was little things, like the way my father acted around my brothers, then treated me like I was the joke of the family. The way people just saw me as this cocky asshole.

I guessed that was all I ever let them see me as, so it was what they expected. It was like all the other roles had been taken, and this was the only one I could do well—the jock, the player, the alpha's son who couldn't control his shifts.

I admit, I'd messed up more times than I could count, but the difference was I was remorseful. I'd made amends with Raff. Fuck, we'd claimed the same girl. We'd done more than just make amends, we were packmates. And Galen... The guy couldn't stand me—okay, that was a lie. He loved having me in his class fucking with him, but I used to hate how he would report back to my father about all the shit I did. Now he was also my packmate. A vampire...the first my pack had ever had in a family, but I was all for being progressive and shit.

If someone had told me at the start of the year that I would be mated to a beautiful angel who'd almost died at the hands of my best friend, have my twin brother express his feelings for our male history teacher—who was also a vampire—and they'd both become my packmates, along with a rogue red wolf that was stronger than any person I had ever met, I would have laughed in their face. I would have bet against that, because the odds were highly stacked against that.

I guessed in the last month I really had done some growing up, but Callum just didn't grow with me. We grew apart instead, and I should have said something sooner, but I didn't think I would find my mate this fast. She jumped right into my life, and I didn't look past my own love for Lexi. Once I had her, I just cut him off without giving him a chance. I never thought things through, Father was always telling me that and punishing me for it. But this time, the consequences were more than I could bear.

I'd missed Zara so much, and I hadn't known how much until now. Having Zara hug me like this, treating me the same as always like I didn't just take everything from her—her son, the chance of her having Lexi as a daughter-in-law—was not what I expected.

Maybe I could make it up to her... *Noah.* Noah was in love with Ada. If I could somehow make that work between them... It wouldn't bring back Callum, I knew that, but if I could help one of her sons find happiness, that might help relieve some of the guilt I felt.

"I miss you," I whispered into her hair. She patted my back as we pulled apart, her hand reaching up to cup my cheek.

"You take care of your mate now. She's one of a kind, that girl. You better treat her right, or I will come whoop your ass, boy." Chuckling at her words, I nodded. She might've been smaller than I was, but she scared me more than my own father. She would whoop my ass, which I knew because she had...many times.

"Pack Kiba," my father's voice called out, and I turned to the direction it was coming from. My father, my alpha, was standing between the two other alphas of Rawlins and Kenneally packs. They all called out to their packs for attention.

"We have some sad news to report. We have fallen pack

members." My heart sank. I knew that we hadn't all make it out unscathed. We had Lexi helping to heal, but there were some who fell, never to get up again. I'd known that not all of us would walk away, but hearing my father say it made it too real.

"Elder John Edwards from Pack Rawlins, Elder Carl Grey from Pack Kiba..." They read out more names, but I wasn't listening. Carl. He was older than my father, never married and usually kept to himself, but he was a good man. As an elder, he was supposed to be protecting the kids.

I looked over to my father, and I could see the heavy weight he carried from being alpha of the pack, something I was glad I would never be. I watched as all three alphas stood tall, then hung their heads for a moment of silence for the fallen. But as everyone hung their heads, I couldn't tear my gaze away from Tobias. He watched us all, his eyes roaming over us, and it made me uneasy. He stopped when he saw Lex in Galen's arms.

I looked over and saw that Galen was staring right back at Tobias. The power I felt between them made my wolf nervous, like I should be running away.

I wanted to tell Galen to stop this stare down, but I knew my father would be upset if I spoke during the silence. No one else was watching this exchange between the vampire and angel. I'd never met an angel and honestly didn't know they existed until Lex. He was very powerful, you could feel that. If he wanted to, he could take Lex from us and there was no way we could stop him. Finally, heads started to rise, and I let out a sharp breath.

"Galen," I whispered, pleading for him to stop.

"Ranger," Galen hissed back. He wanted me to stay out of this, but I wasn't going to. I reached over to take Lex from him. I didn't understand why he was acting like this, but I wasn't about to lose my mate because he wanted to measure dicks with her father.

"Give. Me. Lexi," I growled out between my teeth. Galen took a step back, his eyes flicking to mine, then he glanced down. Lex was still sleeping. She must have used up so much of her powers to be this out of it still. He pulled her up higher and placed a kiss on her forehead before handing her gently over to my waiting arms.

Once she was safe against my chest, I let out a deep sigh. I needed this, I needed to feel her close to me. She was my sunshine on a cloudy day, the light at the end of all of this.

I nuzzled my face into her neck, breathing in her scent, my wolf marking her as mine, letting Tobias know that Lex was mine.

She was never going to be out of my sight. I would keep her safe.

CHAPTER FIVE

RAFFERTY

The crowd had moved away at the alpha's commands. I went to leave when my name was called by Alaric to stay behind. I froze, my wolf vibrating inside, wanting to stay yet also wanting to run. I didn't want to do this—no, that wasn't the truth. I did, but now it was here...how was I going to face them? *My uncles.*

I glanced down to my hands, and they shook slightly as I closed them into fists. I wanted to stay strong and not show how much this was affecting me. I was now a Kiba wolf, no longer from Pack Russet, and I would never have to live in fear again. Yet here they were, my uncles, glaring up at me, and the fear that had left when I joined Kiba returned even stronger than before.

A sly smile creeped over Uncle T's face. He wanted me to lose control, he always did, but my wolf knew better. He held strong as I glanced down at my naked body. After years of his sadistic torture, my skin showed him how strong I was. I wasn't some weak kid anymore, and I could see in his eyes that he knew that. The change in me was all around us. My new pack, they gave me strength, made me stronger and better than Russet ever would be. I could see for the first time in my life, he feared me.

I was so angry at everything—my uncles, the attack on Lexi. *My mate.* I turned and stalked back to where Alaric and Nash were standing with the other alphas and some of the elders. Galen and Maverick were also called forward, but Ranger had left with Lexi since he wasn't called to stay. I was glad, because I didn't want her to see where I came from and the type of people who shared my blood.

I also saw Ranger's face when he'd been included in this. His father seemed to dismiss him often. I'd noticed the different treatment towards him since I moved in. He got away with more stupid things, but if something was serious, he was dismissed.

"Rafferty," Galen said, grabbing my shoulder. I was so tense, I didn't realize I was growling lowly.

A throat cleared, and everyone turned and faced Tobias. When they said Lexi was part angel, it was strange at first, but then it was just a thing. Lexi was an angel. Seeing Tobias and watching him fly with those gold-colored wings...made it even more real. Angels were real.

"I have the power to heal, as I have for all your packs here this day. I am able to control others, but there is a limit to how much. I cannot compel like a vampire can a human, but what I can do is hand you your enemies, the enemies of my daughter." He paused for a second before continuing, "But if let them go, they will tell others and Alexis will never be safe. We must end this now." He turned to Alaric and nodded as he stepped aside, as if he was handing them over to him.

Tobias was an angel, but not like the sweet ones you see watching over humans in movies. No, this golden angel wanted us to kill them all, and with them sitting around like this, they wouldn't even be able to fight back. It would be an easy kill for anyone. I didn't want to let them walk away either. It was the only way to keep us safe, keep Lexi safe.

With them gone, no one else had to die, no more innocent lives taken.

"We can compel them. We don't want all this death on our hands if we can make them forget what Lexi is and to leave and never return," Alaric told Tobias and the others. I could see from the shocked looks on the faces of the other packs that Alaric had really kept Galen's abilities a secret from them. I guessed because he was also a threat to shifters, and if they'd known, maybe they would've tried to take Galen out.

"How?" the alpha from Rawlins asked. He stepped closer, his eyes darting to Galen, and the look on his face was one of shock laced with fear. Galen nodded. I would fear him too, except Galen was my packmate. He would never betray me. *He was my family.*

"I can compel them," Galen said as he dropped his hand from my shoulder and stepped forward. "With Lexi's blood in my system, I can compel shifters." And Galen had a lot of Lexi's blood in his system.

For a while, there were discussions between the alphas and Galen. I wished I was holding Lexi, that she was here with me. I knew in my heart she wasn't trying to hurt me when she dove off that cliff. I could see the way the guys looked at me, especially Galen, like I was going to break. I wasn't upset with her—well, I was, but that wasn't it. I'd been in shock about everything that had happened, and it was just catching up to me.

The thing was, once Lexi got something in her mind, there was no changing it. She was very independent and strong-willed, and that was something I loved so much about her. She was sweet and caring, but sometimes, she cared too much.

I hated to say it, but I would have done that too. I just... *Fuck.* It had broken me to see her so small and delicate in Tobias' arms. We needed her and she needed us, but we'd failed in that moment. We didn't have the strength to protect her, and I felt guilty for it.

I wanted to be with her now to tell her I was sorry, that all this happened because she'd met me. Honestly, I wanted to be anywhere else but here. Maverick was standing beside me, his shoulder touching mine, and it was the only thing stopping me from running. That, and Alaric had commanded I stay.

Finally, Galen broke away from the group and came over to me.

"It has been discussed that the ones who killed our pack members will die. Some of the others...well, there is going to be a vote on it." Galen looked me right in the eyes, and I already knew where this was headed. "The vote is to eliminate Pack Russet. I told them I wanted to speak to you about this, and not the alphas. Your vote will count. If you decide no, no one will talk you out of it. If you vote yes, the same. But I want you to understand that you don't have to vote. You can walk away, or you can stay. *You* are the one to decide."

I tilted my head to see my uncles. They were all that was left of Pack Russet. Uncle T just glared at me, and I took a step towards him, my wolf wanting to rip his throat out. Galen tried to stop me, but I pushed past him until I was standing a foot away from all my uncles. I growled at them and bared my teeth. They all just sat there frozen, unable to touch me ever again. I stood above Uncle T as he had done so many times to me.

"Where did you bury my mother? My father?" I knew he'd killed him, but I wanted to know where my mother was buried. I'd never gotten that answer as a child, and I needed to know it now. Uncle T growled loudly, baring his teeth. He tried to stand up, but whatever Tobias was doing kept him on the grass.

"Where. Is. She?" I growled back. I had no time for his games anymore. I was vibrating, so close to shifting. How would he feel if I bit him? If I injected him with my venom over and over, or rip through his skin until it was scarred? My wolf wanted nothing more than to tear through his flesh, to kill him, but he deserved a slow, painful death. Anything quicker would be too good for him.

"Your mother was a whore." He spat at my bare feet. I started to shake, my wolf coming to the surface. They'd taken the one thing that was important to me as a child. They'd tried to break me, over and over. Then they'd come back and tried again to break me again.

But now...now I would break them all.

CHAPTER SIX

MAVERICK

I had never seen Rafferty this angry. He was struggling to hold it together, and his asshole of an uncle wouldn't answer the question that had us all wanting to know the answer too. Where did he bury his mother?

I knew the pain and loss of losing your mother, but I had never spoken to Rafferty about it, never even thought about the fact his mother was dead and that was why he was in the system.

My father walked over and stood beside Rafferty. He held his shoulder as he looked down at the pathetic pack in front of him.

"Where did you bury his mother?" His voice was calm yet demanding, and there was silence as we all waited to see if this piece of shit would do one thing right in his life. When he spat at my father's feet, I knew Rafferty wouldn't get the answer he was looking for, and that hurt me. He was my packmate, my family, and to see him hurting this bad... Fuck.

"Rose bushes." Everyone turned to Tobias. What? Rose bushes?

"You fucking asshole," the Russet alpha spat out.

"You buried my mom under the rose bushes?" Rafferty asked, more in control now, while his uncle seethed.

When his uncle didn't say anything more, Tobias spoke up.

"Your mother was...cremated. Her ashes were spread over her rose garden." I let out a shuddering breath. Tobias was reading his thoughts. Holy crap, that was so... *Oh fuck.* When Galen looked to me, I knew what he was thinking. This whole time, Tobias was reading our thoughts.

"Your father, he didn't get the same burial. I am sorry." Tobias seemed upset by this as much as I was. Motherfucking assholes. If I had a vote, I'd vote to kill them all now so I could go back to my life, the one with Lexi in it where she kisses me and understands me in ways I didn't understand myself.

I wished I'd been the one holding her when father dismissed Ranger. I could see the look on his face when he wasn't asked to stay. I wanted to show father that Ranger wasn't a screw-up. He was always treating him like he was, and it upset me. Yeah, Ranger was a bit more reckless than the rest of us, but since Lexi had come along, he'd really grown up. He wasn't acting up and messing around, like having a mate grounded him.

Father led Rafferty back over to where I was. Fuck, he looked like shit. I met him halfway and wrapped my arms around him. Raff needed us, and I wanted him to know we were here for him, whatever he chose for his uncles. I had a feeling whichever way Rafferty voted, my father would agree, even if he was outvoted by the other alphas. I pulled back and gave him a bit of breathing room.

"You don't have to vote, son. You can walk inside now and we will take care of all of this, or you can stay if you want." I could see the wheels turning over in Raff's head. This was huge, and I didn't even know if I wanted to stay for it.

"But I would prefer you go and be with Alexis, make sure she's safe. That is very important to me." My father knew how to speak to Raff. He was the alpha, but he was also compassionate and caring, which was why he was so good at what he did. That was the type of leader you needed in a pack.

Raff turned his head back to where his uncle sat among the

others. He let out a shaky breath, and I could see his body almost sag as he said to my father, "I vote yes." *Eliminate*. And with that, he hung his head, his hair falling into his face as he started to walk towards the house, his feet almost dragging him there like at any moment, he would fall down in exhaustion. I felt the same way.

"Maverick," my father said as he nudged me with his shoulder and tilted his head to Raff. Galen nodded at me to go. He couldn't leave here, since he had minds to compel. I jogged after Raff, unsure if he wanted to talk or if we were just going straight to Lexi, so I didn't say anything. I just made sure he knew I was there for him.

When we got inside the house, it was filled with so many shifters. Raff froze and looked around, and a few of them stopped and looked to us, which made my wolf rise. I didn't like being the center of attention and thought Raff didn't either, so I grabbed his shoulder and led him to the stairs.

"Let's go to Lexi. She needs us." I wasn't sure she did need us, but it made his footsteps faster as we moved down the hall. I could smell her in her room, but when I opened the door, I found it empty.

"Lexi?" I could hear the fear in Raff's voice. Shit, where was Ranger?

"Shh, in here." Both our heads turned to the closet. She was in the closet, like when she first moved in? This wasn't good.

We entered and saw a huge pile of blankets and pillows and... "Josh?"

Ranger put his finger to his lips to tell us to be quiet. I didn't mean to be loud, I just didn't expect to find him in here, but it made sense. They might not be blood related, but that was her little brother and she was very protective of him. That made him my little brother. Ranger threw some boxers at us both, so we could be clothed. I was still covered in blood, mud, and dirt, but I didn't want to shower. I was just too tired and didn't want to spend another minute away from Lexi.

"She asked for Josh when we got up here and made me go down and get him. She was in a panic, thinking he wasn't safe. Grayson said Josh was scared and kept calling out for her, so I told him I would take care of Josh and he could stay with us while him and Jack helped out downstairs. But when I got back, she had made her little blanket fort in here...*again*." I could tell by the way he said "again" that it worried him just as much as me. He still blamed himself for the first time she built one, when Father moved her here by force after Ranger told him Lexi was his mate.

"It's okay, Ranger." I hugged my brother, something we didn't normally do, but after last night, I wanted to hug him, hug all my brothers. I wanted to make sure he knew that this was fine, it was just a little step back, and maybe Lexi felt safer in here. It was small and cozy, and others had been staying in her room. Maybe he should have taken her back to Galen's house, since we'd spent more time there than in here. But then this house was full of our pack, so I felt safer here.

Raff had curled up and placed himself against Lexi's back, holding her gently so as not to wake her. I moved in, laying down closer to her legs, and held her. She made a sweet sound as Ranger sat down against the wall beside Josh. He stroked Lexi's hair, and when Josh started to stir, he rubbed his back and made shushing sounds until he stopped.

Ranger looked exhausted, and Raff had fallen asleep as soon as his head hit the pillow. I could hear him softly snoring. My eyes felt gritty and my mind was starting to shut down, but I didn't want to fall asleep. I wanted to wait for Galen because I needed him here. We all needed to be together right now.

"Ranger, you can sleep." He looked down at Lexi. Her sweet lips were parted as she breathed softly, and she looked so peaceful as she slept, not like the sassy mouthed beauty she was when awake.

"I'll wait for Galen. You sleep. I want to make sure Josh is okay. I'm worried about him. He saw so much, and he keeps waking." I nodded. Galen would know what to do. He would help Josh, Lexi... all of us.

CHAPTER SEVEN

LEXI

I felt rested, like I'd slept a hundred hours, and I was feeling like myself again. I rolled over, and something touched my face. A hand? Fingers. "Ugh." It poked my eye, and I rolled away as much as I could into a hard body. I felt a hand come over my hip and hold me tightly, and I opened my eyes. One was slightly unfocused where it had been poked, but I looked down and saw a beautiful sight. In front of me lay my dark-haired Joshy, his mouth slightly parted as he made the softest sounds, and a large hand was on his shoulder. I followed it up and saw Ranger, with his back against the wall, but his head was lolled to the side as his chest rose and fell.

I brushed some of Josh's hair back, and his lips turned up in a small smile. He looked peaceful and so cute with him sleeping here beside me. I pulled him in closer, and he made a funny sound but stopped when I hugged him. Ranger's hand had slid from Josh, and I watched it as it tapped around on the ground until it landed on Josh's back again. My heart felt like it was going to explode as I watched a sleeping Ranger rubbing Josh's back and comforting him, even while sleeping.

I felt a tug around my waist, which was Raff was sleeping behind me. I knew that body anywhere. My big spoon, Raff. I looked down and saw Maverick had his head on Galen's lap, and he was draped over my legs, pinning me down. The weight was welcoming, like a comforting blanket.

The only one not sleeping was Galen. He stroked Maverick's hair like I had just done for Josh, and I felt a flutter deep in my belly. This scene before me, after everything that had happened... This was my family. My mates, my little brother. I felt so loved in this moment, more than I ever had with them all. The events from last night would change us forever, but I hoped it didn't change what we had.

I loved how Josh was so trusting of them in this moment as he slept softly. He was usually afraid of them all. I thought Maverick scared him the most, but as I looked down, I saw Maverick was actually holding onto Josh's ankle. I wondered if he'd had bad dreams, but I hoped not. I didn't think I'd dreamed at all while I slept.

I reached down and stroked Raff's hand on my waist, then he murmured something, and it made me smile. I wiggled my toes, and Galen reached out and held them in his fingers.

"Good morning," he whispered as he smiled, his curls falling into his eyes. I grinned back. God, he was beautiful. My throat felt dry, and I was suddenly thirsty. Morning? It was still early, but I felt like I'd slept so well.

"Do you want me to help you get up?" Galen asked, shifting Maverick's head in his lap slightly, which only had Maverick holding onto my legs tighter. Obviously, he didn't want to be moved.

"Water?" It was hot in the closet with everyone in here. When I'd made the blanket fort, I just needed to feel secure. It was small and safe in here, and after the night we'd had, it felt right to be in here. I felt like I could breathe better in a small space, protected from the outside world.

I watched as Galen tried to move Maverick again, but when his eyes opened and he looked up at Galen, his hand shot out and held onto his sweater. Galen licked his lips as he gazed down at Maverick. They held each other's gaze for a moment before Maverick blinked and looked around the room. He sat up and scratched the back of his head. There was so much love between them, but the confusion in Maverick's face was still there. I wished I could help him, but there was only so much I could do. The rest would fall into place over time. Maverick smirked as he sat up and moved closer to me.

Galen must have showered and changed. I'd only just now noticed that he was dressed in fresh clothes, a sweater and dark jeans.

"It's okay, don't leave. I'll be fine." I didn't want Galen to leave. I thought it was best we all stayed together for now. Galen looked over to me as he tilted his head.

"Someone will get us some water. I think Jack is here to pick up Josh." I pulled Josh a little too tightly to my chest, and he made a sound as I accidently woke him up.

"I'm sorry. Shhh, you can go back to sleep. I got you." I rocked him in my arms as I kissed the top of his head, and he closed his eyes, wrapping his arms around me.

"Lexi, I love you." My heart just about exploded right there. My little Josh.

"I love you, Joshy."

Everyone had woken up now, and I peered back at Raff behind me, then down to Maverick, over to Ranger, and finally settling on Galen as I held Josh close. Now that we were all awake, I could feel the tension in the air. We hadn't talked about what I did, what had happened, and now I could feel it...like the elephant in the room. And this was a small room.

There was a knock at the bedroom door, and I heard it open before anyone said to come in. There was a chuckle, then a loud banging sound, and someone groaned like they were hurt. We all looked to the closet door.

"Cupcake!" Jett appeared with his arms full of bottled water, a huge grin on his face as he stopped and took us all in. Ranger growled lowly, and I rolled my eyes. Really? Of all the days. Jett winked at me as he came in and handed the bottles out, Mekhi right behind him. He shook his head and smiled at me. Saint appeared next, a funny grin on his face. I guessed they were all in a good mood.

"Sorry, Lexi. Jett just can't help himself." Mekhi lightly punched Jett in the arm, and he let out a mock whine. Josh tensed up beside me at this, and I heard him gasp. Jett looked over to us, his eyebrow cocked slightly. He then proceeded to fall to the floor, as if it was some huge hit Mekhi just gave him. He rolled over onto his back and grabbed his chest.

"Why do you hurt me? All I want to do is...tickle you." Jett jumped up with a funny grin on his face, and Josh's whole body pressed against me tightly.

Jett started to tickle a very surprised Mekhi, and I watched as Mekhi's eyebrows rose and he tried to dodge Jett. He was doing a great job at faking the whole thing, a huge grin on his face the whole time.

The giggles that came from Josh were infections, and I started laughing. Jett knew how to break the ice and make people feel comfortable around him. I was happy to be here in this moment with Josh, ignoring everything that had happened, like everything was okay and we didn't just go to hell and back.

"Jett is the tickle monster. I wonder if he can spot anyone else needing tickles?" Maverick said as he sat up on his knees and looked over to Josh. Josh froze up and held me tighter, his eyes widening like he was scared of what Maverick just said. I knew he was still not comfortable with most of them, but he'd just slept in here with my mates and me and I really wanted him to be okay with them. Maverick could sense his hesitation, and a sly grin formed on his face as he winked.

"I think Galen needs tickles... What do you think, Josh?" Josh moved away from me a little, ready to see this, while Galen gave Maverick a look like he'd thrown him under a bus. I wondered when the last time he was tickled. I laughed as Galen put his hands up to Jett, shaking his head no, but I could see by the hint of a smile there that Galen was happy to play along, then Jett dove in. I could now see Jack standing in the doorway, smiling as he watched Josh's face light up when he squealed with laughter again.

"Help me, I need more tickle monsters. Vampires need lots of tickles," Jett said, looking over to Josh. He stopped laughing for a moment before he looked up at me.

"Oh, you need to get him, little tickle monster." I tickled his sides, and he giggled. Josh crawled closer, and Jett stopped for a moment. Galen smiled up at Josh.

"Oh no...another tickle monster," Galen said in a funny voice, and Josh dove in, tickling Galen under his chin. He chuckled and laughed at the little attempts Josh made to tickle him, which just had Josh laughing too...

"Oh no, I've turned into the tickle monster too," I said as I reached around Josh and started tickling Galen, then Josh. My chest felt lighter, and the whole atmosphere in the small room felt better. Josh was so happy to have tickled Galen, and he kept telling us he was the best at tickling vampires as all the boys were high-fiving him and agreeing. The look on his little face was priceless.

I got up and hugged Jack, then took a deep breath as he stroked my back.

"My little fighter. My girl. I love you so much." And that was all it took for the tears to start—happy tears, not sad tears. Jack rubbed my back and told me everything would be good now. I didn't know if it was going to be, but I knew I would do anything to keep my family happy and safe.

"Come on, Josh. Your sister here needs to get ready for the day. Let's go home and see if Grayson has made us cupcakes?" Jack said, and Josh smiled and launched himself at me in a tight hug.

"You'll come home soon?" Josh asked, his little eyes pleading with me. I cupped his cheek in my palm.

"I'll come and watch cartoons with you very soon. I promise." He nodded, and I waved as they both left.

I turned to see Jett with a funny grin spread across his face as

Mekhi pulled him away from the room. Saint shook his head and shoved Jett out the door just as I heard him call out, "Have fun…cupcake."

I rolled my eyes. Jett was such a shit stirrer, but right now, I was thankful that he was. I wasn't overthinking everything, and I felt better, lighter. Happier.

CHAPTER EIGHT

LEXI

I reached my arms above my head and stretched my back. Sleeping on the floor was uncomfortable. I noticed the guys were just wearing underwear, and some still had dried mud on them. I looked down at my feet, and they were still covered in dirt. The only one who had showered and dressed was Galen. I smiled at him as he watched me assessing myself. I loved that army-green knit sweater he wore, since it reminded me of the day he knocked on the bathroom door and surprised me by handing me a bag of tampons and chocolate bars. That was so odd at the time, but so sweet. My stomach rumbled at the thought of chocolate, and I pressed my hand to my abdomen to stop the rumbling.

"I feel like I've slept all day." I stretched again and smiled when Raff yawned and shuffled over to me. He wrapped his arms around my waist and kissed me, taking me by surprise. I'd thought he would hate me... Well, not hate, but not be so...like this. Did this mean we were okay? I hadn't fucked everything up? He hugged me tight to his chest and whispered, "I love you. Are you still mine?"

Did he even have to ask? I was always going to be his. I bounced lightly on the balls of my feet, reached up, and tugged on his hair until he was looking at me.

"I love you so much, Rafferty. I'm yours, always and forever," I said, then kissed him. What was to be a light kiss turned deeper as he ran his hands down over my ass, squeezing gently. Why did our kisses always turn heated so quickly? I could feel him hard against me, and I gasped when he rubbed himself against my core.

Someone made a coughing sound, and we pulled apart, even though I didn't want to. Raff's lips were all red and swollen, and I smiled and chuckled at that. I ran my thumb over his lower lip, and he caught it in his teeth and nipped lightly. Fuck, he looked so ruffled. Bed hair really looked sexy on him.

"You've slept all day and night, sweetheart... You all have," Galen said, and my eyes darted to him, then to the others, my mouth dropping slightly.

"I slept for twenty-four hours?" How did I sleep that long? I'd wanted to speak to Tobias. I wanted to know things, but then again, I also didn't. I was a little unsure what he would say, but I needed to hear it. I needed to know more about my powers, about why I could heal shifters and vampires, and most of all, I needed to know more about my mom. If she was a vampire, what happened?

"I...I wanted to speak to Tobias. I didn't want to sleep this long. Is he still here?" I said, then looked around my room. It was clean, like someone had come in and cleaned while we were all sleeping. It hadn't looked like this when I got here...yesterday morning.

"Where's Ada?" I asked. She'd been sleeping here, and I needed to see her. Oh god, I had to apologize to her and tell her how sorry I was for just leaving her like that. My heart was racing. There was so much to say, and I had so many people to apologize to.

"Hey, it's okay. Tobias is downstairs with Alaric. Ada went home, but she'll be back. She wanted to see her parents and make sure they were okay. She's fine. She was worried about you and visited while you were sleeping." I nodded at Galen's words, but I realized that this little happy bubble we had in here was going to burst when I walked out that door.

I really wanted Ada here, but I didn't want to worry her either. I wasn't going to win gold in the best friend category. If I were Ada, I would've run away and said goodbye to my crazy life long ago, but I felt a warmth in my chest at the thought that she hadn't. She wasn't just going to run off and leave me to this shifter, vampire...angel life. She just rode the same wave I did, and I honestly couldn't think of a better person to be my friend. Plus, she still had the hots for Saint and now Huxley, so I had a feeling that she would be dating a shifter by the end of summer. If not, I was sure she would spend a lot of time here with me. I need that badly. Too much testosterone here.

"I'll have a shower and then go down," I said, feeling nervous. As much as I wanted to see Tobias, ask him all these questions, the whole *he was my father* thing was still just hanging in the air. Did he want me to call him dad? I didn't think I would be able to, plus he looked like he was only five years older than me, so it would be strange. I would call him Tobias. Was I his only child? Did I have siblings?

"Everyone go have a shower, get changed, and we'll meet downstairs," Galen ordered, and I smirked at his bossiness.

"Yes, Mr. Donovani." His face softened from the serious look he had as a sly grin appeared, and he winked at me. He strode over and pressed a kiss to my forehead before he turned to the door. Raff hugged me tighter, then let go as he pressed a soft kiss to my lips and followed Galen out of the room. I licked my lips, remembering that heated kiss we'd just had. I felt like a giddy teenager... Hell, I was a giddy teenager.

I peered over to the twins. I'd never thought about how upset they might be with me. I dropped my gaze down to my bare feet as I skirted the white carpet with my dirty toes. I wasn't good at this. I felt like ever since I got here, I was forever saying sorry to someone.

"I love you, and nothing will change that," Maverick said as he wrapped his arms around me and pulled me tight to his chest. Oh man. I sniffed back the tears as I hugged him back.

"I love you," I replied. He'd been such a grumpy asshole when I first met him, and now he was all soft and sweet. Well, to me he was. Pretty sure he was still an asshole to most people. I stood on my tiptoes and kissed his cheek, then he left the room, which just left Ranger and I standing in here.

My once happy-go-lucky Ranger was looking far from it. He'd been laughing not that long ago, but now he looked so serious.

"Oh, Ranger. Jett was just messing with you." Asshole. I'd told him not to say anything to Ranger about sharing my cupcakes with them. That was it, I wasn't sharing anything nice with Jett from now on. But it did remind of the comment Jett made when he'd called me cupcake about how Ranger would flirt non-stop with Clare, Mekhi and Jett's high-school sweetheart. Which made me feel jealous that he'd flirted with another girl.

Clare was crazy for walking away from them. I would've dragged them with me. Alaric had said they didn't go to college like normal teens do, but I wouldn't have cared. Those guys were so sweet and still hung up on her, *hard*. But had she liked Ranger flirting? Had she wanted him? Was that why she left them, because she wanted Ranger?

"Lex?" Ranger walked over to me, his head cocked to the side, his green eyes questioning me as he rubbed his hand down his chest nervously. Wow, his body was like...so distracting.

"Huh?" I asked. Did he say something?

"I said, I can smell you. What were you just thinking about?" He held my upper arms now, his chest right there in front of me. I tried to lay my head against it, wanting to hear his heart and show him how much I loved him, but he held my arms tight so I couldn't press against him.

"No, you tell me what's making you give off this scent. I've never smelled it on you before." I furrowed my brow. I had no idea what scent he was talking about, but I was happy he was no longer looking at me the way he just was.

"Tell me," he growled lowly into my neck, and it sent shivers down my spine.

"Oh, um...that you were upset? About the cupcake thing. And about how you used to flirt with Clare and it drove Jett and Mekhi crazy." He pulled back and peered down into my eyes. I could see a look wash over his face, and his lips curled up at the side. He chuckled and crushed me to his chest. Did this mean he was okay? I didn't understand what was going on with Ranger. He liked to hide his feelings behind jokes, but this laugh was real, pure.

"You're jealous," he stated as he pressed my hair back. I looked up into his eyes again, and I could see the mirth there. He was genuinely happy that I was jealous, and I wanted to keep this Ranger here with me. He was so real right now. I slapped his chest playfully.

"Yeah well, you're mine, and if you flirt with her ever again, I'll drag you home by your tail." That had him laughing again.

"Okay, fair enough. She was nice and smelled good, I couldn't help it." My eyes flared at his statement, and he let me push him away.

"Aww, babe, Lex, you know I only have eyes for you." I cocked my hip and pursed my lips at him, his cocky grin appearing. He wiggled his eyebrows. "Well, sometimes have eyes for..."

I pointed at him, then at the door. "Out."

He grabbed his chest and said, "I was going to say burgers, but I guess my girl gets jealous of me looking at food too."

"Tease." I smiled, trying to stop myself from laughing, but a small giggle popped up as I quickly turned away. I jogged over to the bathroom just as the room tilted. Two large hands picked me up, and Ranger cradled me to his warm chest.

"I'll wash your back and you wash mine? Or will you be jealous that the water gets to touch me...naked?"

CHAPTER NINE

LEXI

As much as Ranger wanted to shower with me, I kicked him out and showered alone with my thoughts. Now I was in my closet, a clean one at that. All the bedding was gone, and it kinda frustrated me that they were forever cleaning up. I hadn't done the dishes here in like...well, I hadn't at all.

Ugh, why was finding something to wear so hard? I didn't have anything that I felt would be appropriate to wear in front of Tobias, which was stupid because I didn't need to impress him, but I didn't want to look like I hadn't even tried to look nice.

"Hey," came a voice from behind me, along with a knock on the doorframe. I huffed out a breath. This was stupid. Why was I being so dumb about this? It was just clothes, and he wouldn't care. Who cares about looking nice in front of their...ah...angel dad?

"Did you want to borrow something of mine?" Raff asked, and I smiled as I looked over to him. He looked so cute, but he was wearing a black tee and gym shorts. He didn't dress any differently, and neither should I. I would just be myself. I shook my head.

"No, I just didn't want to look...I don't know." I grabbed a tank top and pulled it over my head, then I slipped on some ripped jean shorts. I needed to get some new clothes, even if they were just more tanks and jeans. I walked over to Raff and wrapped my arms around him. I felt him nuzzle into my hair, then my neck, and I giggled at his marking me. His hair was all done and slicked back, so made up...so Raff.

"Marked me up good?" He took a sniff, and I watched the side of his lip quirk when he shook his head no. I rolled my eyes and took his hand before he kept me here all day, marking me as his. The others would want to do that too, and I couldn't leave them waiting.

"Let's go." I gestured, and we walked together down the stairs, where I could hear everyone talking. I took in a deep breath, trying to calm my nerves and the butterflies that had formed in my belly. We rounded the corner and saw Ranger sitting on the kitchen counter, while Maverick was standing off to the side, his arms crossed against his chest. He stood a little taller when he saw me and gave me a sweet smile. Oh man, I loved to see him smile. But when he looked back to Tobias, his smile dropped.

Galen was sitting on a stool beside Tobias, who had no wings. Wow, did they like, retract or something? They were both watching me...maybe waiting for me to say something, but I hesitated. Now that he was here, I didn't know what to say or where to start. Galen must have seen this, as he stood, then he was over to me so quickly, it took my breath away.

"Lexi, I've been speaking with Tobias. He has a lot of information about what you are and your powers." I nodded, not taking my eyes off Tobias. He smiled over to me, but he didn't get up or make a move towards me. I kinda felt...neglected. He'd spoken to Galen, but he wasn't even making a move to talk to me.

I felt sick. As I watched Tobias out of the corner of my eye, I dragged Galen and Raff with me to Maverick. I held my arm out to him and bared my neck, Maverick watching me in confusion. Then he smelled me and almost growled when I pressed my arm to his throat. He nuzzled and rubbed himself against me, marking me, something he didn't do often in the past, but right now, I needed to be marked. I needed Tobias to see they were my mates, and no matter what he said or did from now on, that would never change.

Ranger didn't wait for me. He jumped down and wrapped me in his arms, rubbing against my hair, making it all messy. He tried to fix it, but gave up in the end and kissed me before retreating back to his spot on the counter.

I looked over to Tobias and found he was watching me intensely. I finger combed my hair back and tucked the long strands behind my ears. Fuck it, if he wasn't going to talk, I would.

"Hey," was all I said. He smiled and nodded at me. Ugh, this was a bad idea. He was a total douche. I couldn't talk to him. I took a step back to leave, and Raff squeezed my hand, tugged me towards the counter. I put my hands on the cool black marble and smiled over at Ranger.

"Hey, Lex, so Tob here was just telling us—" Ranger's voice cut off as we felt a weird pressure in the air, and I watched as Tobias turned his head towards Ranger, his eyes boring into him. Ranger's eyebrows shot up as he said, "Tob—" and quickly added, "ias?" The pressure died down, and I could see the worried look on Ranger's face.

Okay, we'd just learned that Tobias didn't like a shortened name. Also, he was scary powerful, and maybe he wouldn't know if I slipped out and ran away. If Galen had all this information, then I didn't need to ask Tobias. I would be fine, right? I swallowed the huge lump in my throat. *Right?*

"Hello, Lexi. Please come and take a seat. I don't bite, unlike your mates." Okay...that wasn't creepy or anything. I breathed out and wrapped my hands around my middle, then turned to Raff and watched his expression. Okay, he was freaked out. Nope, my plan to run was for the best. I took a step back, but Galen stopped me by holding my arm before I got any farther. Fuck, he knew I would run.

"Lexi, why don't you sit beside me. Maverick will make some tea, coffee, *something*," Galen said as he led me over to a stool and took the one beside Tobias. I felt a little better with Galen as a buffer, but I was so tense, I couldn't relax. I didn't think anyone was relaxed right now. I wasn't too sure if Tobias was okay with…well, all of this. Was he going to take me away from my mates? Was that what he meant by them biting? I knew they were wolf shifters…and a vampire, but they were mine. They'd claimed me, and I'd claimed them. I wouldn't leave them, not if I had a choice. I would run away with them.

"Your mates are very protective of you. I can tell you are worried for them and sense your fear of me. Do not be afraid, I just want to help you and get to know you."

I looked around the room, but everyone was just watching us, apart from Maverick, who was in the pantry getting something… maybe snacks?

Did Tobias just talk in my head, like Galen could when he drank my blood? Oh wow. I darted a gaze to Tobias.

"Yes, it's something like that, Lexi. Which is something I worry about, especially for your vampire mate." Everyone turned to Tobias. Oh fuck. He'd just read my thoughts?

"Lexi, I forgot to mention something—" Galen started to say, but Raff cut in and blurted out, "Tobias is telepathic."

"Okay, wow. Is that something I can do? I can hear Galen when he drinks my blood, but he can't hear me." Tobias looked at me, cocking his head, then shifted his gaze to Galen. He scrubbed the scruffy beard on his jaw, and I could tell he was thinking. Ranger shuffled around where he sat on the counter.

"I would like for him to stop drinking your blood, at least until I can find out what happened to your mother after I last saw her. I shared my blood with her, and as you know, vampires do not have children so this is highly unusual."

I didn't want Galen to stop, since I loved the connection I had with him when he drank my blood. I felt safer with him knowing where I was and how I was feeling. I reached down and grabbed Galen's hand and squeezed it. Fuck him. Tobias couldn't tell me what to do. He might've been my biological father, but blood didn't mean shit. Look at Raff's uncles. They sure weren't a great family, and if I had to choose, I wouldn't choose Tobias.

"Your mates are worried that I have read their minds while waiting for you this morning." I could hear the gasps around the room. Did he listen?

"Yes." He nodded to me, and I stood up. I was pissed off. How dare he.

"You cannot just read other people's minds. That's wrong." His eyes shifted to mine, and he smiled. It was a little intimidating, to be honest.

"Lexi, you are my daughter, my only child. Of course I read the minds of your mates. I wanted to make sure their hearts were in the right place." I was shaking, and Ranger jumped off the counter and wrapped his arms around me, shielding me. Raff was next, then Maverick stood beside me. They were all touching me, making me feel stronger than ever, and I stood taller.

Tobias just sat forward, his elbow on the counter now, his amber eyes glowing. It made me nervous. Was he going to say bad things about my mates? His eyes roamed over them all, and his smile grew.

"This one, the chatty one." He pointed to Ranger, who I heard suck in a breath. "He loves you deeply. There is too much going on up there at once, but he is loyal, I'll give him that. But stop thinking about sex while I'm around. Other things might be more useful."

My mouth dropped open. *What the fuck?*

CHAPTER TEN

MAVERICK

Lexi's father could read minds. Fuck, oh shit, I'd forgotten about that. How could I forget that? What was I thinking when I was down here? Not good things about her father, that was for sure. He'd just called Ranger out for his sexual thoughts. I didn't think about sex...well, I did, but I was more concerned that he would take Lexi away from us, and I couldn't stomach the thought. My wolf wanted to come out and show him she was mine. He would have to fight me if he thought he could take my mate.

"You, Maverick." I sucked in a deep breath and held my tongue, waiting to see what he would say. Could he sense my wolf so close to the edge? "You are very protective. You were watching me, trying to find my weaknesses and determine if I was a threat. You were ready to stop me if I tried to take Lexi from you. I like that about you."

My mouth dropped open slightly. I...well, I was doing that. I was always protecting her. I'd been watching him, trying to get a read on what his plans with Lexi were. I couldn't help it, I puffed up my chest a little at his words, and he liked that.

His eyes darted between Rafferty and Galen. His head tilted as he watched Galen, like he was reading his thoughts right now. He'd better stay out of Rafferty's head. He'd had enough shit to last a lifetime. *You better not.* I growled lowly, my hackles rising. I didn't know I would be this protective of a packmate, but Rafferty was ours. My wolf had claimed him when he claimed Lexi.

"Rafferty, the red wolf. So much inner strength. You have overcome so much that you question everything good that comes your way, but know that you are worthy. Your packmates are not happy I'm even speaking to you. They are very protective of you. They love and care for you just as much as you love and care for them."

I looked over to Raff, and fuck, he looked so small. His worried eyes darted to all of us, a troubled look on his face, so I reached out and grabbed his forearm, and the other two did as well.

"You're part of this, one of us. I didn't know you worried about that. I'm sorry if I don't open up more. I just...I'm not big on feelings," I told him, my wolf wanting to jump out and run with him, show him we were equal. Man, my chest hurt as I felt a wave of emotion flood through me.

I gave Galen a smile as I felt my eyes become watery. God, I thought I was messed up, and poor Raff had been here with us, hurting the whole time, and I had no idea. None of us did.

"Galen, you are older...as old as I am." My eyes flared. Fuck, I didn't think Tobias was that old. Lexi looked shocked. I'd assumed he was older, because he looked so young that he must age slower. "Ah, maybe a little older than I am, but still, I see you love and care for them all. You are drawn to Lexi, but you worry that it was her blood that called to you and the wolf shifters. You are correct in that, but her angel side is stronger. That is what called to you. You would have known when you first tasted her blood.

"You wonder if she will ever shift... My mother's blood is not strong enough for her to do so. Neither is the angel blood that runs through her veins, which I am glad for."

Lexi gasped. "You don't want me to be strong?" she asked, almost vibrating with anger.

Tobias shook his head, and I watched as he ran his hand through his hair.

"It is not like that, Lexi. *My father*, your grandfather...he can sense when I use my powers and often times use that to locate me. I'm not someone who interests him, as a half wolf shifter that cannot shift isn't much use for him, so I continue to use my powers. He is not...good.

"He has been searching for my sister for over a decade. She is in hiding and doesn't use her angel powers for fear he will find her. She is half angel and half... Well, her powers are strong, much stronger than mine. So much so, my father wants her, and he does not have good intentions. But my sister, she is the reason I am here. Pack Bardoul reached out and word got to her...warlock, and he sent word to me that I needed to get to Pack Kiba to meet my daughter.

"I think it would be good for him to come here. He could put a protection spell on you, or at least hide your scent. The wolf shifters are drawn by the small amount of true shifter blood that runs through you from your grandmother. Your angel blood might heighten it, which is why so many believe they are your mates."

Everyone just stood there watching Tobias. I didn't have words... Thoughts? I had a few, but I didn't want to think them while he was here.

I felt Lexi start to nod from beside me. She was talking to him... through her mind. I was glad, since I didn't know how much more information I could take.

My mind was already blown.

CHAPTER ELEVEN

LEXI

The fact that my mother was a vampire was taking over all my thoughts. *"How could that be?"* I asked Tobias. I thought the guys knew that we were talking to each other through telepathy. At first, I wasn't sure I wanted to do it with Tobias, since it was Galen's and my thing, but the fact I could talk back to Tobias made it special.

"I don't know, Lexi. That's what I intend to find out and why I want you to stop giving Galen your blood until I do."

My mom ate regular food, when we ate that was. I swore she did, and she drank a lot. I remember all the empty liquor bottles in the house. I remember the drugs too…well, not exactly. I figured out as I grew up that my parents weren't sick and needed medicine like they'd told me, but they were sick with addictions, and one of those came at the end of a needle. I'd just thought it was all normal—Mom and Dad falling asleep on the couch after taking their "medicine," my dad having his "friends" visit for medicine, and my parents not waking up for hours, sometimes days.

I remembered the pain in my stomach that would go away after a day or two without food, and when I'd eaten again, I would feel sick. I remembered feeling cold and curling into a ball on the closet floor to keep warm. It was safe in there, away from the scary friends who visited. I remembered those things very clearly, and I wished I could forget them, but I couldn't.

There were good things I should've remembered, but I just couldn't, like the way she smiled. I knew she did, but I couldn't picture it in my mind anymore. What was the color of her eyes? Were they brown? I didn't know anymore. All the bad things I tried to forget, but I only lost the good memories. Mom, she tried for me. I knew she did, but she was a slave to the drugs and alcohol... The man I called dad, he was just the same. He tried, in his own way, like Mom. He would take me to the park sometimes, and I liked that.

I was numb as I held onto Raff's warm hand. Was what Tobias said before about Raff true? Did he question everything good in his life?

"I can tell you what he is thinking, but I don't think it's right to always pry. Just know you are the thing he cares the most for in this world. Trust... He trusts you and your choice to jump off the cliff. He understands, and he doesn't hold that against you. I know that is something you fear."

Man, the guy was here a day, and he already knew that much. I pressed myself into the guys and took a deep breath.

"My mother, please tell me about her." He was the only person I knew that I could ask this. I'd never thought I would find out more about my mom.

Tobias sat up straighter, and I sat back on the stool. He gave me a gentle smile, and this glow about him happened, which was interesting to watch. He wasn't as bad as I first thought and was starting to grow on me.

"Your mother was strong, one of a kind, like you, Lexi. You look so much like her. She was tough as nails with a wit about her that always kept me on my toes, and she had this throaty chuckle that started deep in her belly. We dated on and off over a century. I loved your mother, I truly did, but she became addicted to my blood." He glanced back at Galen. That was why he didn't want him drinking my blood.

"Addicted? How so?" I asked when he didn't continue

His eyes glazed over a little as he said, "The last time I saw her, she almost drained me. I told her that I could no longer be with her… I'm so sorry, Lexi. If I'd known about you, I would have been in your life. She was the only vampire I had ever been with, and I didn't know she would become addicted to my blood…or that she could have a child."

I nodded. It was a lot to take in.

"Thank you, for coming here." *For catching me.* I couldn't say it out loud in front of everyone. Tobias nodded and reached out to me. I took his hand in mine and smiled.

"I know you have made family bonds here, and I am grateful for that. I honestly don't know where to start being your father. You're now an adult, but I would love to be part of your life, even from the sidelines. I can help you with your powers. Your angel blood allows you to heal and help others. Your powers are not as strong, as you are more human than angel, but if you needed to heal a loved one, you have the power to do so."

Could I do other things? I needed to know. I didn't want to find out after something bad happened. I felt a tingling through my body, and the power in the room changed.

"Healing is your only true power. All others are dull or I don't sense them."

I nodded, that was no surprise at least. Like when I warmed up Galen's arm.

"Wait, what about the tingling feeling I could do to the guys? It felt like ants were crawling on them."

Tobias chuckled. "You are very lucky you do not hold that full power. Have you heard of smiting? All angels hold different powers, some stronger than others, depending on their family line. My father can smite at just a touch, while I cannot. But you do not want to use that power on your mates, even though your power is very weak. That is what you were doing."

"Smiting?" I was a little confused, but Galen wasn't. He'd become ridged, and I watched his face grow concerned.

"The killing touch," Galen muttered.

My heart started to pound as my stomach fell. I felt my skin prickle at the words 'killing touch.' I...I could have killed my mates?

"Just breathe, Lexi. It's okay, nothing happened. Don't worry yourself over what could have been. It wouldn't have happened," Maverick said as he stroked my arm, but I just couldn't breathe. My hands started to shake. I shouldn't have practiced on them. I shouldn't have...

"*You were right to practice, but as I have said, you don't have the full power. I would say it is weaker than mine. But you can heal, and it's your strongest power. Focus on that. Think of how much good you can do. You have a huge heart, Lexi. I can see that through everyone around you. They know you didn't want to cause harm."*

There was a lot of talking around me, but I still was struggling with the fact that if I did hold that power, the same as the healing one, I could have killed Ranger when I first tried it. I had no words... I was dizzy and overwhelmed.

My stomach rumbled, and Ranger chuckled as he ran over to the fridge and opened it. I watched as his huge grin was plastered on his face, but I looked a little uncomfortable.

"Lunch? Pancakes? Donuts?" he asked me. I raised my brow.

"We have donuts?" I asked. I had never seen donuts around here. He shook his head.

"No, but I can go get some. Right now." He closed the door and started moving towards the glass doors. I was surprised at how fast he was leaving to get me donuts. Then I watched him as his eyes darted between Tobias and the door.

I realized what he was doing and tried not to laugh. but poor Ranger. I bet he was trying really hard not to think about anything bad. I couldn't believe Tobias had said he was thinking about sex. Like, that wasn't awkward at all.

This was a distraction…and a good one, because I wasn't thinking about the killing touch thing. I was thinking about food and my cute ass boyfriend trying to escape.

"Pancakes sound like a fantastic idea."

CHAPTER TWELVE

GALEN

I was glad when Tobias left. I knew it was bad to think like that, especially since Lexi had just met her father...who could read our every thought. It was hard being around him and not think about Lexi...or the guys.

I was currently trying to cook a meal for everyone at my house, but I was worried. Not at my terrible cooking skills, which were clearly evident from the smoke pouring from the oven earlier, but about Lexi. She had wanted to watch a movie, but the movie room hadn't been fixed yet. There was broken wood and blood from where some shifters had gotten through. Some of the pack were cleaning it when she'd walked in and seen it, and she'd broken down and cried. It was then that we'd told her about how we had lost some wolves. I'd known we had to tell her, and I didn't want to wait.

Tobias had come in and healed the other shifters that she was so worried about on her way back. Her blood had done nothing to heal them, unfortunately. It just healed vampires. She was upset with herself, but I told her it was the fact that she had tried that everyone was grateful for. I knew I was grateful. If I hadn't had access to her blood, I would have been one of the names read off the list that morning.

I didn't tell her that, nor would I ever. I had given a stern look to Rafferty, asking him not to mention it or how I was a major target to get to Lexi.

"What are you doing to those poor carrots?" I looked to where I was chopping them and back up to Hazel, who had just come up from the basement with Ben. I laughed at the mess. I was using my vampire skills to speed it up, but I had decimated these poor carrots. "What did they ever do to you?" I heard Hazel chuckle beside Ben, her arm wrapped around his as she leaned into him.

"You want to just order in?" Ben asked as I started to clean up the little bits of carrot. I sighed. I'd wanted to make a real meal for everyone, but Ben was right—I should just order in. At least I knew they would like it. It was hard to work out if what I made would even taste nice. Never heard of a chef who couldn't even taste test his food.

"Yeah, I'll grab pizza?" I asked, not sure if Hazel liked it. She nodded as she got a bottle of water from the refrigerator, and I grabbed the menu that Ranger had left here last week. What did they like? Reading off the names, I didn't know most of them. I'd seen pepperoni in the high school cafeteria, which was why I'd asked for that before, and I knew Lexi loved it.

"I can order if you like?" Hazel asked, holding her hand out to the menu. I liked the fact she wasn't afraid of me, knowing what I was, and that she was comfortable here. Ben had found the perfect partner in Hazel. I handed it over and nodded.

"It's probably for the best. Lexi likes pepperoni." She smiled and nodded as she pulled out her cell and started dialing the number.

I was a little nervous having Lexi and the guys over for dinner to officially meet my long-time friend and fellow vampire, Benedict. I hoped they liked him. He was a great guy, and he really pulled through with helping us. I'd known he would without question, as that was the kind of guy he was. Even Hazel, who was human and only new to the supernatural world, had played an important role in helping the injured when they came in.

I heard the front door open and smiled as Lexi walked in without knocking. This was her home as much as it was mine. She was wearing the same outfit as she had been earlier in the day, and her legs in those shorts were long, smooth, and sexy as hell. She flashed me a grin and winked, as if she'd read my mind. I knew I didn't project any thoughts to her, since I hadn't drunk her blood today. After speaking with Tobias yesterday, I was certain that angel blood healed vampirism. I wasn't too sure if Lexi's was strong enough to do that, but I didn't want to find out...just yet. I hadn't stopped thinking about it, to be honest, but that was something for another day.

Raff was right behind her as he entered the house. He was dressed in a white tee, which looked good on him, and his silver hair was in its usual style. Those pale blue eyes scanned the room, stopping when they landed on me. He gave me a nod and shook Ben's hand before he took a seat on the sofa.

The twins were the last through the door, Ranger shoving Maverick out of the way at the last second so he could walk through the door before him. I rolled my eyes.

"Hazel." I peered back over to Lexi as she wrapped her arms around her like they were long-lost friends. I guessed they did have that time to get to know each other. I was glad to see Lexi had a new friend, not that Ada wasn't a perfectly good friend. It was just one that was dating a vampire made me feel better, knowing that as our relationship deepened, she had someone to confide in if she needed.

"Lexi, I'm so glad you're safe," gushed the slightly older blonde, though I wasn't sure how old Hazel was, late twenties I would guess. From the corner of my eye, I could see Ben opening and closing his fists, struggling to keep his fangs in.

"Ben?" I hissed under my breath. I didn't like this. Did he want more of Lexi's blood?

His eye flicked to mine, and he whispered low, so only me and the guys would hear. "Shifters in a small space are setting me off is all. Nothing to be worried about. I won't do anything, just give me a moment to control myself."

Ah, shit. I'd forgotten he was much younger than me and not used to being around shifters all the time. Hell, I still struggled, but had just learned to deal with it. There wasn't much you could do when the love of your life had three wolf shifters as mates. Especially when one of those shifters was also your...well, I wasn't sure yet.

I was attracted to Maverick. I had dated men and women in the past, so this wasn't new to me, not like it was to him. I looked over to where Maverick was standing in the room. He'd noticed Ben and was watching him, being a protective mate, just like Tobias had pointed out earlier.

I wasn't sure if I should go to him or wait for him to come to me. I really wanted to kiss him again, but I didn't know how far he was willing to take this. His eyes flashed to mine, and I saw the glow there. His wolf was close. He shook his head and moved farther into the room towards Lexi.

I had dreams of Lexi and him, them kissing me...me kissing them...me biting them, which was something I couldn't really do with Maverick. His blood wouldn't kill me, but it would make me weak, and that wasn't something I wanted to happen when we were having a good time. I decided to let it happen on Maverick's terms and wait... I had time. We all did.

Pack Russet wasn't ever coming back, and I'd compelled many of the other shifters. Tobias was very strong with his telepathy and had picked out those who'd killed the members from the three packs, and those shifters were eliminated.

I realized the room had gone quiet, and I glanced around. Lexi gave me a puzzled looked, then pointed to the kitchen counter. Oh, yeah. My terrible cooking skills.

"Hazel helped with dinner... She ordered pizza." I felt a little embarrassed and chuckled. I'd told them all I was cooking. The

Lovells made amazing meals, as they were great cooks and were taught from an early age. I had a lot of learning to catch up on before I was even close to their level.

"He murdered the carrots," Hazel supplied, I could see she was holding back a laugh. I shook my head and ran my hand through my hair. Lexi was laughing at me now, which made me chuckle in return as I shrugged.

"I tried, my dear," I said, laying the English accent on thick, and I watched as her eyes lit up and her cheeks heated. She liked that. I'd lost the accent many, many years ago by living all over the world, but if it made her look at me like that, I was going to start using it more.

Ranger walked across the room towards me as he cracked his knuckles and stretched.

"Galen, you need to let a real chef in the kitchen...*old man*."

Oh great. I'd been waiting for someone to mention that, not that he didn't mention it before, more than once. But we'd just found out I was older than Lexi's father, only by a few years, but trust Ranger to pick that to call me. As Ranger strolled into the kitchen, I found a stray piece of carrot and threw it at him. He caught it, looked at it for a moment, then chucked it into his mouth.

"Pizza is going to be awesome," he said, winking at me and turning back to Lexi. He then rushed over to her, picking her up. She squeaked and let out a giggle as he swung her around before putting her back on the same spot and planting a quick kiss on her parted lips. She swayed lightly on the balls of her feet, then playfully slapped him.

"Hey, Ben. You into football?" Ranger asked as he jumped over the back of my sofa and turned the TV on. Ugh... I wanted to hit him over the head for doing that, but then that would show I was an old man. I just really like the sofa and didn't want it ruined because Ranger was too lazy to walk around. Ben walked over to the sofa, his hands still in fists, but he stretched them out and took a seat. He surprised me when he started talking to Ranger and Raff about football.

Maverick made his way over to me and took a seat on the stool. I watched as his eyes darted around the room, like he was waiting for someone to "out" him. He'd already been outed, and I wanted to tell him that ship had sailed.

"You want a beer?" I opened the refrigerator and pulled out a bottle from the six-pack of Blue Moon. I wasn't sure what they liked to drink. I had to admit, I didn't pay attention to the beers they had last time, and well...it sounded like a good beer for a wolf to drink. I smiled to myself. It was what I was thinking when I picked it, though.

"Sure," he said, and I could see the start of a smile. "That would be nice." I placed it in front of him and looked for a bottle opener that I never thought of needing so chances were... But Maverick had already taken the cap off and was drinking the beer. I watched as his Adam's apple bobbed, and my hand wanted to reach out and touch the smooth skin of his throat. He put the bottle down in front of him and nodded at me.

"Not bad," he said, then licked his lower lip as he looked at me. His lips were wet and so kissable, and I felt myself reacting strongly to that, heating my cold body from within. I wanted to lick that beer from his lips, to drink his kiss.

That was it, I lost control.

I needed him.

CHAPTER THIRTEEN

LEXI

There was a clang of glass, and Hazel and I turned to the kitchen. My mouth dropped open at the sight. Holy fuck. Galen had his hand fisted in Maverick's dark tee, and he had pulled him off the stool and over the kitchen counter. Maverick held his hands on the counter, his face only inches from Galen's. What the hell happened? They just stared at each other, and I could see them breathing deeply. It lasted a heartbeat, and then Galen kissed him.

My hand went to my chest as my heart swelled with happiness. I was beaming. Oh hell yeah, this was happening. Hazel bumped my shoulder. I didn't want to look away, but I pried my eyes from my two mates and peered over to her. She mouthed "you lucky bitch," and I laughed as she wiggled her brows at me. I nodded and looked back to see Maverick had his hand in Galen's dark curls, and Galen's hand was now at the nape of Maverick's neck. It was as if they were both fighting for dominance...and I couldn't look away. My body thrummed and came to life, wanting to join but happy to watch just as much.

Maverick tugged on Galen's hair, tilting his head farther to the left. He tugged again, and Galen dropped his hand from Maverick's neck and placed it on the countertop. Dang, that was hot... I couldn't look away as Maverick devoured Galen's mouth.

A sharp knock at the door had the room's vibe shifting. Ranger had jumped up, and I looked over to the door. He glanced back at me and grinned, tilting his head to the now broken up make-out session and winking. I guessed I wasn't the only one watching and... Wait. Ugh, he could smell my arousal. I could see by the way Maverick rearranged his junk that he was very happy with that kiss. Galen too.

"Pizza is here," a voice called from just outside the door. It was Saint, and he came in holding ten boxes of pizza. I glanced to Hazel, and she smiled and shrugged.

"I was told shifters eat a lot, but I wasn't sure what a lot meant so I wanted to make sure we had enough. There's a pepperoni for you in there, Lexi." She skipped over and helped the boys, while Galen grabbed some plates, the smell of pizza wafting through the small house. There were a lot of grown men in here now with Saint as well.

I bounced over to Galen, and he wrapped his hands around me, grabbing my ass and pulling me into his very hard cock.

"I would ask if you were happy to see me, but I think that was all Maverick's doing." I heard a coughing sound and laughed. Looking back over to the guys, Maverick had a deep pink blush on his cheeks. *Oh yeah, you did this.*

Saint looked from Maverick to Galen and started backing up. He had a huge grin and winked at me.

"I'll take that as my cue to leave. Have a great night." When Maverick peered back at him, Saint give him two thumbs up. He was a good friend. Yeah, I liked him...now. He was one of those guys who had to grow on you. I'd probably still call him out for his shit, but he could ask Ada out if he wanted. I wouldn't rip his balls off if he did. I didn't think he would hurt her, and I knew he liked her...at least enough to get jealous. Well, now that she had her eyes set on Huxley Moore, Saint was going to be in for a challenge.

. . .

It was nice getting to really meet Galen's friend Ben. He was nice, and everyone got along. Raff was even talking to Ben freely, and he was relaxed enough that he wasn't shy or holding back. I guessed they both lived in Russet, so they had things in common, and were talking about people who lived there.

Hazel and I spent most of the time together, chatting about movies and girl stuff. We knew they could hear us, but what were you going to do? I had learned that nothing I said was private anymore and that I had to kick them all out of the house when I wanted to do super-secret girl talk. But this wasn't the time, I needed that with Ada when I saw her. She texted to say she would be here today, but then something came up. I hoped she wasn't avoiding me.

My arms were on the kitchen counter and I laid my head on them. I needed this night, after seeing the movie room and learning about the shifters who died...trying to protect me.

I took a deep breath. I needed to move forward. That was what everyone told me, and I was going to do that. I'd told Alaric I would go back to school next week, but Galen suggested I just apply to college with Ada and graduate. That didn't go over well with Alaric. He'd said that he would pay for college, but it would all be online. The thing was, most of it wasn't online, and the stuff that was, I wasn't interested in doing. I wanted the real deal and the experience, not this home school crap.

Ada needed to get into nursing school, she just had to. She was a natural. I was still trying to decide what I wanted to do, but I was also determined to get Alaric to speak to the bear shifters. That was what I was told by Lyell when he was cleaning. He'd surprised me by helping and actually apologizing to me. I'd accepted because I was trying to move forward.

Plus, okay, he was nice to me when we first got here. He just was a little...odd, but in his own way. It wasn't a bad thing. He just maybe didn't like having the same thing thrown back at him, like the whole "test it out on Lexi" thing with Galen's compelling experiment in

Alaric's office. I chuckled to myself... Lyell chasing his tail was so funny.

I found out that Lyell was studying business. Apparently, Pack Kiba had a lot of businesses around the world, and that was where the bulk of their money came from. It trickled down into the whole pack, not just for the alpha and the others in charge. That was where the money had come from when Jack took me out shopping that first day here. I liked that everyone in the pack was taken care of.

I yawned on the sofa. I was exhausted now that Ben and Hazel had gone home and it was just us. This felt so perfect, something we would have been doing before, and I was glad to have this little bit of normality.

We were watching old football re-runs on the TV. I had zero interest, which wasn't helping me keep my eyes open, and they felt like sandpaper.

"Bed?" I asked Maverick as he looked up at me from my lap. He was half asleep with his head lying in my lap. I'd been stroking his hair for a while now. It was so soft.

"Mmm..." he murmured as he shuffled off me and stood, holding his hand out for me to help me up. I took it, and he pulled me to standing, then I wrapped my arms around him and breathed him in. I let go as Galen stood, and Maverick moved away towards the bedroom.

Galen hugged me to his chest, and I felt him stroking my hair down my back, which was soothing.

"Been a long day," I mumbled. Galen grabbed my hand, and we walked into the darkened bedroom. It had to be like two in the morning. I was amazed I'd made it that long. He kicked the door closed on Raff and Ranger, and I felt his hands reach for me. He was warm, since he'd been drinking whisky with Ben most of the night.

He took my chin in his hand and slowly pressed his lips to mine, his kiss sweet.

"Sorry, I just... I've been wanting to kiss you all night." I smiled into the dark, my eyes still trying to focus on him. I kissed him and scruffed up his hair.

"Why would you be saying sorry? I want you to kiss me, all the time. I don't care who's watching. I don't care how old you are, what you eat, or who you pray to. You're mine, and I accept you and love you, just the way you are. Sweaters on hot days and all." I felt his chest rumble at the last words. Yeah...

"Maybe I should call you Mr. Hottie?" I teased when he didn't say anything.

"You can call me anything you want...and I will call you *mine*."

And from the dark behind me, I could hear Maverick shuffle on the bed... "Ours, Galen. *Ours*."

I swayed on my feet before moving to the bed. I needed this, even though I'd slept so long yesterday. Sleep was good.

"Lexi, can I take you on a date tomorrow?" Maverick asked as he wrapped his arms around me.

"Mmm...yes."

CHAPTER FOURTEEN

LEXI

Ranger had kissed me as soon as he got home from school, then marked me. I practically had to shove him in the bathroom. He was all sweaty and gross, and he needed a shower. I smoothed the wrinkles in my top. It wasn't fancy, but it was nicer than a tank.

I chuckled to myself when I heard the knock at the front door. Maverick was taking this date so seriously and formal by knocking. I'd told him I didn't have anything really nice to wear, but he just kissed me and said that I would look good in his tee and pulled it over his head in one move.

My lady parts had tingled at the sight. Fuck, I had seen that in movies and stuff, but when he did it, I was almost a panting hot mess. I couldn't let him see that, not that he couldn't already tell I was worked up, so he left me to do my hair and makeup, returning to his room back in the mansion to get changed. I didn't use his tee, but I may have brought it to my nose a few times just to smell that deep woody scent of pine and male.

Raff had gone for a run with a few of the other Kiba boys, so I only saw him for a few moments. He kissed me briefly, and I laughed when he handed me his clothes. I watched as he ran naked across the Lovells' lawn. His ass was fine, oh so fine. He had really opened up and come out of his shell in the last few days. It was great to see this carefree side to him, and not the hurt, wounded one he had when we first met.

Galen had brought my things over earlier before he left. Not that I had a lot, but it was like he moved me in without asking. Ah...well, he didn't need to ask. I would've said yes. I preferred it here. At least I had some privacy, and it was nice for all of us to be together.

I skipped over to the door when there was a knock again, feeling a little bit giddy. A date was normal. We were leaving shit in the past and moving forward, and I was glad. I didn't like to dwell too much on things, and my mind had been messed up enough. I was done and ready for this.

I opened the door, a huge grin on my face, and my heart flipped when I saw it wasn't Maverick but Ada. I'd been dying to see her all day. She never messaged me back to say if she was coming over, and I'd been worried. A lump formed in my throat as she smiled at me, and I reached out and pulled her in for a huge hug as I choked out a sob. Her arms wrapped around me, and I almost crumbled into a sobbing mess. My mascara was going to run so bad.

"Oh my god, Ada. I missed you. I'm so, so, so sorry. Fuck, that doesn't even cut it. I just left you standing there. I've felt like such shit about it... I was starting to think you hated me." And that wasn't a lie. I'd been starting to think she'd really decided it would be better to not be my friend, and I wouldn't have blamed her.

"Oh my gosh, Lexi, never! You're my best friend. I needed to see you in person after the day I had, so I didn't text. I just came over straight from school."

She had returned to school today, whereas the guys... Well, they were going to be taking it in turns. On Alaric's orders, one got to stay with me here, which was stupid. I was fine, and I didn't need them to babysit me. Plus, I really wanted to go back to school. I hated just being here all day, and this was just one day. I couldn't imagine being here all the time. I didn't want to get behind in my studies, and I didn't want Galen messing with my scores so I passed. I wanted to earn them.

They were still doing patrols here in Kiba, so I felt safe. It was Maverick's turn first to be my knight in shining armor, and as much as Ranger had been upset with that, he'd grumpily agreed. But it was also Wednesday, middle of the week. I'd wanted Galen to stay with me, but he was in Bardoul. They wanted to test his blood, my blood, and Tobias' to see if what they suspected was true—that my mom was cured of her vampirism by angel blood. He'd told me this morning before he left. He'd said he would stay here with me, but I could tell he wanted to know sooner. Plus, I was so curious to find out if that was what had happened that I basically pushed him out the door.

Tobias had stopped by as well to tell me he was waiting on this warlock guy to come meet me and help with my "smell" issue. It sounded so wrong when he said it like that, but I was excited to meet a real warlock. I hoped he would come soon. Did he like...do magic tricks? Could he teleport? Go invisible...

"Let's go into Port Willow and go shopping, have some dinner, maybe at the diner there. You know, just like a girls' night?" Ada asked, and she almost sounded as if she was pleading with me. It snapped me out of my runaway thoughts of warlocks. She was eyeing Maverick from over her shoulder. He had come back and was now standing close by, which meant he would have heard everything. My eyes glanced to Maverick. I'd promised him a date, and I wanted it so bad. But...Ada needed me, and to be honest, I needed her too. Why was this so hard?

"I would love to...but—" I started to say, but was cut off by Maverick.

"We were going to do the same thing together, but if it's all right, can I tag along? I can drive you girls...maybe hold your bags?" I arched a brow at Maverick because...well, he was Maverick and he wanted to hold our bags?

Ada gave a shy smile and said, "Well, I was hoping for a girls only night, but I guess you can talk boys with us."

I laughed as he shook his head and put his hands up, backing away. I was kinda glad she was okay with this, because I wouldn't be able to go with just Ada anyway. No way would the guys let me out of their sight.

"No boy talk from me, I'll block that out. I don't wanna know what girls talk about when they're together."

"Okay...I'll just grab my bag." I ran back inside Galen's house... well, our house. We were all living in it at the moment. He'd told me he would get us a bigger bed, because it was a little tight. It was a cute house, but with four fully grown men and me...it was a little crowded.

I grabbed my wallet and put it in my bag, not that I had much money to my name, but Galen had given me his credit card before he left and told me to use it on anything. I had just rolled my eyes at him when he gave it to me, but yeah...I had ideas on things I wanted to buy.

Ranger chose that moment to walk out of the bathroom, a towel slung low around his waist. His skin was still glistening from the water, like he didn't even bother to dry himself. Fuck, why did he look like he just walked out of some magazine? He really should look into modelling, but then other girls would see him... No, it was best if he just stayed locked up in the house and looked like that for me.

"Come here..." He ran his palm down his chest slowly, and I watched as it slid over the hard plains of his abs... I swallowed. When his fingertips reached the towel, he hooked his thumb inside and tugged it a little lower, but he stopped when he heard Ada's voice outside. My eyes quickly flashed back to his face. Dang... My heart was racing, and I wanted to go to him, strip him naked, and have my wicked way with him... When his nostrils flared, I knew he could tell that too. I took a step back and shook my head.

"No, nope. I'm going out with Maverick and Ada." He cocked his head and swung his hips at me. Ugh... "I'll be back for all of," I waved my hand up and down at his body, "this." He chuckled loudly.

"I should be offended that you're only coming back for this," he said, waving his hand over his chest, and I rolled my eyes but couldn't help the smile that spread across my face. "But I know you only want me for my...personality." He winked at me as he stalked forward, my insides screaming to leave before I got distracted.

His index finger traced a line up from my wrist, across my collarbone, and down the middle of my chest, pulling on my top. I stumbled slightly, my hands reaching out to stop myself from falling, and they landed on his warm, wet, bare chest. I watched his eyes quickly glance down at my cleavage, and the red bra I was wearing showed just how affected I was by his *personality*. My nipples were tight and aching , and it felt like forever since he'd touched me.

"Hello, girls. Miss me?" he said with a chuckle as he let go of my top and it snapped back. I playfully slapped his chest and cursed at him for messing with me.

I poked my tongue out as I turned on my heel, leaving Ranger behind laughing. I didn't turn back when he started laughing harder at how worked up I now was.

"Fucker," I muttered as I walked out of the house. Ada and Maverick turned to me, a surprised look on Ada's face. Maverick cocked his head and grinned.

"You loved it," Ranger called out, and I slammed the door behind me.

"Trouble in paradise?" Ada asked, but I just laughed and took her arm in mine. I noticed she kept looking to the front gate that lead into the Lovell's place.

I glanced over and saw Saint and Elijah, who were on duty there today, were watching us.

"I don't think I'm the one with troubles," I said, and Ada tugged on my arm, shushing me under her breath as we strode towards the Range Rover that was parked out the front. I couldn't wait to ask her what the hell happened to have her practically running away from Saint. He would've had to open the gate to let her drive in here. Maybe he said something. I thought it was best to leave it for when we were on the road before I asked her and he overheard, in case I now had to hurt him.

"Let's go, I'm hungry." Both Ada and Maverick laughed. I stopped and pointed between them both with my finger.

"I am not always hungry. Just now...I am. I had breakfast hours ago, skipped lunch, and I really want a chocolate chip muffin." Oh, a warm muffin, where the chocolate chips were soft and gooey and a hot chocolate with marshmallows... My stomach let out an audible growl, and they started laughing again. But I loved it, even though I didn't admit it. This moment was pure, how teenagers were supposed to be. My best friend and my boyfriend, hanging out like regular people do.

Going out shopping, food and girl talk...with a guy.

That wasn't going to be awkward at all.

CHAPTER FIFTEEN

LEXI

Oh wow, Ada had a lot to say about Saint, without saying anything about Saint. I was struggling to keep up with her code names, since she kept changing them, but I kinda got the gist. I was pretty sure Maverick clued in to who she was talking about, but he didn't say anything if he did. He actually just drove and kept his mouth shut, which was probably the safest thing to do.

We were at a café, but the hot chocolate tasted terrible. The muffin, on the other hand, was good, and I kept eating while listening to Ada as best as I could. She talked really fast.

"Then I was at my locker getting my books, and *H* came up. He like fully came up to me and said hi...and I said hi. Then he gives me his number." I saw Maverick rub the back of his head and the stupid grin on his face. When his eyes drifted to mine, I smiled. Yeah, this was girl talk. *I was learning this with you too, buddy.* Ada took a deep breath, then dove back in.

"I was so excited after. Like, you know, saving *H* was like epic, and yeah, you did most of the saving..." Yep, H was Huxley. She wasn't good at this whole code name thing, but I loved it. She made me happy. "But then I go to my car, and *Ass* is standing right there. I wasn't sure what he wanted, but like, after the whole caveman thing and all, I thought maybe he was going to say sorry or like, ask me out. He tells me to give him my phone. Then I got butterflies, like this is it. Finally, after so long of having this crush, he sees me...like, really sees me, Lexi! So I try and act all cool, like I'm not just dying of happiness inside, and I give it to him. He types something and then hands it back and just leaves... Yeah, he just walks away. Doesn't say anything at all."

Maverick had moved closer, like he was now interested to hear what *Ass* did. To be called Ass already, he'd obviously done something bad. Ada took a slip of her coffee and didn't speak for all of ten seconds, and as it turned out, that was too long for Maverick.

"What did *Ass* do?" She squeaked and looked over to him, her eyes wide. I thought she forgot he was even here, since he'd been quiet for so long. She put her coffee cup down and just stared at him for a moment. Shit, she figured out he knew *Ass* was clearly his best friend, Saint.

"Well, I get in my car. I get excited, but like, I didn't want to text him too fast. But then I didn't want *H* to think I didn't want to text him at all. Like, in case he just saw me with Sai—*Ass*. So I open up my contacts on my phone and scroll to Huxley—I mean, I scrolled to *H* and he isn't there. The whole contact is wiped from my phone.

"So I look to see if *Ass* put his number in, and no, he hasn't. He was just being a caveman and trying to sabotage my possible future of a white picket fence and two point five kids, all because he has some kind of grudge against *H*. And don't get me started on Puppy Dog Eyes. Ugh...he's been following me around school all day, and we share no classes. He isn't even a senior."

Ada took a deep breath, drank the rest of her coffee, then huffed out a strange angry sound. Ugh...what was wrong with guys?

I watched Maverick sit back and take out his phone. I could take a pretty good guess at who he was texting.

"Is it because you're with Pack Kiba, Lexi? And like, 'cause I know…you know. Am I supposed to not like, date people from other packs? Because I don't live in Kiba, and I know that rule applies if you live in the town. But to be honest, the whole 'you can't date her because she is from Kiba' is bullshit. What if your soulmate lived in Rawlins? That's some bullshit right there, to deny her the chance at love because she happens to live in Kiba."

I sat back and watched Maverick's facial expression change from one of humor to horror. His eyes widened as he looked to me, like I would bail him out. I didn't know all the rules here, and Ada had made a good point.

He didn't know what to say, or maybe he was holding back from saying the wrong thing. I just smiled and took another bite of my muffin. Because yeah, I was pissed off for Ada. I was going to have a word with *Ass* when I got home because that was not how you treated my friend. But also, Ada was right—she didn't live in Kiba, so this bullshit rule didn't apply to her. Her eyes looked to his cell.

"Who are you texting?" she asked as she moved forward and reached out to his cell. He had fast reflexes and pressed his phone to his chest before she could grab it. Yep, caught out, buddy. The guilty look on his face made me shake my head. Ada was seeing red. Oh fuck.

"Maverick, why would Saint be such an *ass* to Ada? You're his friend. We had fun in the pool all together and he seemed fine then, happy even. Why is he being all caveman on poor Ada here? If he's interested, he should just say so. But that's so not cool what he did by deleting a number from her phone."

He shoved his phone in his pocket and quickly looked around the café before he stood, nervously running his hand down his shorts and looking anywhere but at us. He turned in a circle and pointed to the front door.

"I need to check the perimeter." And that was all he said before he practically ran from our table. Wow… we'd found his weakness—girl talk. I rolled my eyes.

"Okay, he knows something. You have to get it out of him," Ada said as she played with her empty coffee cup. I felt so bad for her. She didn't deserve boys being assholes.

"Trust me, I'll get it out of Saint. He's back on my shit list." She smiled at me, but it didn't reach her eyes. I needed to cheer her up.

"I have Galen's credit card. Wanna go buy clothes and shoes?" That was right, right? Girls go shoe shopping all the time in movies. God I wished I had more of a clue when it came to this. I wanted happy Ada back, the one who was getting all dressed up just to check on Huxley. That Ada was so happy and crushing so hard. Maybe if I could get Huxley's number back for her, then she could text him and he wouldn't think she was brushing him off.

"Hell yeah, thank you, Mr. Donovani. Let's get you a real swimsuit too."

Yes, the smile was back, and Ada had that look on her face, the one she had when she tried to make me try on half her wardrobe.

CHAPTER SIXTEEN

RANGER

"**A**re you sure this isn't like, *stalking*?" Noah whispered to me as we walked through Walmart looking for the girls. I paused. Huh, I'd never thought of it as stalking. Was it stalking if it was your own girlfriend? Well, maybe if she didn't invite you, then yes... Nah she would love this surprise. She loved me, she'd told me so. Plus, I'd been a little freaked out that I wasn't with her. Like, my wolf knew that Mav could protect her and that there was enough of Pack Kiba here—a few of the guys even worked here—but I needed to see her for myself.

Plus, I had this girl talk stuff down. I'd been around the girls at school more than Maverick. He'd been all messed up when he called and told us that girl talk was scary and he never wanted to be invited again. I'd never heard him so freaked out, and it made me laugh when he said that the girls ganged up on him and he didn't know what to do.

I told Raff, and he laughed too. Then Mav told me he was waiting outside for them to shop alone, and that set my wolf into overdrive. I wanted him to be watching them with his eyes. So when he asked if I was interested in having the rest of tonight with Lex, he didn't even need to finish his sentence before I screamed, "Hell yeah!" I wanted that, but I also wanted to help Noah with Ada. So I called him up to get ready and picked him up on my way, thinking it would be a good idea to start straight away. You could call me Mr. Cupid, because I would have them in love with the big happily ever after in no time.

"Ranger?" I looked to Noah. His face was puzzled as his eyes darted to where we knew the girls were, then back to me. Oh...the stalker thing.

"No, no, it's not stalking if we're going...shopping." I grabbed a tee off a rack and kept on walking, following my nose to find my sexy girl. Noah looked creeped out—okay, scratch that. He looked like the creep that creeped others out. The way he was hunched over, watching everyone. It wasn't like he was small. He was as big as me, if not bigger. You could see him from a mile away.

"Stop with the face and just grab something. Quick, there they are." I could see Lex wearing those sexy shorts she was in earlier, and my wolf growled softly at the sight, my cock reacting too. She was laughing at something Ada said, then her face fell when she saw me and the scary angry Lex face appeared, and I wanted to hide. Fuck. Okay, I wasn't expecting that face. Mav was right—this was not happy shopping girls.

She cocked her hip, her hand going to it, and her brows were raised high. I started to shuffle my feet towards her as I waved, giving her a huge cheesy grin and hoping it would distract her enough that she wouldn't ask why we were here. I distracted her earlier with my... personality. I was sure this would—

"Stalker much?" she deadpanned. Okay, maybe Noah was right, which was surprising for a guy who had never been with a girl. He seemed to know more than I did about this. I stopped suddenly and put my hands up in defense, my heart pounding. I could smell her, and she really wasn't happy.

"No, we were just shopping, and I could smell you from...ah..." Oh, hell. Back the fuck up, *retreat*. I took a step backwards. That was obviously the wrong thing to say as well. From the look on her face, I was not in her happy books. Shit. "Ah...Noah needed to come shopping to get..." I turned to him and looked at what he had. My brows raised up when I saw he was holding a fluffy pink stuffed pig, then I glared at him. What the fuck, dude? I wanted to scream at him. Like, this now looked dodgy as fuck. Why the hell did he grab that?

"You came, to buy...a toy pig?" Ada asked, her brows arched high. She knew... Oh yeah, we fucked up—no, Noah fucked up. If he'd picked something else, it could've been believable. I growled lowly, just for him to hear. If he put me back in the bad books with Lexi, I was gonna hurt him when I got back. I needed to get out of this and not get caught.

"Well, I was getting a tee, and Noah needed some things...for his mom, right?" I looked over to him and nudged his arm when he didn't say anything.

"Yeah, this is for my mom. She likes pigs." They both gave each other a look. I was so out of my element here. I'd had never had a problem with girls, since they usually chased after me. So with Lexi, being the opposite to all other girls, I had no idea what I was doing or how to make her smile and be happy to see me. Was this a believable story, or did we just fuck up?

"Maverick called you, didn't he?" I looked around, my hand going to my chest in mock hurt. I'd promised him I wouldn't tell her about his freak out.

"Pft, no..." Her eyes narrowed on me. "Yes," I squeaked out. Oh fuck, I could see what Maverick was saying. Girls were scary. Lexi freaked me out on a daily basis, more so for the fact that I still couldn't believe she'd picked me as a mate, but right now...I was not her favorite person.

They shook their heads at us and gave each other strange looks. They didn't say anything to each other as they turned away from us and kept on shopping as if we weren't there.

Noah and I stood frozen for a whole minute and watched them walking away and picking up items before we glanced at each other.

He shrugged. I had no idea what was going on or what just happened. Lexi was my first real girlfriend, *like ever*. Did we follow them? Should I run away now and get ready for damage control? Would Galen have been better?

"Are you coming, Stalker? Puppy Dog Eyes?" Lex called out as they disappeared around a corner.

"Puppy Dog Eyes?" Noah asked me. He had this funny look on his face, like he didn't get it, and neither did I—Oh hell, I could see it on his face. He was Puppy Dog Eyes. I chuckled. Oh shit, that made me Stalker.

"Yeah, that would be you, *Puppy Dog*. Ugh, why the fuck did you pick that up?" I pointed to the pink pig. He shrugged, those big blue eyes all sad looking. Oh, Noah man. I didn't think Puppy Dog Eyes was a good nickname, and I was starting to suspect it was going to be much harder than I'd thought to get Ada to give Noah a chance. I probably had a better chance at setting Elijah up with her.

"I panicked, okay? I didn't look, I just grabbed when you told me to. I was just so nervous to see her again, and with you helping me, I just... I just want her to like me so bad."

I felt terrible for the guy. I'd told him I could get him and Ada together, but I thought I overestimated my work here. I took a deep breath and stood tall, then tapped his chest with the back of my hand. "Come on, big guy, not all is lost. Let's go get your girl."

That had his smile returning a little. I nodded at him, and his big smile returned. But man, the puppy dog eyes were still there. I wondered if I'd ever looked at Lex like that.

Well, if I did, it worked for me. Plus, they'd asked us to come with them. This was good—Ada would have to fall for that face. No way she could say no to that big happy grin. We might've been back in the game here with a winning chance. I'd take my odds on that.

"Hey, Lex, wait up. We're coming."

CHAPTER SEVENTEEN

LEXI

Ranger drove us back home. It was very quiet in the car, and I was a little annoyed at Maverick for just ditching us and not saying goodbye. Okay, I got it. Ada could be a little full on, but there were some valid questions there that needed answers. I didn't think Maverick was the type to run away. I looked out the car window and watched as the houses on Kiba court slowly went by. We stopped, and I turned to Ranger, who was looking over to Noah in the front seat.

I'd wanted to ride with Ada in the back. Plus, she'd squeezed my hand when Ranger offered me the front seat, and I wasn't going to leave her in the back without me.

"Thanks for the lift," Noah said to Ranger. He then turned to Ada, his eyes hovering on her for a moment before his face faltered a little. Then his eyes were on me, and I smiled and nodded. He gave me a flicker of a smile, but man... Puppy Dog Eyes was so in love with Ada, and she was the only one who didn't see it. Well, she might've, but she had no interest in him, or so she said. But it wasn't my place to meddle, and Ada came first to me.

The car door clicked shut, and Ranger let out a frustrated sound as he watched Noah run towards his house. It was a huge house and only a couple of houses from the Lovells.

Ada didn't speak at all, and when I turned to her, she was looking down at her phone. Ranger didn't move the car, so I had a quick look around. I saw some people outside their house across the street, something I'd never really noticed before. They were watching us, smiling, and some were waving.

When a familiar looking man came close to the car and waved to me, I didn't know what to do. I sat back farther in my seat. Ranger's arm appeared in front as he waved back.

"That's Nolan, one of Noah's fathers," he said. I nodded and gave a small smile and waved back to Nolan. His grin was huge, and he looked happy to see us. I still felt awkward about the whole Callum thing, and I didn't think I would get over it anytime soon. But I was glad he wasn't upset with me. I really was lucky with that family.

When we finally got to the gate of the Lovells, Jett and Mekhi came into view, almost in a creepy way. They just appeared out of nowhere. Ada was watching them too, and we were lucky it wasn't Saint because she had a strong grip on her iPhone. She might have launched it at him, not that it would've hurt him, much, but it sure would've made her feel better. I knew it would make me feel better, and I wasn't the one who he'd messed with.

Ugh... With the guys swapping shifts, it would make finding Saint and kicking him in the nuts harder. He might've already known what was going to happen and wouldn't show his face for a while. Hell, he was probably with Maverick.

The guys didn't open the gate. Jett rested his arms on the gate and leaned back, looking all...well, hot. Jett looked so much like his brothers, and they were all sexy, like *how are you not already a model* hot. Ranger growled as he rolled his window down, and I just dropped my head back against the headrest. Not this again.

"Oi, open the gate, fucker. You know it's us," he called, and Jett pushed himself from the gate and slowly strode over, a funny grin on his face. I wanted to laugh, because this was doing exactly what he wanted it to—infuriating Ranger. To be honest, it was a little funny.

"Yeah, we know it's you. Just gotta be careful is all. Well, well, well...trying to sneak a cupcake in, are we?" I rolled my eyes. *Jett*. He could see my expression at that, and it just made him smile harder.

"Jett, you're never getting baked goods from me *ever* again," I shouted, and Jett held his hand to his chest, mock dying as I rolled my eyes again. What was with these brothers? They were so alike, pushing each other's buttons all the time.

I couldn't stop the grin on my face. He was so much worse than Ranger. How did I think Ranger was the cheeky brother? Jett won that title hands down. Mekhi just shook his head and grabbed Jett's shoulder, jerking him back from the car.

"Sorry, Lexi. You know how dumbasses lose more brain cells around their own kind," Mekhi said, and Ada started to giggle, while I did too. I nodded as the brothers tried to defend themselves.

"Can you tell me where Saint is?" I asked and heard Ada as she sucked in a breath.

"Home, I believe. Did you want me to go get him?" Mekhi asked. I could see Ada shifting in her seat and turned to her. She was shaking her head and mouthing 'no' to me. I turned back to Mekhi and gave a huge grin.

"Oh yes, please. Tell him I really want to see him. Right now, at Galen's," I said in a sickly-sweet voice. Jett's brows went up as he whistled lowly. Mekhi just shook his head and laughed as he backed away from the car. Jett gave me two thumbs up as Ranger closed his window, then he turned and looked at me.

"Why do you want to see Saint, Lex?" he asked, driving me crazy with his jealousy.

"To give him a cupcake," I snapped back.

Ranger's eyes glowed as he growled low. Oh, I'd pushed him a little too far with that one. Jett and Mekhi opened the gates, and the car almost screamed through to Galen's. When the car stopped, Ada hugged me quickly and, without a word, jumped out. Before I could even get out, she was in her own car and driving away. I didn't even get a chance to even really tell her thank you for today, that I'd had a great time and after the past week, it felt nice, normal... That this was really needed, not just for me, but for everyone.

I smiled. I'd really had a great time. I didn't wait for Ranger as I walked into Galen's house. I could smell popcorn, but no one was here. I walked into the kitchen and saw a huge bowl of popcorn, just waiting there. Yummy. I popped one in my mouth. It was still warm-ish.

"Hello?" I called out...but there was no reply. Where was everyone?

The door to the house slammed shut, the whole house groaning at the force of it. I spun around and watched Ranger drop my shopping bags on the floor. His eyes narrowed on me, a hint of the wolf peeking out and making me a little nervous now we were alone. I let out a little squeak. Okay, I'd admit I might've pushed him a little too far with the cupcake thing, but the way his lip pulled up on the side as a sly smile appeared on his face made him look devilish. Okay, it was totally worth it for that look. He was so badass.

Ranger's eyes flashed between the green I knew and the glow that happened before his shift as he slowly stalked his way over to me. Prowling, his wolf was close to the surface and looking at its prey. Oh, fuck... My body was thrumming, and everything felt heightened, as if all the air was sucked out of the room.

I didn't speak, I didn't move. I hadn't seen him like...this. He was normally playful and sweet...in his own way.

But now he looked deadly. He looked ready to possess me...and my body.

"I'm very angry with you, Lex," he purred. He was so close to me now. He took another slow calculated step towards me, and couldn't stop myself, I took two steps back. He cocked his head as a smirk appeared on his face, then disappeared just as fast.

"What's the matter, Lex? Wolf got your tongue?"

I couldn't believe he was so...so alpha. Just like Maverick was alpha when he wanted to be, Ranger could turn it on as well. I knew he wouldn't hurt me, that wasn't in his nature, but this Ranger, he was oozing in power. The way he stalked me, the way he looked at me like he was going to possess me, body and soul... I wanted him like this. I didn't know my usually playful Ranger could be so dominant.

"You want me to spank it out of you? If you keep pushing me, I will."

Was that a threat? My body didn't think it was... My fingers tingled, wanting to touch him. His hand hovered near my face, and I wanted to lean into it. I wanted him to take me. But I was also stubborn, and I wanted to see how far he would go with this. Was this all an act? All the other times, he'd wanted to touch me, never wanting me to touch him, claiming the pleasure was all mine.

I realized in that moment that was why he held back with me. All those times, it was all about me. It was because he didn't want to scare me with his alpha side.

He growled, and it was so deep, it went straight to my core.

Oh god, I was so wet just from the way he was looking at me. Did I want him to spank me? No? Yes? I had no idea. He licked his lips slowly as he stepped even closer, our bodies only an inch apart, my chest rising and falling quickly with my racing pulse.

His face lowered to mine, our warm breath mingling in the air between us. His nose ran up my throat, and he licked the rim of my earlobe. I let out a shuddering breath.

"Ranger," I whispered. My hands found his hard chest through his tee, and I clung to it desperately, wanting more, wanting it all. His skin was so taut over all those muscles as I ran my hands down to the waistband of his shorts, and he let out a small growl as my fingers curled under the elastic and pushed them lower.

His hand wrapped around the back of my neck as he took my mouth deeply, our tongues meeting in a wild fight so possessive, so raw, my body shivered from his touch. I moaned and held on to anything I could grab just to keep myself upright. Fuck... Everything in my brain left as my need for climax took over.

This was what I needed right now. I needed him to take charge and give me the pleasure I so desperately wanted.

He broke our kiss, and I was breathless, my nipples aching as I rubbed myself against his hard cock.

"Take me," I begged. He growled again, and I felt it through my whole body. The corner of his mouth curved up, and heat flared all over my body.

"Big bad wolf," I taunted him, wanting to see what he would do. I didn't want this to stop. I wanted it.

His eyes found mine, and I could see the hint of a smile in them as he wrapped his hand in my hair and tugged a little roughly to tilt my head back, exposing my throat to him. I gasped slightly as my hands grabbed onto his ass to press him harder to me. Oh, that got his attention. I saw the glow that time that said the alpha was here to play.

"I'm too worked up, Lex. I can't take you...gently." He ran his fingers down over my lips and throat. "Sweet. Oh, so sweet, Lex. I want to do that with you, take my time...bring you pleasure over and over until you're a withering mess beneath me. But right now...I can't. I'm too worked up... I want to punish your ass with my palm, stop you from giving away *my* cupcakes."

His palm came down hard on my ass, and I felt the smarting of it through my jean shorts. Need throbbed in my core as I clamped my thighs together to chase the feeling. Maybe I did like to be spanked. His hand came up, grabbed the hem of my top, and pushed it down, exposing the red bra my nipples so desperately wanted to break free from. His warm palm ran over the top of my breasts, and I pressed in closer to him.

"I do *not* share with anyone but my packmates. Stop pushing me, Lex." I nodded as best I could. It wasn't a question, but a statement. All the cupcakes were his, there were no more for anyone else. If this was what I got in return, I'd bake for him every day.

With one hand wrapped in my hair, the other came up the

column of my neck. His thumb pressed against my bottom lip, and I parted my lips.

"I want to eat your pussy until you scream my name, then I'll eat it again. I want to push your body over and over until you're begging me to stop, but I won't. But first, I need to be inside you. I need to mark you and let everyone know that Lexi Turner is *mine*."

I swear I orgasmed just from that alone. I licked his thumb, his eyes flaring slightly as he pressed it farther into my mouth. I swirled my tongue around it, and I could feel his body tense. *Fuck*. Oh, he likes to talk the talk, but would he really do these things, or did he just have a way with words?

"King of dirty talk, put your money where your mouth is." I raised my brow, ready for anything.

That growl deepened as he lifted me off my feet and spun me. I squeaked as he threw me over his shoulder and slapped my ass...*hard*.

I was glad it was just us in the house. I'd wanted this one-on-one time with Ranger for so long, and now it was here, it was better than I could ever imagine.

When my back landed softly on the bed, Ranger took a few steps back to admire me. I was still clothed, wearing jean shorts that were so short, I knew he could see my underwear... He sniffed the air and palmed the hard bulge I could see through his shorts.

"Oh, Lex. I can smell and see how wet you are from here. This pussy..." He leaned in and cupped me through my shorts, sending thrills of pleasure flushing through my body. I was drenched, I could feel it, and he could smell it.

"This is mine," he growled out lowly, "and the big bad wolf is gonna eat it all up."

CHAPTER EIGHTEEN

LEXI

Ranger's fingers trailed down my chest, my body arching up to meet his hand, but I wanted the fabric between us to be gone. I pulled my top up and over my chest, and Ranger moved over me. His hands gripped my waist as he ground his erection into me.

"Lexi...fuck." I pulled it up and over my head and reached for him. He came to me, his mouth crashing down on mine, his hands touching me. They weren't gentle. They were rough, hard...needy, stroking my heated skin like they were fireworks.

"Ranger, that feels so good," I told him. I wanted him to know how good he made me feel. His kisses got lower and lower, then a hand slipped behind my back and my bra was undone. Ranger skimmed his fingers over my breasts, avoiding my nipples, teasing me...torturing me by not touching me where I wanted him to.

"Ugh, you're killing me," I groaned out, and he chuckled before his head dipped down and he took one nipple in his mouth, his warm, wet tongue gliding over the hard nub, then sucking and licking before switching to the other, making sure they had equal love and attention.

I was so worked up. He took off his tee as I went straight to his shorts, my fingers grabbing at the waistband and slowly pulling it down over his bare ass. No underwear...as usual.

"A little worked up, are we?" His cocky chuckle teased me, and I rolled my eyes. Yes, yes I was seriously worked up. His hands went to my shorts, and within twenty seconds, we were both naked, our eyes gazing over each other, taking in the sight of each other's bare bodies. And fuck, what an impressive sight he was.

"You're mine, Lex." Ranger bent down and picked me up, gently throwing me a little higher on the bed before crawling on after me, and my legs parted as he came up between them.

His hand reached between us, and he slipped his index finger through my folds. I was so wet, so worked up, that when he touched my clit, I almost bucked off the bed as I saw stars.

"God, Lexi, you're so sensitive." He kissed me deeply as he inserted a finger and stroked me from inside. I reached between us, trying to rub him back. It was a hard angle, but I got my hand on that hot silky cock. I didn't want what had happened last time, so I was careful not to make him come.

He reached for the drawer, the one I knew was full of condoms, and dropped two on the bed as he tried to open a third with his teeth. I laughed when it didn't tear open and reached for it.

I ripped it with my teeth and spat out the little bit of silver wrapper, then handed the opened condom back. Ranger chuckled as I pushed my hair out of my face to watch him slide it down.

"I love you, Lexi. You know that, right?" His body was heavy above mine as he pressed his cock against my entrance. We were so close, just one move and he would be inside me. His hand stroked my cheek as he ran his thumb over my swollen lips before taking my mouth, thrusting his tongue deep at the same time he thrust his cock to the hilt, and I gasped. I felt so full, so good.

"Fuck, Lex. Did I hurt you?"

Ranger's eyes bore into mine. He looked so concerned, not like the alpha Ranger I had just come to know. I shook my head.

"Would feel better if you moved." At the grin I saw on his face, I knew I would keep that memory of our first time. He started off gentle, so I slapped his ass. He'd promised me a punishment and he was giving sweet, but it didn't take long for him to get the hint. I wanted this. I wanted him to take control and give me the pleasure I needed.

"Harder," I demanded, and that spurred him on as he growled. He pulled out, and I whimpered at the loss. I was so close. He sat back on his heels, picked me up, and turned me over until I was on all fours.

The sound of his slap on my ass echoed around the room before he was filling me again, and I moaned as he hit all the right spots over and over again. His hand reached under me, thrumming my clit until I tumbled over the edge, my body giving me the climax I needed over and over as Ranger continued to drive into me hard. I could feel him panting against my throat, and I turned and kissed him as another intense orgasm washed over me, my body trembling and clenching around his.

"Fuck...I'm coming. God, Lex... I'm..." He let out a sound that wasn't human as he jerked and shuddered in his orgasm. His grip on my ass would've left marks for days if I wasn't a fast healer. I was almost disappointed in that moment that I wasn't fully human. I wanted to wear the reminder of how amazing that just was on my ass so that I'd feel it every time I sat down. I guessed I'd just have to do it again...and again.

He flopped down next to me and pulled me in close, brushing my damp hair from my cheek as he breathed me in. We were both covered in a sheen of sweat, and our chests rose and fell heavily.

"You smell so fucking good, Lex, like me and you. I love you so much. So, so much, babe." He let out a deep breath as I felt him remove the used condom. I turned in his arms and watched as he peered down at me.

"I love you, Ranger. That was amazing." He kissed me, gentle and sweet, and I smiled as he wrapped me in his arms, close to his chest. I liked this about Ranger, that he could be sweet and caring and dominant and alpha too. He was a balance of both worlds, and I knew right then that this between us had gone to the next level, that this was official between us. He had claimed me as his.

He was mine, and I was his.

CHAPTER NINETEEN

MAVERICK

I felt like shit for leaving her. Lexi was the one person who scared me the most in this world. Even my own father didn't put the same fear in me. Yes, it was a different kind of fear. She could leave me at any time, by choice or by the hands of someone else. We saw how far people would go to have her. Until this warlock guy came and did what he could to hide her scent, I was on edge all the time. My wolf was really struggling with control since the night Lexi had almost died, and now it was almost uncontrollable.

But I worried the most that she would tell me she didn't love me anymore, that she didn't want to choose me. I knew this was a normal feeling. Everyone had fears, and I'd found out mine was losing her. But I just kept thinking I was fucking everything up, over and over. I was in my room when Saint slammed the door open, and I jumped a little at the sound, not expecting him to do that. He kicked the back of the door with his foot, and it slammed closed.

I rolled my eyes and looked back to my painting, then added another stroke of white. This was the same painting I'd been doing in art class. The same class I shared with Lexi.

"Lexi is gonna kill me. You have to help me, man." I glanced up from my painting, dropped the paintbrush, and raised my brow at him.

"Kill you? You almost cost me my balls. Lexi is pissed, and I wouldn't go near Ada, man. I'll even kill you if you do. You need to figure out your shit before you speak to her."

He huffed and sagged onto my bed. He dramatically flopped back and ran his hands over his short dark blond hair, then down his face, making pained sounds as he did. I tried to ignore him, but he was acting like a two-year-old. His eyes peered over to me.

"I fucked up." I didn't say anything to that. Yeah, he did, and I didn't know what he wanted me to do. The only thing I know about relationships was from my short one, and that had been spent mostly with my girl as a target to other shifters. So it wasn't a regular type of relationship, and I had no advice to give.

I picked up my paintbrush again. I'd realized since Lexi got here the painting had started to change. It was once dark, black and purples swirling. It was supposed to be a painting of emotions, and I had been painting mine. But now it had changed. There was light in there mixing with the dark, pulling and changing it for the better.

"Man, what do I do? Lexi wants to see me." That had me sitting back in my chair.

"Why?" My brows raised, why would Lexi... "Oh fuck, she's really gonna kick your ass. She told you. She warned you not to fuck with Ada, her *best friend*, and you were an asshole to her. I would know, I had to hear about it all afternoon from the two of them."

He jumped up and moved to me, his eyes wide...pleading.

"Look, I don't know why I did it. Noah called me and told me that fucking Rawlins *asshole* gave her his number, and I don't know what happened, okay? I just..."

He started to pace my room. I was actually surprised to see him so worked up. We hadn't really talked about girls before, and now here we were. I had a mate, a girlfriend, the most amazing, beautiful... stubborn Lexi.

I would never officially claim her. To do so meant I had to bite her and she would become a shifter, something I was glad wouldn't even be considered now that we knew that she couldn't. But I had claimed her, even without the ceremony.

Well...not fully claimed all of her. There were few things I would love to do with her, but I'd heard from Rafferty that my brother was doing that now, so I'd stayed here to paint. One day, it would be the right time and she would be mine... Galen too. A vision of Galen and Lexi on their knees flashed before me. I quickly shifted on my chair and tried to ignore the blood rushing to my cock at the thought. Fuck, Saint would be able to tell I was aroused.

But when I looked up, Saint had moved back to pacing again, too caught up in his head to have noticed my scent change. Mr. Untouchable, all the girls chasing him, wanting him, and he never settled down or chased them back. He was just happy to have a night, then move on to the next one.

"You like her?" I questioned, and he stopped and snorted at that, like it was a joke. I rolled my eyes and continued with my painting. If he couldn't figure out if he liked her, then I had no idea why he was still in my room, pacing and looking like he wished he had longer hair to pull out.

"Fuck, you're my best friend. You gotta help me here, Mav." I shook my head, not even looking up. He growled low, challenging me to a fight, but I wasn't in the mood. I was already upset with myself before he came in. Now I was just pissed off at him for putting me in a position where Lexi's only friend was getting fucked over by my best friend, just because he had no idea if he liked the girl or not.

"Fuck, I like her, okay? I do. She's so...ugh." I sat back again and watched him as he just looked to the ceiling. "She isn't what I thought I would have in a mate, okay? She's different from the girls I normally hook up with. I don't know if I want her or if it's because I don't want Rawlins to have her."

I was glad he admitted it, even though it wasn't exactly what I wanted to hear. But he needed to think, and I needed to as well. I got up, marched over to him, and punched his shoulder. His head snapped back at me, his eyes glowing as he growled at me, and my wolf responded to his.

"Let's go for a run."

We sat down on the grass overlooking the cliff. I didn't know if I wanted to be back here, but I almost felt like it was important for me. My wolf needed to see it was the same cliff as it had always been. Lexi was safe at home…with Ranger. I was glad Galen's house was set up so we couldn't hear what was going on inside. I loved Lexi and was glad to have Ranger as my packmate, but I also didn't want to hear him having sex with her either. Well, not yet. I knew it was unavoidable, but I didn't want to listen in on their first time.

Like with Raff. That was something private, a special bond they were making with each other. I knew I didn't want others hearing us when we had our first time together. I wished that I had never been with Olivia. I'd been wishing lately that I could've had my first time with Lexi, that I'd saved myself for my mate.

"Hey, so do you think I should go see Ada?" I hung my head down between my legs and let out a deep breath. Fuck, the guy was giving me whiplash.

"Are you gonna say sorry?" I really wished he would pick someone else to date…because he was my best friend. He was closer to me than anyone, and I didn't want to a day to come where I had to choose Lexi or Saint. Not that Lexi would make me choose, but it would just be awkward and uncomfortable and I didn't want that.

When he didn't answer my question, I added, "You need to think this through. Do you want her in the long run? Is she someone you see as a mate? If she's just someone you want to hook up with, then pick someone else. Ada deserves better than that.

"If you want her as a mate, then look at getting a packmate. Noah, I guess, would be the best option there. I already saw the way the two of you work together around her. I know she has a thing about his age, but he's almost sixteen. That's the legal age of consent here in Washington. So the two of you ask her out on a date, a real one. No sex, just a date. See how things go, and if you think she's the one, then tell Huxley you're with Ada and you're going to put a claim on her. Don't go shifting and attacking him. She likes him, so I'd be careful around that. She might pick him over you, since she seemed to really like him."

Saint just blinked, so I pushed his arm and he caught himself before he fell.

"That's it? You've changed. Not in a bad way, but that didn't sound like the old Mav. I'll go talk to Noah, I think... You know, to make sure he's onboard with me."

I nodded, since I didn't think Noah would say no to that. If he was Saint's packmate, it was probably the only way Ada might give him the time of day. But then, look what happened to Callum. Maybe it wouldn't work out. I didn't want to overthink it.

"To be honest, I would go see Huxley and explain what you did. *Apologise,* get his number, then go to Ada, tell her you're sorry, give her the number, and then walk away. Think about it, truly think, and if you can't live without her, go ask her on a date."

He stood up. He was naked, since we didn't bring our clothes out here, not when we were going for a run.

"If I ask her on a date, maybe it's best if we double dated. You and Lexi, me and Ada."

I threw my hands up and said, "Why not?" I'd soon find out if I would regret it or not when I asked Lexi.

"This is gonna be great." Saint shifted and took off into the woods behind me, and I sat there. The sun had gone down, and the stars were out.

I heard the call of a wolf and knew it was Nash. He was out on patrol, just reaching out, letting us know all was safe.

CHAPTER TWENTY

LEXI

"Sleepy head, time to wake up." I felt the bed dip and the covers being pulled away. I quickly snatched them and heard the throaty chuckle of Galen.

"Ugh..." I groaned. "I don't wanna get up, I have nothing to do." I made whiny sounds to annoy him. "You won't let me go to school. I feel like you all bubble wrapped me, but you've forgotten I don't need that. I can kick your ass, Galen."

I felt the weight of him over the blanket as he lowered it from my face. I opened a sleepy eye and saw his beautiful smile. I couldn't help the grin that spread across my lips.

"I know you can kick my ass, and I'm not the one who bubble wrapped you. That was Alaric. We have a meeting with him and Tobias, so maybe you should go get dressed and you can go kick his ass, my little ass kicker."

He pressed a warm kiss to my forehead, and in a blink, he was gone. Fuck, I hadn't mentally prepared myself for seeing Tobias today, but I was going to tell Alaric what I thought of this home prison thing. The school was full of shifters. What could happen?

. . .

There were a lot more people in Alaric's office than I'd thought there'd be. It was a huge office, so it was meant to hold a lot of people, but I wasn't expecting it. He didn't say anything to me when I entered, he just pointed to some chairs, and I took Galen's hand and led him over there. I wasn't sitting by myself while they spoke about me. I assumed that's what this meeting was about—me.

You could tell when Tobias entered. It was like a powerful feeling washed over the room. His whole body turned to me, like he knew exactly where I was, and I sucked in a small breath.

"Lexi, how are you, my child?" I was almost jarring. This guy was my father, spoke like an old man, but he looked more like he could be my brother. When I didn't speak quickly enough, he added mentally, *"I hope you are well."*

Oh wow, yeah. He could do that—talk in my head. I nodded and smiled, but tried to keep my thoughts to myself. I felt Galen stiffen slightly beside me, then nod, and I shuffled on my chair. What did Tobias say to him for that reaction? My fight or flight was kicking in, and I hadn't really had this feeling in a while. What was going on in this meeting? My heart started to pick up a little, and Galen grabbed my hand and stroked it lightly.

This wasn't like when I ran to the cliff. That was me trying to protect everyone. No, this feeling was like when I ran from the police back in Seattle. Or when I tried to run from Jack and Grayson's house because I'd just learned boys who turned into wolves was a real thing and I couldn't fight that. If I knew I couldn't fight something, I ran. I wasn't like those heroines from the books who stay and slay the monster. I was the one who preferred to slink away, hoping someone else would slay it and I wouldn't get caught up in the crosshairs. That was how I always dealt with danger.

"What's wrong?" Galen whispered. Everyone was still looking at us. I was tense, on the edge of my seat.

"Okay, now that we're all here, could we all be seated? We have a long list of items we must address. I want to thank Tobias for coming to this meeting. Also, to the other packs, thank you to Erick, Alpha of Pack Rawlins, and Mackenzie, Alpha of Pack Kenneally, for joining us here today. It was a tragic event that brought us all closer, and I wish for our packs to be united together to help us all heal."

Alaric stood behind his desk as he started to talk about stuff I had no idea about, and my mind wandered a little. Nash was there beside him, nodding, watching. I guessed he was learning from his father.

He looked a lot like Alaric. The genes in the Lovell boys did not take after their mother. They all looked like different versions of their father. When Nash's eyes met mine, I quickly looked away. How embarrassing, to be caught staring at him.

"Lexi." I blinked and looked over to Alaric. Huh? Oh shit, I wasn't listening. Did he ask me a question?

"We want to thank you for everything you did for the packs, and to Tobias for your help in ending all the carnage."

Tobias stood up. He didn't have his wings again. Actually, I didn't really look at him properly when he came in. He wore a dark blue suit, and a black shirt with a yellow tie. It really made his eyes pop.

"Thank you all for having me here today. As you all know, I have come to learn I have a daughter, Alexis Turner. Her mother was a lover of mine and a vampire. I spent time with Pack Bardoul yesterday, trying to find out why and how Elizabeth turned human.

"The warlock who lead me to find my daughter will be here in a few minutes. He will help with her...calling to your shifter sons."

Oh wow. I looked around the room, then to the door. I was so excited. This was why I was here—to meet this warlock. My knee started to jiggle a little. I was excited now. Once he helped me, I could go anywhere and just smell human, and no more weirdos sniffing me everywhere I went.

"Then I can go back to school. This is great, thank you," I said, a huge grin on my face. As much as what had happened only a few nights ago was very scary, I didn't want to live like that, dwelling on it, depressed. I'd had my moment, and it was time to live again, like all the others around here. No one had stopped, they'd buried the dead and mourned. I'd noticed this was how they were here. It was time to move on. We could remember them, but we had to keep on living. The reason why we fought in the first place was for freedom, because if they had my blood, all the supernatural would be controlled by them.

I needed to start really living, instead of being home all day. I'd already taken enough time off, and I was itching to get back. I felt Galen rub my back. I hadn't realized that I'd almost jiggled off the seat. I was just so excited to be back to my normal and so close to being "mate" scent free.

"You will not be returning to school, Lexi. Not until we deem it safe," Alaric said, and I looked over to him. He was seated now at his desk, and I felt everyone's eyes on me. Say what?

"Yes I am. I'll go tomorrow. There's no more threat, and when the warlock comes, I won't even smell. This is perfect."

Alaric shook his head, that scary look on his face, but Tobias nodded his head from where he was standing beside me.

"No," Alaric said at the same time Tobias said, "Yes." I stopped moving as the air prickled my skin.

Oh fuck, was Tobias mad? Or was this Alaric and Tobias just using their power to show the other they were in charge?

"Lexi will be free to go to school tomorrow. There is no threat to her."

I heard chair legs scrape against the wooden floor as Alaric stood.

"She is Pack Kiba, and my sons' mate. I say when she will or won't attend school."

You know that feeling you get when your wool sweater becomes static and clings to your body, zapping you as you move, and your hairs all stand up off your body? That was how I felt in that room with the two of them, their powers fighting each other. Tobias was much stronger than Alaric, and you could see that from the way Alaric took a step back when the intensity was turned up. This was a standoff, one that Alaric wasn't going to win.

A bright white light flickered from the corner of the room, and I blinked at the area where there had been nothing before, but now there stood a man. Wait, that couldn't be right... Wow yes, he had purple eyes. They went straight to Tobias, and I watched as he rolled them. Then I realized what had just happened.

"Just in time to see you messing with the wolves, brother. I'm here now, put away the powers." The feeling in the room went down heavily, like a blanket being dropped, and I could tell everyone felt it from the sounds they made.

"Oh my god, you can teleport?" I blurted out just as I realized what he'd done. He was the bright light. Galen chuckled as I stood up. I was... This... *Oh my god.* This guy had already gone above and beyond what I was thinking he could do. This was amazing.

"I am her father, and I say she will attend school." I turned to see Alaric and Tobias still arguing as the warlock approached me. He was slim, the same height and build as Galen. His hair was jet black, shorter on the sides and long on top, but the top had been dyed a deep purple. He rocked that purple so hard. He wore a black leather jacket with a dark purple shirt, no tie, and a pair of black faded jeans.

"Hello, you must be Alexis. I'm Eiji, and I'll be your warlock today." He cocked a funny smile my way, and my mouth just dropped open. No words... I had no words as he shook my hand, and I could feel his power run up my arm and tickle me like little fireworks beneath the skin.

"Hi," I squeaked out. He gestured with his free hand to walk with him, his other hand still holding mine as he led us past two very angry men and out the door of the office. Holy crap, Eiji was so gorgeous, and he really liked purple.

Galen was hot on my heels. He wasn't just going to let me walk away with this warlock. I was glad, since because he could teleport, he could just zap me somewhere if he wanted too very easily.

"Let's go to the living room, shall we? Leave the men to do their... business." But I couldn't hear them once the door had closed. I was glad, because I didn't care. I was going to school and not because Tobias said so, but because I said so.

I couldn't place his accent, but it was different. He seated himself down opposite to me, and Galen hovered nearby.

"Where do you live?" I asked. That was a reasonable question to ask, right?

"I'm from all over the world. I age a lot slower than a human and I can prolong my life, but I'm not immortal like your mate, Galen. You are very much like your father in that way, taking a vampire as your mate, except you are not as strong as Tobias. You do realize your mate could kill you, yes?" I nodded.

Yes, I knew he could, but he wouldn't. I trusted him with my life. I looked over to Galen, but his eyes didn't meet mine as he gave me a weak smile.

"I bet you have a lot of questions. I will help for as long as I can. Feel free to ask away while I work my magic on that delicious scent of yours."

That had Galen hissing out a warning, and I couldn't help the smile on my face. Was Galen a little jealous?

CHAPTER TWENTY-ONE

LEXI

I watched as Eiji moved his hands over me. At first, I wasn't sure what he was doing, since I didn't feel anything. When a small pink glow appeared on his palm like smoke, he bent forward and blew on it.

Immediately, the smoke surrounded me, and I tensed up. "What is this?" I hoped it was safe because it was all gone now. Galen moved closer and held my hand.

"This doesn't last forever unfortunately. I haven't mastered that yet. But then, I don't often need spells to mask scents. You and your aunt are the only two I have done this for. When it starts to wear off, your mates will know to ask Tobias to summon me."

I looked around the room. I wanted a shifter to come and tell me he couldn't smell me. But for the first time, the house seemed quiet, except for all the shifters in Alaric's office, and I didn't want to go back in there. But there was something Eiji said that had me bubbling full of questions.

"What is my aunt like? What's her name?" I had only just learned about her and that she was hiding from my grandfather. I didn't need to know why. It seemed pretty serious, based on the way

Tobias was happy I didn't have strong angel blood. But I wanted to know more about her.

"Oh, your aunt was very excited to learn about your existence. She goes by many names, but those she is closest to call her Cate. She is one of a kind, that is for certain. Beautiful...strong, like yourself. But she is your grandfather's most favorite creation, and this is why she couldn't come be with you today. She wanted to meet you so desperately."

I nodded. It felt nice to hear she wanted to meet me. Aunt Cate... That sounded strange, but I'd never had an aunt before. I wished I could've met her.

"She gave me a gift to give to you."

He put his hand in his leather jacket and produced a silver chain. When he opened his closed hand, a purple stone, the size of a quarter, was attached to the end of it. It was amazing. I reached out and gently cupped the stone in my hand.

"It's a rare stone from the Underworld. If you look closely, you will see it's not just a stone." I looked closer. This stone was from the Underworld? What the hell? Were demons real? Before I could ask, I saw inside the stone. It looked like a...galaxy. I felt Galen move in to get a closer look. Inside the stone it was moving, swirling around a glow in the center. I gasped, my eyes going to Eiji's purple ones. From this close, I could tell his eyes weren't just purple, they held some blue flecks in them. They were mesmerizing.

Galen must have noticed my distraction. He cleared his throat. "I've heard of this from the mage I did my time with. It's a Dragonor stone, right? I've never seen one. Is it true that if you make a few smaller ones from a larger stone, it communicates with the others?"

Eiji sat back and nodded.

"Yes, this is why Cate has given this to you, Lexi. She wants you to wear it. If you are ever in danger again, it will call to her and she will expose herself to her father to protect you at all costs.

"She hopes to one day meet you and your family here, but until we can find a safe way for her to travel... Well, I hope it will be soon."

I nodded. I didn't want her to expose herself to him if he wanted her for something bad. I didn't even want to think about what that could be. I wanted her to stay safe, and hopefully, I could meet her one day. Or couldn't he use his powers?

"Ah...I see the question in your mind, and the answer is no. I am extremely powerful in my own right, but there are others in the world who are older and more powerful than me. They work for your grandfather. He is not an angel of life, he is the bringer of death. Most know him around the world as Diablo Angelo, or the Devil Angel, because that is exactly what he is.

"I hope you never have to meet him in your lifetime, that you will be here, safe. You have a good bond with your mates, I can sense this. This is a good place for you and your future. Now I must go before I am tracked."

Eiji stood and took a few steps back, then he smiled and tipped an imaginary hat.

"It was a pleasure doing business with you, Lexi. Until we meet again."

The bright light flashed for only a second, and then Eiji was gone before I could even thank him or say goodbye. I had so many questions still, but I knew that it was for the best I didn't know too much about Cate. I assumed Eiji was her warlock? Boyfriend? He was hot.

"Hey...those thoughts better be for me," Galen teased, and I laughed.

"So I still smell good to you?" I wanted to make sure I wasn't too different. Hell, I never asked Eiji that. Would the guys not feel the same way?

"Hey, you honestly don't smell different to me. I know Eiji has changed your scent to others, but Tobias made sure it wouldn't change for Raff, Ranger, Mav, and me. Okay?"

I nodded as I let out a deep breath and looked down to the Dragonor stone in my hand. I was glad Tobias had made sure I wouldn't change for them. I hoped I was never in trouble and needed to call on Cate, but I also hoped to one day meet her. She sounded amazing.

I clutched the stone to my chest and laid my head against Galen's chest.

"Can we go to Jack and Grayson's house? Do you have their number?" He stroked my hair, and I felt him move slightly, then he handed me his iPhone.

"Tell me, why do you own a phone if you never take it with you?"

I laughed. "Ah...well, I guess that's because I didn't want to see the messages from the guys having a great day at school while I'm stuck here." I heard Galen make a mock gasp, and I chuckled as I elbowed him in the ribs.

"You know what I mean. I love being stuck here with you." I kissed him and looked back to the phone.

"What's the password?" When he didn't answer, I thought he must've had something bad on there that he didn't want me to see. I looked at him, and he was blushing...well, as much as a vampire could blush. "What?" I asked.

"Nothing. It's five-three-nine-four." I typed them in and unlocked it. Nothing bad was on his screen, just a photo of the beach. I was thinking he had a photo of me on there. Oh shit, we didn't have any photos together. I pushed the camera app, and the screen popped up and I spun the camera around to be facing me.

"Selfie time." I didn't give him time to react as I leaned back and took a photo. I sat forward and had a look. I laughed, and he snatched the phone out of my hand.

"Hey, that was cute. You look scared, like it will take your soul."

"Maybe it does take my soul?" His brows wiggled at me as he pulled me back to him and took multiple photos. I was giggling and poking my tongue out, then kissing him on the cheek. I liked his expression in that one. He looked so happy, we both did.

"Okay, call Jack so we can go see Joshy and watch cartoons."

And hopefully, Grayson had baked muffins.

CHAPTER TWENTY-TWO

LEXI

I got to Jack and Grayson's house just before school pick-up. I was excited to surprise Josh. Galen said he would wait with Grayson and help cook some after-school muffins. I loved that, and it made me so giddy inside that Grayson was eager to teach him, my little heart burst. I quickly kissed Galen and ran off to the car with Jack.

"I am so glad you came over today, Lexi, and that you felt comfortable bringing Galen. You know we accept him as your mate the same as we accept the other three. You don't need to hide your mates from us. They're just as welcome in our home as you are."

I laid my head back on the headrest and glanced over to Jack. The sun made his salt and pepper hair really shine, and I smiled.

"I know. Just...now with Tobias, and you and Grayson—"

"No, don't you worry your little head over that. We'll be whatever you need us to be, okay? We'll always think of your as our girl and never treat you any differently. Tobias is a good man—angel. He came to see us yesterday and thanked us for being there for you. Even though it was only a short time, he made it clear that he wasn't trying to push us out. He wants to be a part of your life, Lexi, he just doesn't know how."

Wow, I didn't know that. My throat felt a little tight. I hadn't been the friendliest to him, but I guessed I never was with someone new. I never wanted to let my guard down and let someone into my life that would then take me away or disappear. I'd learned to keep people away...but I would try to let Tobias in. I thought the fact he was my real father scared me more than anything. If he was to just leave, my own flesh and blood... I never wanted that feeling. I quickly changed the subject.

"So, Grayson said that Harry and Jaxon have gone back to their mom," I said, and Jack nodded.

"Yes, that's been the plan since day one. They haven't been here too long. They were from a pack in New York, where there were issues with drugs among the family, and their kids ended up in the system. But their mom is now free of it all, did rehab, and has been accepted by a pack down in Nevada. She has the support she needs down there.

"Not all packs are bad with rogue wolves. I know it must seem that way here at times, especially with Rafferty, but we take in shifter kids. They're part of the pack here, even if it doesn't seem like it at times. Kiba, Rawlins, and Kenneally all take in lost cubs. Some stay, some leave, but they're all loved and wanted."

I reached over, grabbed his hand, and squeezed. Fuck, they were amazing. Those boys were so well cared for, and I was glad they were now with their mom. But what about Josh? Oh my god, I never thought. Was he...going to leave me?

"Joshy? Is he leaving?" I felt a lump form in my throat at the thought. I felt like I was waiting forever for Jack to answer. He squeezed my hand back and dropped it to use the indicator as he turned onto a street.

"No, but we would love it if you could stay for dinner. We have some...news." That didn't sound good, but before I could say something, he quickly added, "We're here."

I watched as all the kids walked through the big blue doors at the front of the school. This was a much smaller school than I had realized.

"It's a Kiba school, since the packs don't mix the young ones up. It would be helpful if they did, so there was less...aggression and fighting. You've seen the way they act in high school. It might stop some of that if they were able to socialize early." He was right—that would probably help stop some of the hate and fighting from the crazy teen hormones that likely mixed with the fact they'd just started shifting.

"Oh, there he is..." I looked over where Jack had pointed and saw little Joshy walking with his big bag on his back. Oh my gosh, he was just the cutest. His dark hair whipped around to see something behind him, then a big kid came out of nowhere and shoved him to the ground.

"What the fuck?" I opened up the car door and could hear Jack hot on my heels after witnessing the same thing. When I got over to Josh, more boys had surrounded him and one of them kicked him.

"Hey, who the fuck do you think you are? Get the fuck off my Joshy," I yelled, shoving the kid out the way. I didn't care that I was older and I'd cussed at him. Little asshole was picking on a kid half his size.

"Lexi?" Josh's sad little voice almost broke me as Jack picked him up.

"Boys, this will be reported. You have been warned. Stop with this bullying behavior," a teacher said, coming out through the big doors, a little too late if you asked me. She started asking questions and taking names as Jack let Josh down to go to me, and I hugged him tight. I wasn't letting him go, ever.

"Hey, buddy, I'm staying for dinner. Wanna go home and watch our cartoons?" His little face lit up as he sniffled and wiped the tears from his eyes. I kissed his head and ruffled his hair. I didn't want him to see the tears that were forming in my eyes. Fuck, why did kids have to be like this?

"Yeah, just you and me. Teen Titans, go!" I laughed and nodded and held his hand as we started to head towards the car. Jack was still talking to a teacher when one of the asshole kids ran past us.

"Watch out, orphan boy."

I felt my blood boil as I watched the back of his head disappear around the corner.

That kid was going down...*hard*.

CHAPTER TWENTY-THREE

GALEN

I left before they had their meal. Jack and Grayson were going to share some news with Lexi, and I thought it would be best if I left them all for a while so they could be together as a family and also to give Lexi some space. I was sure she would see too much of us before long, and even I liked to be alone at times. Hell, I'd never had this many people around me at all times.

I drove around for a while, lost in thought, until I ended up back at the diner, the same one I had taken Lexi to the night she ran away. The memory made me smile. I'd proved to her she wasn't just team wolf. Fuck, my life had turned around so much in the last month. I hadn't realized how mundane everything had become, how I had shut myself off from so much.

I'd had so much fear in me, that no one could ever love me, not fully, and so much hate for the monster who scarred me. My scars were my punishment for being an arrogant asshole, thinking the world owed me because of my status among my peers. That was another time, another place, but that was the true reason I was a vampire and why I'd felt that I wasn't worthy of love for so long, why

I was drawn to the wrong people in the past. Because I believed they would be the only ones who could love me. I was wrong...and Lexi had proved that to me.

Life became the same routine—school, home, school, Ranger shifting in front of humans, me compelling them to forget, home. I hadn't had a close friendship, ever. I spoke to Shelly and Ben, but not often enough to be a good friend. Lovers... I hadn't had sex in a long time. Shit, if I truly thought about it, it had almost been a decade since I'd been with anyone or felt touch from someone, even a hug.

The last woman I was with was a night vamp, who was envious at my walking in the sun. She was demanding and cruel at times, and would making fun of my scars, telling me that no one would love me like she did. In the end, I walked away, but not before I lost all hope in love and of being loved in return. When I looked back, I knew I hadn't loved her. I knew that then, and now, I could call it what it was —an abusive relationship. I'd stayed with her for so long because I just didn't want to be alone. She'd broken what little faith I had in relationships. Smiles and happy times were not for me, not for the broken.

It all turned out for the better, though. At the time, it didn't feel like that. It felt like another failure in my life, but what I didn't know was it was the path I was meant to walk. Of all the places I could have gone in the world, I ended up in this small town in Washington state.

Kiba.

When I'd gotten here, I was a mess, but I met Laura and Alaric of Pack Kiba and their five sons, all little mini clones of their father. They invited me to their house, even though they knew what I was. Couldn't hide the smell of a bloodsucker. They let me stay at the cottage for a few days until I knew where I was going, the same one that was now my home. I couldn't believe these people would offer me this. And of all people...shifters. I was at my lowest point then, but Laura didn't care. She treated me as if I was...human.

I travelled a lot after that, between homes. I had places in different parts of the world, and most of the time, I leased them out when not in use. But no matter how hard I tried, I always ended up back at Kiba. It was like I was drawn here, and at the same time, they were good to me. Laura especially. She didn't ever treat me differently. She knew what I was, and she'd seen me at my lowest. I knew what she was, but we never spoke of it. It was something we silently agreed on without ever bringing it up.

Every year for five years, I would visit with Ben, then come up and visit Pack Kiba for a few days. When I was here, it was the first time I felt like I could breathe in a long time.

I'd always been living on the edge, looking over my shoulder, not knowing if I was going to be killed. I hated living like that. Shifters of any kind didn't like vampires. I guessed if there was a possible threat living near you, you would remove it. But vampires were just as bad.

When I heard from Shelly that Alaric needed a vamp at Kiba and that he was looking for me, I didn't hesitate to go. I had a good relationship with Alaric already, but I was shocked and saddened to hear about Laura. She truly was an accepting woman, sweet and beautiful. Her life ended too soon. She would have loved Lexi. I liked to think she was looking down at her boys and proud of the men they'd become. All of them, even Ranger, who was so much like her at times.

Alaric had needed me here to keep the pack safe from other vamps, like those who'd killed Laura, and at school to keep the *secret* safe from humans when teenage boys shifted in front of them. They'd managed quite badly before I was on the scene. But no other shifter was as bad at keeping his wolf under control like Ranger Lovell. I chuckled out loud. He was the real reason I was hired. No other packs had a shifter like him.

In the last five years, I'd had to clean up after Ranger more than anyone else. The only other Lovell I'd had to help was Jett, but that was something different.

Alaric had asked me to stay on at Kiba for protection after I told him my intentions with Lexi. He wasn't happy with me being one of his sons' packmates, but he wouldn't voice that. They were men, and it wasn't his place to say. They could make up their own minds, because I was staying with Lexi for the rest of my life. She was my world now.

I thought the real issue lay with Maverick and his feelings towards me. It wasn't the fact we were both male and attracted to each other, that had never been an issue among the shifters, and I really was attracted to him. He was gorgeous, everyone could see that. But the fact I was a vamp and he was shifter had everyone so caught up on, especially with him being the alpha's son.

I knew this was going to be new for a lot of shifters. I was happy to wait it out on Mav's timeline, but he set it in motion and we were moving forward. Shelly and Keene were out in the open about their relationship, but I hadn't seen how his own pack responded to that. They had been working with Shelly for a century, maybe even longer, but he was the first shifter she'd dated from their pack.

Alaric had asked if I could find a replacement day vamp for the school. Until then, he needed me to go there and fix the messes made by the shifters. Well...honestly, it was going to be Ranger problems. Though, I didn't think there would be many problems, to be honest. He'd been pretty good lately.

At the rate I was striking out, I'd probably end up back there in the new school year after Lexi graduated, not that I wanted to go back. I actually enjoyed the larger role I'd been given within the pack and the research at Pack Bardoul.

Trying to find a vamp was proving to be impossible. For one, they had to be a daylight vamp, and we made up about a quarter, maybe even less, of vampires. They would have to move to Washington and be part of a wolf shifter pack, which wasn't the friendliest environment, and work in a high school with *assholes*—I mean shifter teenagers. But in return, they could live here safely, without worrying about being jumped by other supes.

Plus, you were paid very well by the packs. I was paid by all three for my working at the high school, and from Kiba for my work within the pack, not that I needed any more money. I was trying so hard to give it to Lexi. I was glad she used the credit card I'd given her yesterday, even if it was only a small amount. I had enough money to last many, many lifetimes.

I sat in my car for an hour, watching the patrons enter and exit the diner. Some families, some truckers...some lowlifes. I was hungry, since I hadn't drunk Lexi's blood today. I had some older blood in my basement fridge, which wasn't nice, but it filled me. I needed to eat before I returned to Lexi. I waited until I saw a young waitress emptying some trash out the back of the building and the dark figure of a man walking towards her.

I was out of my car and over to him within a second.

"Wow, da fuck," he slurred, and I could smell his breath— stale beer and cigarettes. It made me want to heave. That was the worst. I preferred to pick people who were not upstanding citizens if I could, like this guy, but because I did, I had to smell this foul odor. Even his body odor was gag worthy. I felt myself getting dark and thirsty as my vamp senses kicked and I was ready to compel.

"You need to learn about personal hygiene, buddy, but today isn't that day. You are going to stand there and not make a sound while I drink from you. Do you understand?"

He nodded slowly before I took his wrist. I almost didn't want to do this, but I knew I would be hungry later and I didn't want to mess with that, didn't want to lose myself in hunger and attack Lexi. Even though her scent had changed, it didn't change for me. She still smelled amazing, and I just couldn't trust myself.

My fangs descended, and I brushed my tongue over them. I could feel all my senses heightening, hearing the sound of chatter in the diner, dishes being washed, the dishwasher dropping a knife, a rat eating leftover scraps in the bin...

My lips met his wrist as I sunk my teeth in, and he didn't move or flinch. He just stood there as I tasted the fresh, iron-filled blood, the metallic taste of it spilling into my mouth, my body screaming for more. I had been so deprived lately, since I wasn't eating as much as I should and I wasn't eating fresh. I was ashamed to admit to Lexi that I didn't just have donated blood... I didn't want her to find out, but I didn't want to keep this secret from her either. I would tell her. Later...

I pulled away, trying to keep myself as clean as possible, the blood still seeping from the two puncture marks. I pricked my index finger on my fang and used my blood to heal him. When he looked the same as before, just with a little blood on his sleeve, I compelled him again.

"You will forget about me, what has happened. You will become a decent human and take regular showers. Now leave."

It was always fascinating to watch them come out of being compelled. They looked like a deer in headlines at times, blinking, looking at their surroundings as if they didn't know how they got there. I walked away and got back into my car. That had killed some time, but it was time for me to go back and pick up Lexi.

I hoped whatever Jack and Grayson were telling her was good. She needed some great news to keep her mind full of happy thoughts. I had been waiting for the other shoe to drop with this happy Lexi, for it all to hit her, but it hadn't yet. I was wondering if I was worried for no reason. She was strong, just like Eiji had said, but that didn't mean she wouldn't be affected.

That was my second time meeting the guy, Eiji. There was just something about him that rubbed me the wrong way. I thought it was his lack of urgency in helping us find an angel, and then the way he looked at Lexi. I hissed under my breath. If I could avoid a third encounter with him, I would. But we needed him, Lexi really needed him. So I would ignore his existence for as long as I could.

The one nice thing I could say about him was he scrubbed up well and he knew how to work the color purple.

CHAPTER TWENTY-FOUR

LEXI

I had the best afternoon with Josh. We watched our shows and played Twister, which I'd figured out early on wasn't exactly fair, so I made sure to lose a couple of times as Grayson spun the little arrow and laughed at us.

"Dinner is ready," Jack called out. He was cooking tonight and I loved that, but I was worried I wouldn't have enough room after all the muffins I'd eaten. They were so good, and Galen had helped, so I had to eat them.

"Come on you two," Grayson said as he put down the board that told us where to stick our hands and feet. "Let's not keep him waiting. He cooked us dinner, and we have news to share with Lexi."

Okay, I'd been nervous about what this news was, but the way Grayson said it sounded good, not bad. I pretended to fall down, grabbing Josh on my way down and tickling him. It was a little hard, as he was slipping around on the Twister mat, but he got me back just as good. When Grayson made a sound that said we better hurry up or we'd be in trouble, I rolled off the mat and jumped up.

"Let's go eat," I said, reaching my hand out to Josh. He took it in his, and I pulled him to standing. I ruffled his dark silky hair, and we walked together to the table.

"Take a seat next to Josh, Lexi. He's holding in a big secret, and we wanted you to be the first to know."

I sat on the bench seat, the one I remembered so well from when I first met Josh...who told me I smelled...like a shifter. Not shit. Josh sidled up beside me, and I held onto his little warm hand.

"Okay, I'm ready." I didn't know if I was or not, just that I didn't want to wait any longer. Grayson smiled and turned to Jack. He did that often. It was sweet, and Jack had a way with words like no other. He could make you feel better with one of his speeches. I watched as they both held hands and then faced us.

"As you know, Harry and Jaxon have returned to live with their mom. But our little boy here, Joshua... We are adopting Josh, and we finally received the papers. We wanted you to be the first one to know, apart from us, Josh and Alaric. But it's official."

My mouth dropped open. Holy shit. This was the news, and it was huge. My heart was exploding. Josh really wasn't going anywhere. He would be here forever, with me. I wrapped my arms around him and sniffled.

"This is the best news I've heard in so long, I'm so excited for you all. This is amazing." Josh started to cry, then Grayson was wiping tears away, and even Jack was tearing up. Fuck, I was crying. They stood up and came over. We all ending up in a huge group hug of happy tears and giggles. I felt Grayson brush a tear from my cheek.

"We love you, Lexi. You will be our girl, no matter what. Paper or not, you are ours." That got the waterworks on heavy, and I tried to stop, but it was just too perfect.

"If we could've adopted you, Lexi, we would have. You are our girl, okay? Nothing will ever change that. You might be Lexi Turner, but in our hearts, you're a Rawson. We wouldn't have changed your name, that is who you are, your identity. We love you, and Josh adores you. We are all so lucky to be a part of your world."

I sucked in a deep breath. Would I want to be adopted now, so close to being eighteen? Maybe... Yes. But paper or not, these three guys were my family.

"I...I don't even know who I am anymore. I love you all so much. I'm not sure if I ever told you that, but it's true. I'm so happy, and I'm glad I was sent here. I gained a little brother...but more than that, I gained two dads."

That set Grayson off badly, with full body sobs, as Josh turned his little red splotchy face to mine.

"It's next week on Friday. Will you come?" he asked, and I nodded. I wouldn't miss it for the world.

"Um...I, well... Can you..." He looked so nervous. Oh, my little bubba. "I call Jack Papa, and Grayson, I call him Dad. Did you, like... maybe, like, wanna call them that too?"

Oh, those eyes peering up at me... He was so nervous to ask me.

"You don't have to, Lexi," Grayson said, squeezing my hand.

Jack quickly added, "We weren't expecting it or anything. Like, we weren't going to ask, but Josh wanted to. And we said he could, but—"

"Be quiet, Dad and Papa."

The smile on Josh's face lit up his eyes. I didn't do it for him though. I did it for me. It might take me a while, but I was sure one day, hopefully not too far in the future, I wouldn't even have to think about it and they would just be Dad and Papa. Tobias... Well, that was a hurdle I would prefer to jump another day.

"Okay, enough crying for now. Let's eat some dinner. It's probably all cold now, but I can reheat it," Grayson said, and we laughed at that. It cleared the air, and I felt lighter. This had truly made my day.

CHAPTER TWENTY-FIVE

LEXI

I was all smiles, since I was going back to school today. I'd texted Ada, and she was going to wait for me at the front so we could walk in together.

"I'll drive, everyone eat up," I heard Galen call out. Huh? I walked out of his room, the one that I'd slept in last night with Raff and Maverick. I could see the sofa still had a lumpy blanket where Ranger was still sleeping. He groaned.

"The couch is so uncomfortable. Please, let's get a bigger bed. I don't wanna sleep alone here... again."

Oh man, I felt bad. When I'd gotten home last night, I just collapsed. I didn't want him to feel left out, so I ran and dove on top of him.

"Ugh," he grunted out, flipping me over. I didn't get a chance to think before I was under him, his body pinning me to the sofa. The gleam in his eyes told me he'd planned this, and I quirked my brow and eyed him.

"You tricked me, didn't you?"

Galen was the one who laughed and said, "He got you—he didn't sleep alone. He had me, and it wasn't as if he didn't sneak in halfway through the night, only to be kicked out a few hours later."

I smacked my hand on his chest that was practically on mine. "You ass." He tickled my sides, and I started to giggle and squirm. "Stop. It. Ah." I needed to pee so bad. I heard the sound of a door closing, so I tilted my head back and saw the bathroom door was closed. Raff's hair was all disheveled as he rubbed his eyes, then his lips twitched into a smirk.

"I don't know how you did it, Lexi. Mav snored like a freight train." Everyone laughed. I hadn't even heard it, but I was pretty worn out from the day. Ranger moved up my body a little more, and it was impossible to miss his hard cock between my legs. He planted a kiss on my lips and wiggled his hips, showing me he woke up happy...everywhere.

"Have some nice dreams, did we?" He ground his erection into me again, waking my body up with little fireworks going off in my core. He murmured, "Yes," as he kissed me. I was a little nervous sometimes to kiss them all in front of each other, but when I looked back over to where Raff was, his eyes were watching us, and he readjusted himself in his boxers. Holy crap, how was I ever going to leave this house if they all looked at me like that? Even more so when I was with another and it affected them like that? I was still amazed by this whole sharing thing. I'd been waiting for a fight, someone to say it wasn't fair, but nothing.

Ranger kissed me again, and I grabbed his ass and wrapped my legs around his waist.

"Come on, Ranger. Lexi is going to school today, and you're distracting her. You're all gonna be late if you don't start getting ready."

Ranger just chuckled and sat back on his knees to look over the couch at Galen. I sat up too and saw Raff was now on the stool eating bacon. My stomach growled, and he smiled at me as he took a big bite. *Tease.*

"Okay, *Dad*. You're showing your true colors, *old man*," Ranger quipped, and I smacked him harder this time. "Hey," he said, grabbing his chest and rubbing the spot. If that didn't hurt him, it did hurt me. I shook out my hand, then pointed at him.

"Don't 'hey' me," I said, but before I got a chance to get up, he grabbed me again and tickled. With the strange angle we were in and the fact I was trying to get away, especially from his tickles, it made my knee go up involuntarily and—

"Ah, fuck. You kneed me in the nuts," he said with a groan as he rolled off me onto the floor, clutching his junk. At first, I felt a little bad, but then I didn't. I laughed.

"Well, that'll teach you to not be an ass, *young man*," I snapped back. Maverick had come out of the bathroom just in time to witness what had happened. He was wearing only a towel, his hair dark and damp. I watched as a water droplet rolled down his arm... Dang, his muscles were so tight. He looked to me, then to his brother, and winced. I could see the amusement on his face at the pain of his brother, and I snorted. Maverick crouched slightly, then ran at me, and I giggled as he wrapped his arms around my waist and swung me on the spot, kissing my cheek. I felt his hot damp skin against my own as he dropped my feet to the ground, not letting go as he dipped me back, and his lips touched mine gently before turning back to Ranger.

"I can see now why Saint ran to me instead of coming here like you asked. That looks nasty, brother. Stop upsetting our girl and go put some ice on it." I looked over my shoulder down to where Ranger was still lying on the floor, tears in his eyes. He flipped his brother the bird, then looked to me and growled low. I felt that deep in my core.

God, Galen was right—we would all be late if I kept getting distracted, and I didn't want to be late. Ada would be waiting for me. I just shook my head and peeled myself from Maverick. He made a protesting sound, and I felt the same way. I loved the way he felt against me... Maybe I should stop looking.

I quickly ran to the bathroom before anyone else decided they needed to go and closed the door behind me.

I couldn't believe this was my life now. This was happiness.

CHAPTER TWENTY-SIX

LEXI

I was so excited, I almost forgot my backpack, which Galen had packed for me. I couldn't help but think yeah...maybe Ranger's teasing had a little truth to it. Not that I would ever tell either of them. Plus, it was why I loved them both, for who they were. Age didn't play into it at all.

We all jumped into Galen's sexy black car, the four-door one. I'd heard Raff talking about cars with him earlier, and he really knew a lot about them. The way he almost hugged Galen when he said he could drive his cars around anytime made Raff and Maverick both whistle low as they smiled.

"You trust this guy?" Ranger jumped onto Raff's back playfully. It was funny to see because Ranger was bigger than Raff and it really showed when I saw them like this. "You've never let me drive." Maverick laughed and shook his head. What was I missing?

"Oh Lexi, I see you wondering why Galen refuses to let Ranger drive his cars. There's a very good reason behind that... Ranger?" Maverick turned to the guys, and I laughed when Ranger did the mock "who me?" expression.

"Ranger stole my car a couple of years ago... I miss her." My mouth dropped open. What, Ranger stole Galen's car? And...

"Miss, as in gone?" I asked.

Ranger jumped off Raff and held his hands up. "To be fair, I didn't know how fast a Shelby Cobra was. Plus, it was harder to handle than the Jeep. I told you I was sorry, Galen. Shouldn't you be happy I didn't die? I'm a great driver now... like, could I please play a little with your Mustang?"

Galen just rolled his eyes. I was pretty sure Ranger would have just healed quickly, so he wouldn't have died.

"I'll think about it, Ranger. Can you run in and hit the button on the wall? My garage door opener batteries have died, and I haven't had a chance to replace them."

Ranger saluted Galen as we all jumped into his four-door car, me in the front with Galen, and I rolled the window down like Galen had since it was a nice spring morning. Was this a Chevy? Cars were not my strong point. It wasn't as loud as the other one, but still black and sleek. And from the sounds of it, Galen liked to collect cars...ones that were irreplaceable from the sounds of it.

We backed out of the garage, and I watched as Ranger hit the button and the door started to come down. He started to strut towards us, then as the door was close to closing, he rolled out underneath, jumped up, and fist-pumped the air. The door started to go back up.

"Ah, fuck. I really thought I had that. Hold on." Ranger ran back to the wall and did it again. This time, he did a stupid dance, then rolled out under at last second, but the door went up again.

"I really thought he didn't touch it that time," I said, more to myself than anything. Must be a sensitive door.

"Come on, asshole, stop fucking around, Ranger," Maverick called out, which just set Ranger onto more funny dance moves. This time, he hit the button and did a catwalk strut like a model would. I laughed, which was probably encouraging him more. Then he dove down and rolled under, and instantly, the door went back up.

"We're going to be late! Just hit the button and come on." Maverick growled. This was a little funny but frustrating at the same time. Ada was waiting for me.

"Come on," I screamed out. He hit it again and ran straight for us, but the door went up again. I looked over to Galen and saw a goofy grin on his face. "Galen?" He turned to me as Ranger started to cuss and head back for the button, when I saw a small dark controller in Galen's hand.

"Oh my god, give me that." I reached over, but he was too fast.

"What the hell?" Raff called out to me as I snatched the controller out of Galen's hand and he cracked up laughing. Had the tables been turned? Was Galen becoming Ranger?

I shook my finger at Galen. "I cannot believe you did that." I wasn't angry, if anything, I was smiling. Ranger jumped in the car and laughed.

"Man, that door is oversensitive." I held up the controller and pointed to Galen. The look on Ranger's face was priceless.

"Oh, you asshole. You were fucking with me the whole time. I knew I made it the first time... Was this about the old man thing or the Cobra?"

Galen put the car in drive and laughed before saying, "Both."

I smiled the whole way to school, while the guys all chatted away about cars.

I jumped out the car and ran straight to Ada, her arms open wide for a hug. I wrapped my arms around her and smiled. This was going to be so good.

"What took you so long?" she hissed under her breath. We pulled apart, and I was about to explain about Galen and how he'd messed with Ranger, but I felt a tall figure move to the side of me.

"Hey, Ada, Lexi. I heard about the...you know. And it worked. You don't smell anymore... Oh wait, I mean like you don't smell like a

—" Noah's eyes went wide, and his hands were doing a lot of gestures. I looked to Ada and held my tongue. Noah was so cute, and I had a feeling the guys were telling him off.

"I'm sorry, Lexi. I'm gonna go now." He pointed his thumb to the school doors and ran up the stairs as fast as he could.

"I assume that's the reason you needed me here earlier," I said, and Ada raised her brows at me, then looped her arm through mine.

"Maybe... Let's go. School just got better now you're back."

I'd noticed that none of the shifters sniffed me or even looked at me. A few did double takes like they weren't sure it was me. I recognized a lot of them, some Kiba, some Rawlins...ugh, even that asshole Parker Tolson from Kenneally. I saw the bright pink banners in the halls, with 'Prom' written on them in big silver writing. Oh wow... fuck. I'd missed a bit while I was away. Ugh, the dreaded prom.

"So...do you take one or all of them to pr—" Ada started to ask before I cut her off.

"No, no...prom. Like, totally forgot about prom, and like, I'm busy then and I can't go." Her eyes widened, and her mouth dropped open.

"Lexi, they already got their tickets and yours. Even Galen." I froze. They what? They'd already gotten the tickets? Even Galen had bought one? Like, how was that even going to work? He couldn't be at prom with me without having everyone on his case about the fact he was in a relationship with a student. Even being an ex-teacher of the school, I was pretty sure that would turn heads and have the gossip mill running wild.

"We're gonna be late, hurry. English is boring, but it's gonna be fun now you're here."

She wasn't joking about class being boring. Turns out, Galen didn't just compel the teachers to pass me, but he did it for Ada too. This meant the teacher didn't ask us to do anything and didn't give us work, saying we'd already passed. I was going to speak to Galen. I wanted to at least feel like I'd spent the last four years trying to pass and get into college. Exams...my birthday. College. Well, community college. I didn't care what Alaric said, I was going to study on campus. So far, I was in school, I just need to enroll with Ada and then we could go together. I just didn't know what I wanted to study. Maybe I should look into the medical field...

"Look, I don't mind he did that. It's given me heaps more time to organize the prom." I turned in my chair to face her.

"You're on the prom committee?" She gave a "well duh" shrug. And really, I should have known. Ada had lived for extracurricular activities when I first met her, and I didn't expect that to change at all. Just...*ugh, prom.*

"So it was a hard choice, but we went with the masquerade ball. But only because I was thinking about you when the time came to vote." Me? Why was I the reason behind the theme?

"Oh, wow. Thanks?" I wasn't sure if I wanted to thank her, and I still didn't get it.

"For Galen? This way, everyone is hidden, mysterious. Well, I'm pretty sure you'll still be about to tell most, but I thought he could wear a mask, and that way, all your mates can come. You can celebrate together without worrying about the one left behind."

I stuttered, unable to form words, so I just hugged her. She laughed a little as she hugged me back.

"You are truly the best friend ever." I got all teary from that, man. She was good.

"Okay well, if I'm the bestest friend, would you come to dinner at my house tonight? Mom and Dad keep asking about you and when you're gonna come over to meet them. I can drive you home after?"

"Of course I will. I'll tell the guys." I could tell this was important to her, so it was important to me. I hugged her again. Wow, I was a little emotional today, but in a good way... Ugh, maybe I was getting my period. Oh crap, it was due soon. I was a regular twenty-eight-days girl. I just had to count back the days...one, two...twenty-nine. *Fuck*...thirty? Nope, wait, that couldn't be right.

Oh my god.

CHAPTER TWENTY-SEVEN

RAFFERTY

I felt better today with Lexi being alone. Well, as alone as she thought she was. The pack was watching her, protecting her, she just didn't know. It was the only way Alaric was going to let her come today. I loved how happy she was when she woke up, all bright and cheerful.

The day went smoothly, which really shocked me. I could still smell Lexi. Her scent didn't change at all for me, and Mav and Ranger had said the same thing. It was a little different for Galen, but he'd said nothing had changed. Yet every shifter I'd seen had told us the same thing—they couldn't smell her anymore, and she just smelled human to them.

That made the stress of her being here lessen. We all scent marked her once she was out of the shower and dressed this morning, and I loved that. We had been doing it for a while now, but not like that, with all three of us at the same time. I was getting so close to my packmates, our own bond growing between us. Knowing when to give space, when to join in, who got the bed that night. It was like how I'd been told Pack Russet did things, how I'd seen the families in Kiba, especially Noah's family. I'd wanted to speak with one of his fathers, just to get some advice on how to navigate this new world, because this truly was a new world for me.

"Okay, so Noah and Saint are gonna watch our girl while we go take care of our little brother's bullys," Ranger said, clapping me on the back.

This was Galen's plan and why he drove us. He wanted to come with us, help us after school to get the little assholes that had been pushing Josh around at school. He was just like me—an outsider trying to fit in with a new pack. They just wouldn't let him be, but they were gonna learn today.

"Why are Noah and Saint going? Seriously?" Maverick asked, rolling his eyes. I'd heard all about that conversation, and I even thought the same thing. If they got caught there...well, all hell would break loose and Saint would have to watch more than just his balls. I'd be there watching...wouldn't miss my girl kicking his ass for a moment. Yeah, we might be a pack and friends now, but I couldn't forget that night he attacked me. That was a wound too deep to fully heal, but we'd both moved on. I didn't know if I was rooting for him to get the girl or for Ada to kick his ass with Lexi.

When the growling rumble of an engine got closer, most of the students in front of the school were looking in the direction it was coming from. I'd heard it coming, but I wasn't sure if that was Galen, because it sounded different from the Cobra this morning.

"Fuck yeah! Oh, hell yeah," Ranger exclaimed as he ran down the stairs and towards the sound. Maverick just shook his head.

"Galen ain't gonna let him touch that. That's his baby...well, after the Cobra. It's beautiful, you're going to love it."

Oh, hell yeah, a Mustang. I couldn't believe the cars Galen had. I felt like I'd won the lottery having him as my packmate. Old vamps were loaded, who would've known? Not me. I didn't really know any but Shelly.

"I wonder if he would buy me one?" I mused as Mav chuckled.

"Sugar daddy?" he asked, and we both cracked up. Oh fuck, that was too funny.

"Maybe if you called him that, but it wouldn't work for me." Mav just winked at me as I watched the deep green Mustang with bronze stripes come to a stop, Ranger bouncing around to get in the driver's door.

"Okay, so here's the deal—we don't want to be arrested, not that it would make much difference, but still, let's avoid that. Just a little scare, you know, to let them know we're waiting for them if they hurt him again. Then we're gonna take Josh out for ice cream and drive him home for dinner."

Galen had it all planned, and Ranger got kicked to the backseat for trying to drive, while arguing that he was this amazing driver and it was only one time he messed up...a costly mess up. I slipped into the passenger seat and stretched my legs out. Of course, Ranger had a little hissy fit, saying he was taller than me and needed the leg room.

"You snooze you lose," I told him as he slid into the back next to his twin. He grumbled something, and Galen clicked his fingers as we took off for the elementary school in Kiba.

"I told you I would think about it. I did and decided that you weren't going to drive her," Galen said, and I could see the wheels turning in Ranger's head. He was about to say something when we arrived at the school. Galen parked right out the front, like he had prepared an empty spot to be there when we arrived. Hell, maybe he did organize it.

The four of us all piled out of the car and stood in front of the school. We leaned against the Mustang, gently, waiting for the bell to ring and to scare some little kids.

When the bell finally rang, we had a crowd around us...of moms. They were looking at us, some reeking of concern, some looking as if they were mentally stripping us, and others... Well, you didn't want to know what scent they were giving off.

"There he is," Ranger said, pushing up from the car and making his way towards Josh. I could see now five boys coming up behind him, and they didn't look like they wanted to be his friend.

"Show is on," Mav said, and I followed him and Galen to Josh. Were these boys were about to have the shock of their life.

"Hey, Josh," I said as I eyed the largest boy in the group. He stopped and looked at us. Mav was on his own mission, his finger pointed at the big kid as he stormed right past us to him.

"Fuck," Galen hissed, chasing after him. I followed as backup... like we needed backup from a ten-year-old. I heard Ranger tell Josh that we were busy and would he like to come sit in Galen's car, that he could sit in the front seat.

"You little fucker. You know who I am?" The kid looked up with big eyes. Was he a shifter? I thought I'd seen him before.

"You're gonna leave Josh alone. You go near him, speak to him, or touch him...hell, if you even breathe on him, I will be back. I know where you live, and we are all Josh's brothers. We will destroy you." Mav's approach was very to the point, a little scary, but still, highly effective.

"That goes for all of you. You see something happening, you see him being bullied and don't stand up for him, we'll know and we'll be back," I said. I totally wanted to say that last bit in the *Terminator* voice but was worried it wouldn't hold the same warning if I did.

The kids ran away, nodding. God, I hoped this helped. I couldn't stomach the thought that he'd been bullied for so long, suffering without anyone but Jack and Grayson to talk to.

We headed back to the car, and the little dude was in my seat.

"Let's get ice cream. What's your favorite flavor, Josh?" I asked him.

He smiled and cheered as the car jerked forward with a loud rumble.

"It's chocolate."

CHAPTER TWENTY-EIGHT

LEXI

As soon as we got into Ada's car, I freaked out. Like, I swore I got this shit wrong. I was never late with my period, and I'd used protection.

"Hey, do you remember how long ago it was that Ranger asked you for things to buy me when I got my period?" I could see her brow scrunch and her lips purse.

"Um...like a month ago?" My heart started to hammer, and my mouth went dry. I had to have messed up. So much had happened in such a short time, it was hard to keep track of the days.

"Oh fuck! Wait, do you think that you—Oh shit. Wait, let me think back. That was the day you weren't at school because of your period. Like three weeks ago? Not a month. Like twenty-three days? Maybe twenty-four?"

I let out a deep breath. "Oh man. I think you're right, I just... Every day has been something huge, and I just lost track of time. Wow, I think I deserve a treat after all of this."

Ada reached over and patted my leg. "You really should use your iPhone more. You can then track when it was last and set an alarm for when it's due. That's what I do. As for a treat...go to prom!" I laughed at her determination to get me to prom. She was so organized. That was a good idea, though. I'd figure that out later when I was home. I really should've used the iPhone more. Then I wouldn't have ended up with mini heart attacks.

"Yes, okay. I will go...if they ask me. But you know they haven't asked me yet, or I would have known about prom. Plus, I saw Olivia hanging around Ranger again. He tried to brush her off, but she is very...*persistent*." I ground that last word out between my teeth. I trusted them and I knew they wouldn't cheat or do anything to hurt me, but it didn't make it any easier when other girls were touching them and flirting with them. I guessed these were all the feelings that came with being in a relationship.

"You know she doesn't just do it to Ranger, right? I saw her flirting with Noah." That had my attention.

"Noah, huh? So is he taking her to the prom?"

"No," she snapped back. I tried to hide the smile from my face, but I couldn't.

"Don't you even start... I have no idea what's going on between us. Wait...not us. Like, I mean with him and with me. There is no *us*." Her shoulders lowered, and she let out a small huff. She tapped a few times on the steering wheel before asking, "Is it weird he invited me to his sixteenth birthday dinner with his family next week?"

He did what? Oh my gosh, that's too adorable.

"Oh, it's weird. I knew it," she said, and I shook my head and turned to her. Her cheeks were pink, and I knew deep down she liked him. She was just hung up on the age...maybe his immaturity as well. I could never forget Noah playing fetch with her.

"It's not weird. Nothing is if you're happy and he makes you happy. I was just thinking how sweet it was. Like, you're going to dinner with his family? That's a big move. Did he ask you to go to prom? Actually, maybe he's waiting for you to ask him. Or are you waiting for Huxley?"

She didn't speak as we turned onto a residential street and drove into the driveway of a nice little suburban home. It was very similar to

Jack and Grayson's house, except this one was more brown and cream colored.

"Let's not talk about what happened at Kiba, school, or boys. Let's pretend they don't exist for today and go paint our nails and watch trashy shows. Girl time, no stress." I couldn't agree with that more. Hell yeah, no boy problems. Not that I had any, really. Finally, I had the freedom I needed, and if it meant painting nails, I was in. I needed some pamper time, to slow down and chill for a while.

When Lexi's parents came home, I could see where she got her looks from. She looked so much like her mom, Michelle. Her dad, Graham, was a little older than I thought he'd be, with a full head of gray hair, but he was very friendly. He wore a dark suit and had taken the tie off when he sat down. He asked me some questions about school and what I might like to do after graduation. He chuckled when I said I didn't really know and said I was just like Ada.

As the meal went on, I could see Ada had grown up in a very loving home. Both her parents asked questions about her day, she asked them about theirs, and they laughed and joked. It was better than I'd imagined it would be. She had an amazing family.

"Ada tells me you were invited to Kiara's wedding next weekend. Destiny is flying in for it on Thursday, wouldn't miss it for the world. Only six more days till I can see my girl." Michelle said with a huge smile.

I nodded. I'd almost forgotten that they had to postpone the wedding…well, ceremony. I was surprised they allowed outsiders to come, knowing what it was really for. But then, maybe they didn't bite the female in front of everyone. Maybe that was done privately. I just…didn't want to see it. I'd already experienced it, the bad effects of it anyway.

"Well, we'll have to have you over again for dinner when Destiny is here so you can meet Ada's big sister."

"Mom, she's only a year older than me, not that big." Ada smiled and shook her head. Her mom got up and kissed her hair, then started to clean up the table.

"Oh, I can help," I said, grabbing a few plates, but her mom was over to me, asking me to please put them down and telling us to go have fun.

On the drive back, we blasted songs, some I had never heard of before, but Ada told me they were a K-pop band called BTS. I was having such a great time, I didn't want it to end.

"Hey, like, I don't want to freak you out, but there's a car that's been following us and they're still there." I looked up ahead, and saw that we were really close to Kiba court.

"It's okay, just keep going. If they follow us down, then I'll call Galen."

Her hands were a little shaky on the wheel. Shit, I didn't know how badly affected she was. Shit. I kept looking, trying to say positive things, but as I felt the car turn, I watched the car follow us too. *Fuck.*

My hands were now shaking as I reached into the pocket on my bag and pulled out my iPhone. I quickly hit Galen's name, and he picked up on the first ring.

"Are you okay?" His voice made me feel so much better. He would come. He was fast.

"There's a car following us. We're almost at the gate, but I don't know who it is." I could hear him yelling out something, so he must've been with the guys. As the gate got closer, I could see Jett and Nash there. The gate was open, and they were ready for us.

"Just drive straight in. You're safe, okay?" Huh? My heart was hammering. There shouldn't be any more of this. It was over, we'd won. They were all gone. Did Galen's compelling not work? Did it wear off after a while? These were things we didn't experiment with.

"What about the car? They can just drive through the gates," I said.

I heard some more background noise, and someone said, "Don't."

"Ah... Love, please don't yell...but that is Saint and Noah following you."

What the fuck?

CHAPTER TWENTY-NINE

LEXI

"Stop the car, Ada. It's Saint and Noah. I'm gonna go ask them why they're stalking us tonight." Like that wasn't creepy. As soon as the car door opened, Galen was standing in front of me, his hands up defensively.

"Look, I can explain. Please let me explain."

I held onto the car door and cocked my hip, pretty sure there was no explanation needed. They had them watching us. Then they'd followed us back here and made us believe we were going to be attacked again. After what had happened, after everything, they thought it was okay to do that and not tell me. Instead, poor Ada was a mess and I was still shaking, but I was more mad now than frightened.

"It's just, we wanted to make sure you were safe. Ada, too—" I held my finger up and gave him the most blank stare I could. He shut his mouth, and his eyes widened slightly. I hadn't really told Galen off since I'd chosen him as a mate.

"If you ever, and I mean ever, do that again, I will never speak to you again. That is a line you crossed. Having protection is one thing, but not telling us and we panic thinking we are being stalked, that's another thing. I thought you would be smarter than that, Galen."

Ada had gotten out of the car and came around to defuse the situation.

"It's okay, at least they weren't crazy killers… Maybe crazy, but not killers."

I cracked a smile. She was trying to put a positive spin on this, and it didn't take long before Maverick, Ranger, and Raff were beside Galen. I had a feeling that they were all ganging up on me.

"We just wanted you to feel like you had space, but also know you were safe," Maverick said, trying to add to Galen's reasoning, but it wasn't working. I was actually mad. Not that they wanted to keep me safe, but to lie to me and say that I could go to Ada's house, that they weren't going to be there, I was fine. Yeah, because they had people watching me.

"Look, we're going to talk about trust when I get inside, something I thought we had in each other. I trusted you when you said I was safe to go to Ada's without you all, but having others watch me, that's a breach of trust."

I could see Saint and Noah walking towards us, and I rolled my eyes and shook my head at their approach. Ada saw them but didn't jump in her car like I thought she would.

"Hi, Ada. Hi, Lexi," Noah said, looking bashful. His hands were in the pockets of his shorts, and he looked up at us through his lashes as he kicked the gravel with his shoe. He looked like he'd gotten caught with his hand in the cookie jar. And well…he had. Kinda.

Ada gave a little wave. Ugh…I wished I wasn't so angry so I could watch this. It was so sweet. I had a feeling Noah was wiggling his way into her heart, just like Ranger had. But I was angry, and I just needed some space to think.

"Thanks for the lift, Ada. Your parents are super nice, and tell them again thank you for having me." I hugged her, and she nodded.

"Anytime, my parents loved you. See you on Monday?" she asked. I nodded and started walking towards the gates that weren't too far away. I could feel the guys behind me, Ranger walking slightly ahead of me. I watched him...and his ass in those jean shorts was— Nope. Not going there. I looked away. He was doing that Ranger swagger thing, hypnotizing me with his ass.

Jett smiled at me and nodded. He was smart. I wasn't looking for any smart-ass comments tonight.

Nash, on the other hand... "Is that trouble in paradise I see?" When I shot him a death stare, he shook his head. "They should've known better is all. They should've told you, Lexi."

Yeah, they should have.

So, turns out being mad at your mates ends up with a lot of chocolate, a bubble bath in my room back in the main house, and whatever movie I wanted to watch. I picked *Frozen*. Pretty sure the guys were internally screaming as they plastered on smiles and we watched all together in the movie room.

There was popcorn, a big blanket fort, and Ranger shifted and snuggled with me on the lower floor. This was nice, and they did apologize a lot about the mistake they made. I may have let them suffer a little more than needed, but I was just glad to be back here in the movie room. It was all fixed now, and you wouldn't have even known it was damaged at all.

We all fell asleep together, and Ranger stayed in wolf form. Pretty sure Alaric was gonna be mad that he shifted and stayed like that, but we could vacuum later.

When I woke up, I was happy. Everyone was sleeping still...even Galen. He was so close to me, his arm wrapped around me. I moved and sat up, and his arm dropped to my legs. He didn't wake up, so I tentatively reached out and touched his skin where his sweater had ridden up. The scars there were white and raised against his already pale skin.

He was cold, but I had gotten used to it. I liked it. It was Galen.

He wasn't a real hugger or really initiated physical contact with me. I thought he was worried about the temperature of his skin. But now, like this, touching him, I thought it went deeper than just the temperature. I thought he had some deep emotional wounds.

"Hey," he whispered, and my eyes flicked to his. It was enough to stir Maverick, who rolled over and started snoring...badly. We both glanced over to him, and I pursed my lips to try and stop the giggles from coming out. Galen had a beautiful smile on his face, and I looked down at him and stroked his cheek before running my fingers through his curls.

"Hey," I whispered back. I liked that we were the only two awake. It was nice, a little one-on-one time. I tugged a little on his dark curls, pulling him towards me. His brows raised, and a little spark flashed in his eyes as he sat up and kissed me, then pulled away. Oh, hell no. I wanted to be kissed by him. I pulled him to me, our lips crashing together, his mouth opened, and I slipped my tongue into his mouth, deepening the kiss further. We were waking everyone up, but I needed this. I needed to kiss Galen right now.

"Get a room," Ranger grumbled and threw a pillow at us. It broke us apart, and I giggled as I threw it back.

"No, you get a room. Or go back to sleep."

He didn't, he sat up and rubbed his scruffy mop of hair. It had grown heaps. All of theirs had. Even Raff needed a haircut. The shaved sides were really long.

"You need a haircut," I told him as I wrapped myself into Galen and stretched my feet out to Raff. He took them in his hands and started to massage them.

I moaned, fuck. "This is like heaven."

Then we heard a huge snore, and all of us looked over to Maverick and laughed. His eyes popped open, and he looked stunned. Oh, poor thing.

"What?" he asked, his voice deep with sleep as he rubbed his eyes.

"You snore like a freight train." He smiled sleepily and dropped back down to the pillow. I smiled as I rolled away from Galen and Raff, and lay my body down on Maverick's, the blanket between us. He groaned and said I was heavy, so I laughed and tickled him.

"Get up, sleepyhead. Let's go in the pool today."

CHAPTER THIRTY

RAFFERTY

It was amazing that a week ago, we were all preparing to fight. That I was protecting my mate from my uncles, who thought it was their right to take her from me the same way they took my mom. I remembered Uncle Jordy told me once they'd snatched her from the street and forced the change on her. That was one of the many reasons why I gave the go ahead to wipe out the whole pack. There were no redeeming qualities about them. Drugs had taken over their lives, and they'd done too much hurt, delivered too much pain to me and to others. They needed to be wiped out before they slipped up and showed themselves to humans. Exposing us all would be the downfall of our world.

"Hey, you've been really quiet. Wanna talk?" Lexi pulled herself out of the water and nudged her arm against mine. I'd come out here to watch her learn to swim. Maverick was teaching her today because yesterday, we found out that Ranger was not the best teacher for Lexi. He was a jokester but had the patience of a two-year-old.

"Just thinking." She nudged me again, and I almost fell in.

"Yeah, I can see that. You haven't really been yourself all week. Like, I know no one has been, and it almost feels like a bad dream the way everything is back to normal around here. Even the patrols are less. But it did happen, and I think you should talk to someone. Doesn't have to be me, maybe Jack? Or Grayson?"

I shrugged. I knew I should, and talking with Lexi had been good for me in the past when I opened up a little to her. But how do you tell your mate you don't feel any guilt for signing off on your pack's death warrant? That because they were all gone, and I was the only living heir, all the Russet land was now mine. I wanted to go there and burn that piece of shit they called a home down to the ground. I wanted to wipe all those memories from my mind and start to live again.

"Let go back inside for a while. Just you and me? Out of the sun." she suggested.

We went to Galen's. I was happy we were more or less living here, even if I had to share the sofa. It was better when we were all together. I felt...whole, and even though at times, I felt alone, I knew I wasn't. They could tell when I needed to be by myself, or with Lexi, like now. She wanted to try and help me, but I didn't think I could be helped. I wasn't broken, yet I wasn't whole either.

"Is it about your mom?" she asked really softly as she held my hand. I guessed it was a part of it. I didn't like to think too much about it, and my wolf didn't like that, didn't like the feelings it brought. But it was something I had been struggling with.

"It's okay, you don't have to tell me. Just trying to help."

Her eyes, so unusual and so unreal. They were big and bright, like they were looking into my soul.

"It's not that I don't want to, I just find it hard to control my wolf when I think too much about it. It's like a trigger for my shift almost, and I'm scared I'll shift and accidently hurt you."

I bent forward, dropping her hand and resting them both on my knees.

"Oh, Raff, babe. It's all right, I can heal fast, remember?" she said. Not fast enough for my liking, but Galen would be able to speed it up. I took a deep breath and sat up straight.

"It's just I keep thinking about her, what they did to her. And to find out they murdered her...my mother." I growled low, my wolf itching to jump out and rip their throats out. But they were no longer here, they were dead. When I didn't speak for a while, Lexi rubbed my back softly in circles. It calmed me down, and I relaxed slightly.

"Do you think maybe you would want to go back? Like, you know, to Russet?"

That I didn't know. To burn it down, yes. But then, my mom's roses... They'd said she was buried with the roses.

I looked over to Lexi. It was funny, the first thing I really noticed about her was the way she smelled. Not just like my mate, but she smelled like my mother's roses. I was drawn to that—the good memories in springtime when they blossomed, their fragrance on the wind. She'd loved those roses. I did everything I could to make sure they were looked after, but now, no one was there to take care of them.

"Yeah, actually, I would. Maybe after Josh's adoption? I can go there on my own after. Or if you want..."

She kissed me, and I didn't realize I'd been crying until her thumbs came up and wiped my tears.

"I'll be there with you. We all will."

I sagged down and let it all out as Lexi held me tight, stroking my hair and saying soothing words. Eventually, I felt them all home. They were quiet as I rested with Lexi, but each, one by one, came over and held my shoulder, letting me know they were there.

We are all in this together.

This was my family.

CHAPTER THIRTY-ONE

LEXI

It had been a few days since Raff broke down in my arms, four days to be exact. It had been good for him to let it out like that, and he'd been doing better. Tomorrow was adoption day, and then we would be going to Russet straight after. It was cleared with Alaric, and I was excited. Plus, my period had come, which I wasn't expecting the guys to notice, but as soon as I woke up yesterday morning, Galen had told me everything I needed was in the bathroom.

I'd laughed when I walked in there. He was right—everything I needed was there. As soon as I'd walked out, all the guys asked how I was feeling, and Ranger rubbed my back and asked if I needed a hot water bottle, chocolate, or to take the day off school. I just blushed under all their attention. It was sweet, and they did load me up with chocolate before we left for school.

It would've been even sweeter if they learned how to put the lid down on the toilet. Like really? Was that asking for much? Probably because I had mentioned it a few times, along with their aim! Ugh... didn't even want to go there. Boys were gross.

As soon as Ada saw me, she grabbed my arm. Her eyes were wide, and I knew she wanted to talk and exactly what she wanted to talk about.

"So did Noah have a good birthday dinner?" I tried to whisper, but it was hard in the school halls with so many students being loud. Her eyes widened more, and she slapped me gently as she shushed me. "That good?" She rolled her eyes, then stopped suddenly in the hall. I turned back to her and saw she was red in the face. Oh crap. I looked over to where her eyes were trained, and yep, Noah was standing there watching her. From the huge beaming grin on his face, he was happy to see her. He was standing with a few other Kiba boys, Luca and Harley, and they were all watching us. I smiled and started to wave as two big arms wrapped around my waist from behind and lifted me in the air.

"Ranger, put me down," I protested. He laughed and dropped me to my feet, but not before he walked up to Noah.

"Hey, man. How was your birthday dinner?" I pursed my lips and rolled my eyes. Ugh, couldn't they just let us girls talk for one minute without listening in? I peeled myself from Ranger and went back to where Ada was still standing, students walking around her. I grabbed her hand and took off with her in a different direction until I found the restroom and dragged her in with me.

"We can't be late for class," she protested as the warning bell rang.

"Because we won't pass?" I replied, but she didn't say anything. Her face still looked like she'd seen a ghost, but when she cracked a smile, I knew she got it. I hugged her, something I noticed I was doing a lot of lately. The door slammed open, and the sound bounced off the tiles. Olivia and her little group of bitches were here.

"Oh, gross. It's contaminated in here. Don't want to get any stripper or nerd germs." For fuck's sake. Who the fuck told these bitches about my former employment? Whoever it was, I was going to kill them. But first, if she didn't want stripper germs, she should've walked away. I moved over to where she was looking at herself in the mirror and pressed my body against hers.

"Hey, back off. Don't touch me, stripper whore." I grabbed her ponytail and yanked, hard. Her hand flew to her head as she crumbled to the floor. The other two girls pulled their claws out.

"What, you both gonna take me?" Olivia was whining on the floor and cussing at me. Why did girls find the need to do this to each other? Why bash each other down? She infuriated me, and I lashed out. I shouldn't have, I should've been the bigger person, but she'd pissed me off.

"Look, I don't know why you bother to be nasty. Like seriously, you obviously like the Kiba boys. You were at their parties. You know I'm with Maverick and Ranger. Yeah...you know. They aren't going to leave me for you. So you might as well accept that."

She got up and spat at me.

"They were mine. I had them first, and they'll come back to me. I know they will. They're only with you because you're new. They don't actually want to be with you. They just see a stripper who can perform." My blood was boiling. It was like talking to a dumbass.

"Stop being such a bitch, Olivia. We all know they wouldn't leave Lexi. You can keep trying, like you have all week, but they're with Lexi. They want her. I'm sorry if that's hard to understand, but you need to back off," Ada said, her hands on her hips. I felt so proud of her in that moment. She'd stood up to them, and I smiled to show Ada how good that was. In the corner of my eye, I saw something blue whip past, then Ada was flying down onto the tiles. My hand reached out, but I couldn't grab her in time.

She hit her head hard and made a pained sound as I moved to her. Fuck. I turned back to see Olivia straighten up her blue dress and brush her hair from her eyes. My eyes flared as she laughed, but the other two girls didn't. They were smart, because I was going to make sure she hurt...bad.

"You think I'm gonna hurt you? That would be too easy... I'm going to destroy you." She put her hands up in a fighting stance and I chuckled. "I ain't gonna fight you, no. This is worse. I'm gonna freeze you out. You are done with Kiba boys."

She stood tall, her hands on her hips, and just laughed. You could tell she was worried, and the other two girls just watched on, not saying a word.

"You think your magic pussy is going to stop all the Kiba boys from wanting me? Ugh, pathetic piece of trash. You'll be the one they kick to the curb, bitch. Not me. Let's go, girls." The other two ran to the door. I guessed they didn't have anything to say as Olivia strutted out of there like her shit didn't stink. Ada moaned as she sat up, and her hand on the back of her head came away stained with red.

"Oh shit, you need to see the nurse." I moved behind her and saw her blonde hair was now stained with sticky red blood. She'd hit the floor hard.

"You're bleeding, Ada." I jumped up and grabbed some paper towels and wet them, then quickly put it to the back of her head. She flinched.

"I have a headache. It's like a little army of soldiers marching in my head." I didn't know if her describing it that way meant she had a concussion, but I wasn't going to wait to find out.

"Hold on, I'll get help."

CHAPTER THIRTY-TWO

LEXI

Poor Ada went home. Her parents were going to get her checked out, but she would be fine. I'd thought of using my powers on her, but when she saw the way I looked at her, she told me not to. She knew how much pain it put me through, and that she was okay. Just a headache, mostly.

"Ah, Lexi. Hi. Um...is Ada okay? I tried calling her, but she didn't answer." I turned and saw the concerned look on Huxley's face, his dark brows all scrunched up.

"Oh, yeah, I think she'll be fine. She hit her head pretty bad. Olivia started shit with me, and Ada... Well, Olivia didn't like what she had to say."

I watched as his fists clenched and his dark brown eyes glowed for a moment. Oh, shit. Fuck.

"It's okay, don't... Fuck, don't shift." He shook his head.

"I'm okay. Just, when it comes to Ada... I don't like seeing her get hurt is all." I nodded. I could see a few other Rawlins' guys standing off to the side, obviously waiting for Huxley to return.

"I also wanted to thank you for saving me. Twice." He rubbed the scruff on his face as he looked everywhere but at me. "I tend to act before thinking. So you really saved me, and I owe you my life. If there is anything you need, not that you would need something from me... Ah fuck. Yeah. Ranger is coming. I should go." I reached out and grabbed his arm to stop him. His eyes glowed again, but I didn't think it was me he was worried about. It was Ranger.

"Look, there's something I need. Would you guys, the Rawlins boys, would you freeze Olivia out? Don't look at her or speak to her. I hope this way she gets the idea that you don't just go hurting other girls to get what you want. She might learn her lesson."

He nodded and looked down to where I was still holding him. I let go fast, as if his arm was on fire.

"Oh, sorry. Try calling Ada after school. I know she would love to hear from you. I don't think she has a date to the prom..." I didn't wait to see a reaction from him. I just turned and made my way over to where Ranger was waiting with looks that could kill.

"Babe..." I ran my hand up his chest. He blinked, and a slow smile crept over his face.

"Aww, Lex. You called me babe. I love it, even though I know you're trying to distract me. I can't help myself. I see you touching someone else, and I get all..." He growled low in my ear and nipped at it, and I laughed.

"You heard what I said about Olivia, about freezing her out?"

He growled low again, before whispering, "She doesn't exist to the Kiba boys." I smiled, not that he wouldn't have done it. I just needed him to spread the word.

He wrapped me up in his arms, and I loved the feel of being trapped there. He rocked me from side to side before the bell rang again. Ugh...class.

When I made it to art, Maverick was sitting at a table with his work in front of him, looking at it intently. I thought I'd be able to sneak in without him noticing me, but the curl of his lip as he turned his head to me told me otherwise.

"You think you can sneak up on me?" His hand pulled on my hip, and I stumbled into him.

"Oh, I can try." I kissed his lips, and he slapped my ass. I jumped. Wow, that kinda display in front of classmates was new. He wasn't very affectionate outside of the house. If anything, he seemed to be scared of public displays of affection. I used to hate being the center of attention, but I was slowly learning to ignore it. Heads would always turn when I was kissing three of the hottest guys in school, displaying our relationship in the open for everyone to see.

I sat down beside him and looked down at his painting, the one I remembered he was creating when I first started this class and he hated me. Well okay, he didn't hate me. He just wasn't a big fan of my being here because I smelled like his mate and he was scared of me and what I meant.

"Oh wow, Maverick. It's beautiful." He wrapped his hand around my shoulder and pulled me in close. I reached out to the artwork. The dark purples and blacks I remembered, but the light colors were new.

"This is you," he said, pointing to where he had painted a star. It was big and glowing with yellows and reds. "This is Galen." Another star connected to mine with star dust. It was smaller than mine, but only slightly.

I pointed to another star farther down that was more red than yellow and asked, "Rafferty?"

He nodded, then pointed to another. It had green swirled into it. "Ranger."

My stomach fluttered. Oh, Maverick. This one was so dark, so sad and lonely. Now he had these bright stars. I was his star. We all were.

"Mav—" He cut me off with his finger to my lips, then shook his head and smiled.

"You don't need to say anything, just know that I didn't realize how lost I was until you came into my life. And now I've seen how bright my future is, there is no more dark. Only light."

My throat was thick with emotion, and Maverick knew, his hands cupping my face as he brushed his lips against mine. When his tongue brushed along the seam of my lips, I opened, reaching for his tee as I pulled him to me. Everything around us evaporated, and it was as if we were the only two people here and the whole world disappeared.

A throat clearing had us returning to earth. It was a huge drop back when I felt like I was floating.

"Love birds, there is a time and a place." It was our art teacher, an older woman who seemed to wear the same paint-stained smock every time I saw her. She tapped on the table and returned to the front of the class.

I giggled a little as Maverick held my hand under the table.

When the bell rang, we walked hand in hand to the lockers to get our bags. Because yes, I'd started using my locker. Olivia walked past. She saw Maverick holding my hand, but it didn't stop her from running her fingertip down his colorful tattoos. *Oh, hell no.* I went to move, but he held my hand tight.

"Something freaky just happened," Maverick called out for everyone to hear, and all heads turned our way. Olivia, with her huge smile aimed my way, tilted her head towards me as if to say "you're the freaky thing."

"What was it?" Harley called out as he walked to us, a funny grin on his face as he pushed back his shaggy hair. He looked like a true surfer boy with that hair. He was in my English class, but we'd never really spoken before. Even though he did sit at the same table as the Kiba boys, he was usually at the end.

"It was something horrible, and it touched me," Maverick replied.

Olivia's mouth dropped open, then she screeched out, "Horrible? I'm not the horrible one. Your pathetic girlfriend is the horrible one. Do you know what she did to me? She provoked me." It was eerily silent before Harley spoke again.

"Fuck, man. I hope it didn't contaminate you or shit." Olivia stomped her foot, and everyone looked away. Holy fuck. Everyone was in on this. I'd just wanted to ice her out of Kiba and Rawlins for a bit, until she learned how to play nice, but even the humans were doing it too.

"You can all see me. Stop looking away. I didn't start this, that dumb bitch did." She was pointing at me, but I ignored her, just like everyone else. Everyone went back to packing their bag and going home, and she was still in the hall, yelling at students.

It felt good, even though I knew it was bad. But bullies needed a taste of their own medicine sometimes, and this was hers.

When we got to the Jeep, Maverick opened the door and Raff called shotgun and jumped in the front.

"Hey," I said, trying to shove him over. He laughed and hoisted me up into his lap.

"Hey, back at you." He kissed me as Maverick jumped in the front. We were waiting on Ranger, and then we would be home with Galen. He was going to make pasta tonight. He'd told me he was preparing it today. I didn't know what that meant exactly, since I didn't think pasta took all day, but I was excited to try it.

"Ugh, where's Ranger? He's taking forever," I asked as I crawled between the front seats and into the back and sat down, waiting for him.

"I'll call him," Maverick said, his cell to his ear. When Ranger didn't answer, I heard him cuss under his breath.

"What's wrong?" I asked. Maverick shook his head, then gave me a smile that didn't reach his eyes. I shook my head.

"Ranger being Ranger is what's wrong."

Oh fuck, what has he done now?

CHAPTER THIRTY-THREE

RANGER

That asshole had to be told to stop hanging around Ada like a lost puppy. He'd approached *my* mate to ask her about Ada. He shouldn't even have her number. That needed to be taken care of before the weekend. I knew he would see Ada at the mate ceremony that Lexi had been invited to, the one I wasn't happy about.

My wolf was even more unhappy about it. I had gone for more runs this week than usual. Not fighting was getting to me. It was how I let out this anger, this emotion I couldn't contain. I used to spar with Callum back at home, but now he was gone, that wasn't possible. Noah wasn't a fighter, since he didn't care for it. Saint would, but he'd said he was busy...every night this week.

I didn't voice that to Lexi or the guys. I didn't want her upset with me about her going to Rawlins for the ceremony, but it was hard when they were all cool with it. I thought I must be overreacting, but really? Not one of us were invited, only Lexi. We were just going to let our mate go to another pack without us? That set my wolf on edge, and I had felt it building up all day. Then seeing her touch Huxley, it took great control to not shift and rip his throat out.

It was Noah's birthday yesterday, when he finally hit sixteen, and he'd invited Ada to dinner. He was so nervous when he asked her. He thought she would say no, but she'd told him she would think about it. He'd called me over to his place on Monday to tell me that Ada had said she would come. Zara was so excited, she was fussing around the house, asking her mates to clean up in case Ada came over. But when they gave Noah a Jeep—the same as mine and Mav's—he said he wanted to pick her up and drive her.

They all ate out in Port Angeles. He'd told me how he picked up Ada and took her to the restaurant, and then he dropped her off at home. He walked her to the door, like I told him to, and she kissed him on the cheek. I was proud. That was my boy there. His moves were totally sloppy, but he was learning, and a kiss on the cheek was better than a slap in the face. Small steps.

"Hey, fucksley. Woods in five," I said, slamming my shoulder into Huxley as I strode past and out the door. He gave me a warning growl. Good, I needed a good fight.

I was ready when he approached, bouncing on the balls of my feet. I'd been itching for this all day. He was alone. Good, didn't need his pack here trying to stop him.

"What's your problem, Lovell? I didn't touch your mate, she touched me, and I did as she said. Olivia is out. Didn't you see what happened back there with your brother?"

Yeah, I saw him and Harley fucking with Olivia. I didn't stick around for long.

"No, this is about Ada. Back off, she belongs to Noah and Saint. They're gonna claim her, and you're fucking with her head."

He backed up, his hands in fists as he shook his head.

"Fuck you, they've made no claim. She's fair game, and she isn't Kiba. I've liked her since freshman year. Never had the guts to talk to her, but after she saw me dying and shit...well, she didn't even blink at my scars. You just don't get it, pretty boy with all the girls chasing after you. Fuck you."

My wolf was prickling beneath the surface. I needed to strip before I destroyed my clothes and Lexi found out I was fighting. I ripped my tee off, and my shorts dropped just as the pain flashed through me and I was on all fours. I growled at Huxley, who was undressing. He was big, matching me for size. I had never challenged him before. He was quiet, usually kept to himself when there were fights, but today, I would find just how much better I was than him.

He let out a long howl, fucker. I didn't let him finish as I launched at him, going straight for the throat, but he dodged me and I grabbed onto his flank. I sunk my teeth in, tasting the metallic of his blood seeping out from the wound. He yelped loudly in pain and pulled away, snapping his teeth at me, but I held on, sinking deeper. I lost myself in my wolf as I let my venom flow into him.

"Ranger." My name was being called. "Ranger." It was screamed this time, so I let go. I could smell her now…my mate. Huxley whimpered as he moved away from me, limping badly. Fucking asshole was putting that on. It wasn't that bad.

I looked over to Lexi. She thought it was bad, and she looked at me with disappointment in her eyes. I hung my head, my wolf even feeling the sadness of upsetting our mate. Why did I do this? I had so much anger that built and built. Why didn't I walk away? Why did I do stupid, dumbass things?

"Huxley, do you want me to heal you?" Lexi asked, and I looked over. She was crouched behind him. I didn't want to shift, but I knew I had to.

"Ranger, what the fuck were you thinking?" Mav asked, his old monotone voice back, the one that told me he cared I was fighting but didn't care I was going against Father's orders. But this time, this time was different.

"He started it," I protested when Lexi shot me a look that said I would be on the sofa tonight. Fuck, it was my night to snuggle. Why did I mess things up for myself like this?

"Ranger, I...I really don't have words right now. I don't understand why you do this. Was this because I touched him?"

I shook my head no, but I knew deep inside it was one of the reasons I told myself that he deserved to be punished like this.

"He's lying," Mav told her, and my mouth dropped. She looked to Raff. He wouldn't meet my eyes as he nodded.

"Oh, fuck you both. Lexi, babe, I just wanted to tell him to stay away from Ada is all. Because she is—" Before I even finished, she had stood up and stormed over to me, her beautiful hair all wild...like her eyes. Her index finger poked me in the chest.

"Don't you even start. That's just another excuse. You just can't help yourself. Why? Tell me. Why not go join a gym or do kickboxing? Why do you pick on others like this?"

I didn't have a clue why. I hung my head. I could smell the fear and sadness coming from her. I didn't want her to feel like that, and I was the one who'd caused it because I just didn't think. I couldn't be here any longer. I shifted, the pain over in seconds, and I took off running.

I needed time and space. She needed to cool down before I told her why. I just had to find the reason why I did these dumb things. I just hoped she could forgive me.

CHAPTER THIRTY-FOUR

LEXI

The pasta Galen made was amazing, but it didn't help my stomach. I was worried about Ranger. I was mad, and I had a right to be. He was fighting with another shifter, all because he thought that Kiba owned Ada, as if she was some cattle.

"Where do you think he is?" I asked. Maverick was shoveling in the pasta, so he didn't answer me, red sauce dripping all over his chin. "Galen?" He looked worried, his brow creased, but he shook his head.

"This is really good," Raff said before adding another forkful to his mouth. I assumed Ranger was out running around somewhere, and we had his clothes so he would need to come home eventually. I decided to just let it go. He would be back soon. He had to be. We had Josh's big day tomorrow.

"So does everyone know what they're wearing tomorrow?" I was glad that Jack and Grayson had invited the guys. They said family was to come, and they were my mates, so they were invited. It had made this even more real, that we were a family to outside eyes. Oh, except they weren't invited to Kiara's ceremony. I didn't know exactly why I was going, since I had only met her a few times, but she'd invited me and I couldn't be rude. Us wolf lovers had to stick together, even if our wolves didn't like each other.

"I'm going to wear a grey suit, but I couldn't decide between a tie or a bow tie," Galen said with a smile and wink. I looked up at him through my lashes. He had a bow tie...

"Bow tie, it wins every time. Can I see it now?" He jumped up and took off toward the bedroom.

"Oh, he looks hot in a bow tie." Maverick winked at me before more food was shoveled in his mouth. Honestly...where did all that food go? I knew where mine went. I had gone up a bra and jean size since being here and was happy for it. I finally had fat on my bones.

Galen returned with a white shirt on and a bow tie. It was red. Oh, hell yeah. I clapped. "Yes, this. So, this. You look hot as sin, Mr. Donovani." His eyes narrowed, and I could see the dark creeping in. I giggled when he pounced on me. He swept back my hair over my shoulder, and his tongue on my throat had my body shivering. Oh yes, that felt amazing. Fuck, why did I still have to have my period?

"Is that all you need to say to get some action? I've been calling him that for years and not once did he lick my throat," Maverick teased, stretching back on his chair, his tee rising up and showing his abs and the trail of hair leading down to the impressive bulge I could see in his gray sweats. He'd put them on when we got back, and I told him he wasn't allowed to wear them out of the house. They were for my eyes only.

"Maybe it's the way you say it?" Galen teased back. "You need to go low, deep."

He pulled away from me and stalked over to Maverick, his dimples appearing as he cocked a brow.

"Mr. Donovani," Maverick said, and fuck, that was so deep...it had me getting wet. Galen pulled on his hair, exposing his neck, and licked a line from his collarbone to his ear. I watched as Maverick's eyes closed and he shivered at the sensation. I knew that feeling, I'd just had the same thing. I watched as Maverick's hand moved to his crotch, and he palmed himself through the tight material.

"It's good...isn't it?" His eyes slowly opened, and they were hazed over with desire. He looked to me, then Galen. Oh, I wanted this. Just being a female was in the way today.

"Soon..." Maverick whispered, then grabbed the back of Galen's head and pulled it to his mouth. I watched as they vied for dominance once again. The kiss was heated, full of power and passion, and once again, Galen was the one to concede. Giving in to Maverick, he lowered to his knees before him, and I rubbed my thighs together. I was so worked up from watching, I thought I could just orgasm from the visual alone.

The front door slammed opened, and we jerked and turned as one to see Ranger standing there, covered in blood and mud. The look he wore on his face scared me. The scene in front of me played out like the night of the blood moon. That was what I had heard Jett call it the other day. It upset me that people had to lose their lives to protect me, but everyone kept telling me they would do it again. I still held that emotional baggage, but it didn't trigger me to fall down a deep hole. I didn't feel as upset and scared about that night as I did right now.

"Ranger?" Maverick stood up so fast, the chair fell over. The sound made me jump as it hit the floor. My heart was racing. "Fuck, what happened?" Ranger's beautiful green eyes looked lifeless as he scanned the room until his eyes finally settled on me.

"Ranger?" I asked, my hand going to my throat. What had he done? Where had he been this whole time? He was not okay, that I could tell. We all could. I took a step to him, my hand reaching for him. God, was he hurt?

He closed the door behind him and walked straight to the bathroom and slammed that door closed. When I heard the shower turn on, I turned back to very worried expressions.

"What does this mean?" I asked the three of them, and they all looked like me.

"I've never seen him like this before, ever. Animal?" Maverick asked Galen, and he shook his head. Galen walked over to the door, before turning to us, his curls bouncing as he nodded.

"It's animal blood, not shifter or human."

We packed up the meal, Galen making a bowl for Ranger and placing it in the fridge. When he finally emerged from the bathroom, he strode out...naked. His shouldered sagged, his eyes darting to us.

"I've been wandering around most of the night, trying to come up with a reason for doing what I did." He took a deep shuddering breath, his eyes unfocused. "I have an anger in me, a rage of sorts. I used to fight to let it out, but when I don't, it just sits in me. It festers until it explodes. I don't know how to stop it...and I don't know if I want to. That scares me more than anything."

No one said anything for a really long time. I didn't know how to respond, so I did what I thought was best. I went to him and gave him a hug. At first, he didn't move, but he slowly wrapped his arms around me, holding me tight. He whispered into my hair, so low I almost missed it.

"Please forgive me, Lex."

CHAPTER THIRTY-FIVE

LEXI

We were at the courthouse. Last night had been pushed to the side for later as we all came to be with Josh on his special day. I gave him the biggest hug. I was so happy for him. He was officially going to be Josh Rawson today.

"You wore the blue dress?" Jack asked as he pulled me in for a hug. I smoothed my hands down the front.

"You told me I might need it for a special occasion, and I couldn't think of anything more special than today." He chuckled and wiped a tear away. Oh no, I had mascara and eyeliner on. If he started with the tears, I was going to follow too. I didn't want to cry, not yet anyway. Happy tears later.

Jack and Grayson shook the guy's hands, and I saw Shelly talking to someone, maybe a judge or lawyer. Josh held my hand and Grayson's as we walked up the stairs and into the courthouse.

It was big inside the courthouse. I had never been in one. Well, I didn't remember if I had. Maybe when I was little.

There were a lot of people around, and children too. I assumed they were here today to get new families also. It made me smile. I took a deep breath. This was something I had always wanted, but I didn't hold any jealous thoughts for these kids. I didn't think, *why not me?* anymore. I knew that I just had to wait to find my family. These lucky, amazing kids were getting families that would love them to the end of the earth.

"So many people... Do you think we're first?" I asked. The appointment time was midday, so I thought we had a while to wait.

"No, I think some other kids might be first, but that just means we get to sit together longer. Maybe if we're super nice, Galen will buy us some orange juice and maybe some chips?" I said. Josh turned to Galen, those big eyes pleading. Little did he know that Galen would do it without the eyes, but they had me adding, "Maybe some chocolate chip cookies?" Josh jumped up and down.

"Yes, please. Galen, can we please have cookies?" he asked. Oh shit, maybe I wasn't supposed to give him cookies? Like, Grayson gave him all those muffins. That was sugar. I looked over to him, and he shook his head.

"We just didn't want him eating too much before. He can get overexcited and sometimes make himself sick." I turned back to Galen and shook my head.

"We'll have cookies after. Maybe when we all go out to lunch and celebrate?" I asked Josh, hoping he would agree because nothing would be worse than him throwing up when we get into the courtroom.

"Okay, but I still get chips, right?" I nodded. That was safer, and I would limit that...by eating more. Not a hardship at all.

Oh my god, there wasn't a dry eye in the courtroom. Even Shelly shed some tears. When we had all taken photos and thanked everyone, we left the courtroom and made our way outside. I saw Galen speaking to Shelly. They were laughing, and she nodded a lot. I guessed he was catching up with her, because she came over to say goodbye, and when she said she would call Galen, I eyed him.

"Call you for what?" He chuckled and wrapped his arms around me.

"Oh, you know. For a night on the town." I smacked his chest lightly, then played with his bow tie.

"Hell no, the only night on the town you will have is with me." I pulled on his tie, and he came with it as I planted a kiss on his lips. I saw a woman in a business suit, smoking on the stairs of the courthouse. She smiled at me and gave me two thumbs up and nodded.

I smiled and then wondered how far could I go... She was telling me she thought Galen was hot, which even a blind man could see he was, and so were my other three. I grabbed Raff's ass, and he turned, a smile on his face as I kissed him. When I pulled away, she had forgotten her cigarette, her mouth agape. She pointed between Galen and Raff, and I nodded. I could hear her whistle from here as she fanned herself with her hand. Galen had caught on.

"Stop teasing the common folk, they can't handle four mates," he said, putting on that thick English accent that he has, and I laughed. I loved it, and with a bow tie, it was like he'd wrapped himself up as a present to me.

"Hold those thoughts, love, we are off to lunch." He took my hand, Raff held the other, and I looked back over my shoulder at her. She wiggled her brows at me, and I winked.

At least some people weren't judgmental assholes.

Ranger tagged behind, looking so sad. He'd been exhausted last night when he got back, so it didn't surprise me he was like a zombie today.

"Babe?" I called, and that got his attention. He gave me a smile that didn't reach his eyes. Ahh...we needed to sit down, really talk and find out what was going on with him. But we all had to just push this aside for today especially. When we got to Raff's old house, I expected there to be some hidden anger underneath all these happy smiles today too.

I was worried, but I knew he needed this, to confront the past and say goodbye to his mom. I had made something with the help of Jack.

I couldn't wait to give it to Raff.

CHAPTER THIRTY-SIX

GALEN

The drive to Russet was solemn, especially after what happened with Ranger last night, the way he came back to us. We needed to talk about this. He had demons inside that he hid beneath his smiles. They were convincing to most, but we all knew.

We took the twins' Jeep, since it was more comfortable on a long drive than any of my vehicles. I'd told Ben we were coming, but with how things were right now, this tension I could feel between us all, it wasn't the best time to be catching up with him and Hazel.

Raff drove us from Seattle, and it wasn't a long drive, only forty or so minutes before we were winding up through the trees on a road that was full of potholes.

"This is Russet land. There is a fence around the property to keep hunters out...or keep them in," Raff said with a shrug as he went over another pothole and the Jeep bounced.

Lexi had fallen asleep, and Mav was trying to hold her head steady so as not to wake her.

"Are the fences intact? Did you need me to get someone out here to take a look?" I asked, wanting to make sure his land was protected.

Even though he didn't seem happy about being back, it was up to him. He could sell the land if he wanted, but he hadn't indicated that was what he would do. I suspected that his mom would be the reason behind that.

He didn't answer me, just shrugging. I would ask him again another time. Leave the ball in his court. If he wanted to sell, I would help him, or if he wanted help fixing it up, I would help him with that too.

When the trees cleared, there was a big open space. Old cars littered the sides with old machinery and a large rusted barn with the roof caved in. There was also an old cottage that might've once been white but now was a light gray. A smashed window was boarded up from the inside, and to the side of the cottage, an overgrown garden sat. I could see some white and red roses poking through. That must've been his mom's roses, where her ashes were scattered.

When the car stopped, everyone just sat, waiting on Raff. Lexi was blinking and rubbing her eyes as she took in the area around her. Her mouth dropped a little at the way Raff had been living. She quickly closed it, not wanting to let on how she felt, although I suspected she was giving off a scent.

Raff opened the door and dropped out onto the dirt below. Everyone took that chance to get out and stretch their legs as we watched him walk towards the house. It was eerily quiet here, like animals actively avoided this spot.

When Raff stopped by the garden, he started ripping out weeds, and Lexi ran to him. He froze and watched her as she started to do the same, then we all went over to help. No one had said much as we almost cleared it all. It looked so much better once it was all cleared. There were five different rose bushes, and one looked sick, but without the weeds, it might get better. I would call someone who would know when we returned home.

Raff pulled out another weed and landed on his ass in the long grass. He didn't make a move to get up, and everyone stopped as he broke down, throwing the weed away, his head between his knees.

Lexi was the first to him. She wrapped her arms around him and laid her head on his back. I moved over to him and held his arm. He didn't flinch away like I thought he might. He took a deep inhale and let it out slowly. Mav and Ranger sat down beside him, reached over and touched him. I felt like a current passed through my body.

I gasped, and the others did as well. I could feel his pain., could feel it all—he hurt, the loss. He grieved for a mother he lost so young, for all the pain his uncles inflicted on him. His strength, the amazing will to live, his love for Lexi, that was so deep and strong, and his love for us, for all of us, it was all so powerful. How could we feel this? My fangs had descended, and I wanted to harm those who had harmed him.

"Lexi?" Raff's voice was thick, husky from the tears and sobs. "Is that you doing this?" I looked over to her, and saw her eyes were bright, almost glowing as she looked to me, tears tracking down her cheeks. My mind cleared as I retracted my fangs.

"I...I think. I don't know." She dropped away from Raff, and the connection was lost, her eyes returning to her amber ones. I took a few breaths to try and center myself. That was a lot to take in all at once. I knew she didn't mean to do whatever she did. Ranger stood and brushed his shorts out. I saw him wipe his eyes, and Mav was doing the same as he watched Raff.

Raff cleared his throat. "I'm gonna go inside and see if there's anything of mine left." His shoulders hung low as he opened his hand and let the long grass dance over his palm.

"I'll go with him," Lexi said, jumping and following him. I didn't get up, instead, I lay back on the grass and looked up to the sky, the white clouds floating past slowly, revealing the blue sky.

I stayed like this for what felt like forever, while Mav hadn't moved from where he was sitting. He just stared off, not looking at anything, just thinking. When I smelled gasoline, I turned to see where Raff and Lexi were. I could hear them outside the house.

"Raff, I understand why, but...just, maybe we should have some water on hand?" she said.

That had me up fast. Maverick and I ran over and met with Ranger as we watched Raff lighting a match and throwing it into the open door of the cottage.

A powerful wave of heat engulfed us as the house went up in flames.

Fuck... I wasn't expecting that.

CHAPTER THIRTY-SEVEN

LEXI

I didn't know how or what happened when we all touched Rafferty. I just felt all his hurt and pain run through me, and I couldn't breathe. So much pain at being back here, at the place he grew up in, and no happy memories without his mom or his uncles...

When he wanted to go inside, I knew I had to go with him. I couldn't let him do that alone. He had suffered so much in this place. The cottage was small, so how it housed so many of Russet surprised me, as there were no other places around here, only this one.

He just stood in the doorway, staring at the old sofa and the coffee table littered with what looked like drugs, needles, and beer bottles. It smelled bad as I followed him in, stepping over the broken floorboards, and the kitchen looked just like the coffee table. The tap was dripping into an overflowing sink of used dishes, like no one around here washed or cleaned.

"Did you want to wait outside?" he asked, and I turned to face him. Fuck, he could smell how I was feeling, and I knew he didn't want people's pity. I knew he was better than this, that this was just his circumstances were. He didn't do this to himself, this was done to him.

"Did you want to show me your room?" I wanted him to be the one who chose. If he didn't want me to see, I would leave. He looked up at me through his red-rimmed eyes, the pale blue of his eyes glistening as I watched them crinkle at the sides.

"Yes," he whispered with a half-smile. This was important for him to show me. I knew that. I wanted to see, but I was glad he wanted me to.

He took my hand and led me to a closed door in the back. It had a hole through it and some claw marks, like someone had scratched at it, trying to get in. I held my breath and waited to see what was beyond. It might be different to how he last saw it. He'd been gone for a while, so his uncles could have done anything in here.

He let out a sad sound. The room was destroyed, everything ripped up and the mattress on the floor, with massive claw marks in it. Oh fuck, if they weren't dead, I would've killed them myself. They were going to hell for what they did to him.

"I'm sorry." I didn't know what else to say. He just stood there, my hand in his unmoving for so long. He shook his head and dropped my hand.

"It's okay," he said finally. I wanted to scream that it was not okay, but I nodded instead. No point in getting angry and upset again. He needed to do this, he needed to heal from these wounds that ran deep. He started picking things up, looking for something, I guess anything that belonged to him. I started moving large pieces of wood, which I assumed were the bedframe, out into the hall to help.

He pulled up a bag. It was covered in dust, and as he dusted it off, the particles floated around, landing on everything around him. He looked inside and nodded, grabbing my hand and leading me back outside. He put the bag beside the Jeep, and I stood there and watched as he went into the barn. I would've been worried about it collapsing on him if he wasn't a shifter who healed fast. He came out with what looked like two jerrycans in his hands.

He didn't look at me as he walked directly to the cottage. When he went inside, I realized what he was doing. Fuck. I ran over and went inside as I heard him sloshing the can around. The smell of gas was strong as he walked into view.

He turned to me, but the look in his eyes was wild. I didn't say anything as he dropped the now empty jerrycan on the floor with a thud and picked up the other one, dousing everything with gas. I stumbled as I made my way outside. He dropped the second can, then came to stand beside me, a box of matches in his hand, and one single match he played with between his fingers. I watched as he clenched and unclenched his fist.

My heart was thundering. Where were the guys? This was going to turn out badly. We were surrounded by forest, so this could get out of control. I was hoping Galen would at least have heard him, or hell, even smell the gas he was pouring through the place.

"Raff, I understand why but...just, maybe we should have some water on hand?" I asked nervously. I understood, I knew why he wanted—no, needed to do this, but maybe there was a safer way to do it. After the heat of the moment, he might regret it. Maybe not.

Galen was beside me, and Mav and Ranger stood beside him, as Raff lit the match, strode up to the house, and threw it in the open door. The house went up with a roar, the heat scorching my skin, and within a few minutes, the entire cottage was up in flames.

Raff didn't say anything, he just stood there, the flames dancing so close to him. He was going to burn himself. It was Ranger who grabbed his shoulders and pulled him back to us. He didn't let go of Raff. He held him there as we all watched the flames licking the walls, eating everything in its path, destroying everything bad.

We stayed for half the night, just watching the glow of the embers that remained of what once was Raff's home. Ben ended up meeting up with us. He'd brought a hose, which was helpful to catch any embers lighting up around. Plus, he said that Hazel's house backed onto the forest here, so we really didn't want to lose control of this.

When it was safe to leave, Ben said he would take care of it, and I was grateful. It had been a long day, with so much going on. I'd thought things would be easier after the blood moon, after Eiji changed my scent ...but now was the hard part. This was what we didn't get to do before. It was where we learned about each other, grew with each other, and hopefully, be able to move forward together as a family, as one. Because if we couldn't do those things, we wouldn't be whole, and I didn't want anyone to hurt or feel left out. After last night, I realized we had a lot of growing to do, and I was ready for it.

I wouldn't give up on any of my mates. Ever.

CHAPTER THIRTY-EIGHT

LEXI

After the night we'd had, I wasn't ready for today. It wasn't that I didn't want to go, it was just that I was so tired. Kiara was so nice, although we didn't get too much time together when we met. But she'd been with me through so much that I wouldn't miss this special day of hers, even if I needed some more sleep. She was having her ceremony at eleven, and it was almost ten and I hadn't showered or dressed yet, but Galen was on the ball. Thank god one of us was, the rest of the guys were in bed sleeping.

We'd all crammed in there last night. It was uncomfortable and hot, but I didn't want anyone to leave, and I thought they all felt the same. After what had happened with my powers, and everyone feeling what Raff was...we needed to stay together.

"Come on, get up. I have your clothes ready and hanging up in the bathroom. Jump in the shower, wash your hair, and get dressed. When you come out, I'll do your hair for the ceremony." My brows raised at that.

"Mmm...do you know how to do hair? And you're only just telling me this?" He looked a little sheepish as he smiled.

"YouTube." I chuckled. Oh, he was seriously the best. I gave him a hug and ran off to the bathroom. I could smell the smoke on my hair from last night, since we'd all just collapsed when we got home and didn't even have a shower.

The dress that was hanging behind the door was floral and to the knees. It wasn't me, but I could see how it would suit today. When I saw the underwear he had left me, I laughed. Oh, naughty Galen. I hoped the wind didn't blow my dress up, or everyone would see my ass in this little thong. The bra was gorgeous, with little bits of pale green laced through the white lace of the cups. I smiled as I turned the shower on, thinking I would strip that dress off for him when I get home... No more period, and I was horny as hell. Plus, it would be nice to get lost in each other, just for a while.

There was a knock at the door as I was zipping the dress up, my wet hair wrapped in a towel. "Come in," I called out. My makeup was done, and I went with a more natural look, no smokey eye, and I'd sprayed some Britney Spears perfume I found on the counter. I assumed it was for me, unless Galen used it, which even if he did, I wouldn't care. I'd still use it, and then we would both smell nice together. Galen opened the door and popped his head in. I watched from the mirror as his eyes roamed up and down my body. A smile crept over his face, and he winked before clearing his throat.

"Love, you look amazing." He walked in and wrapped his hands around my waist, and we looked into the mirror at each other. He kissed my neck before pulling out a necklace. It was my Drongor stone, the one from my aunt. I hadn't worn it yet, since I'd been too scared to lose it. When he draped it across my throat, I touched it. It was beautiful.

"I would love to stay in here with you all day, but Ada is here and Tobias has dropped in also. He didn't realize you were busy today, but he's waiting with Ada." My eyes widened. Tobias was here? I turned in Galen's arms, and he kissed my cheek before running his hand under my dress and grabbing my ass. I grabbed his ass back and winked at him as I walked out to see Ada staring at Tobias, but like, not just staring. She had her elbow propped up on the counter and her cheek in her hand as she gave a little chuckle at something he said. I rolled my eyes. Didn't she know who he was?

"Tobias, I didn't know you were coming." That sounded normal, right? Like, he didn't tell me, so I didn't expect him here.

"No, sorry. I thought I would pop in. I wanted to see if you'd like to go to lunch with me, but I see you have plans here with your friend, Ada." I nodded, and she smiled at me, like she had forgotten he was my father.

"Ada, I'm so glad you got to meet Tobias, my father." She sat up straighter and nodded.

"I forgot. Wow. Hi, Lexi's dad, it's nice to meet you. I didn't realize you looked so young. Like, well, Lexi told me, but like, wow. What kind of moisturizer do you use? It must be amazing for wrinkles. I missed meeting you last time you were here, what with the whole saving lives and stuff, but..." She kept on talking, like Ada does when nervous.

"I like your friend. She is very amiable."

"Okay, so I just have to get my shoes. I'm sorry we can't stay long. We have to be going," I said, grabbing Ada's arm, and she jumped off the stool and giggled. I almost laughed at that.

"Wait, I didn't get to do your hair." Galen pointed to a spot he had a brush, comb, and pins laid out. Wow, he was really prepared.

"Shut the front door. Galen is doing your hair?" Ada exclaimed. Just then, the bedroom door opened and Ranger walked out, yawning and scratching his chest. He was wearing black boxers and nothing else. He sleepily looked at me and then his eyes scanned the room, and he stopped.

"Ah, hey Tobias. Ah...it's a beautiful morning." I could see the nervous look in his eye. When his eyes met mine again, he winked. "You look good, babe. Not sure when Galen picked that out, but then, anything looks good on you. Ada, you look very nice too." He kept walking to the front door, and Galen pushed me to sitting. My hair was still damp as he took the towel off and it fell around my face.

"Hey, come on in." Who the hell was Ranger talking to now? I pushed the hair out of my eyes and watched as he invited Noah, Saint, and Zara into the already small room. What the fuck was going on?

"Hey," Noah said as he smiled and waved to Ada, then me. Saint gave a strained smile and nodded, and Zara had the biggest beaming grin like she was up to something.

"Hi, girls. Oh wow, Galen. You're doing Lexi's hair. That's so wonderful. I was coming over to see if she needed any help, as I have lots of experience. Ada, did you want me to do your hair?" I could see Ada standing to the side, squirming a little. She looked over to me, and I shrugged. I had no idea.

"Your hair is beautiful like it is. I just thought I would just offer if you wanted."

Galen reached down to grab a comb. "I have plenty of supplies. I went to the store earlier in the week and got everything." My mouth dropped open. He'd planned this a week ago?

Ada dropped to the couch, looking between Noah and Saint, and I thought Zara caught on when she said, "Boys, go wait outside. Your friends aren't even ready yet. They're all in bed. Let the girls have some space." She was so tiny compared to Noah, it was cute watching her shoo him away. Saint grumbled something and left, but not before she smacked his butt. Ada and I were a little surprised at that.

When Zara looked back to us, she must have seen our expressions, and I heard Galen chuckle.

"Oh, he needed a smack on his ass. You don't talk back to a momma."

Tobias made his way to the front door. I had almost forgotten he was here.

"I shall call you later in the week, Lexi. We can have dinner then. I hope you both have a lovely day. The weather will be perfect for most of the day, but I do believe a storm will pass through in the evening. Please wish the happy couple my best, and if there is anything I can do to help, don't hesitate to call me."

When he left, the atmosphere in the room relaxed, and Zara started to brush Ada's hair. "Tobias is very attractive. I wonder if he's dating anyone?" Ada mused, and I almost choked on my own saliva.

"Ada, that's my father," I said, turning to her, and Galen tsked at me and pulled my head back to where it was.

"What? I was just saying out loud what everyone is thinking it. To be fair, he looks like your big brother, not your dad."

Zara laughed and added, "He's a DILF, but don't tell my mates I said that."

My mouth dropped open, and I heard Ranger yell out, "I heard that, Zara."

CHAPTER THIRTY-NINE

LEXI

Galen really did an amazing job on my hair. He had curled and put it half up, half down, and he'd even wove little flowers through it. Zara was amazing at braids. She had done this braid across the top of Ada's hair, but it was soft and slightly messy. She'd put the same flowers in there and curled the rest. She looked amazing. If someone didn't ask her to prom soon, I would, since the guys had made no move to ask me. They did all rush out of the bedroom just as I was leaving to mark me, which wasn't as nice when they smelled of smoke. When they were happy, they let me leave, which was good because we were probably running late now.

"Did you lovely ladies need a lift?" Noah asked as we walked out to Ada's car, then it dawned on me.

"You've got to be kidding me. Are you going to follow us again?" I exclaimed, but Zara quickly intervened.

"No, they are not, and they have something to say about that. They should've told you. No one will be following you girls today. Rawlins pack will keep you safe."

Noah looked to his feet and scuffed them on the ground.

"I'm really sorry about scaring you both," he said. "That wasn't what we meant to do. We just wanted to keep you safe." I nodded, that was a nice apology. When Saint didn't say anything, Zara reached up and smacked the back of his head, and my mouth dropped open.

"I'm sorry too," Saint said, and Zara growled. That was the first time I'd heard a female shifter do that. It was scarier than Alaric. "I am very sorry that I scared or upset you. That wasn't my—our intention. We just wanted you both to be safe."

I didn't know what to say back, so I just nodded, and Ada did too. Zara was scary when she was mad.

"All right, now that's done, you boys can go wait inside. I think Galen was about to start fixing up a big breakfast for the boys." Aww…I didn't want to miss that. He'd become so domesticated in the past week. I thought him not having a full-time job, plus the pack stuff, was giving him spare time to do other things. They ran off to the house, Noah waving at Ada before taking off.

"Now, girls, tomorrow you come to my place around this time. Just bring yourselves, casual clothes, a swimsuit, and some pajamas. We're having a ladies' day with all the females of the pack…well, the ones under fifty at least. We do this once a month, and you're invited as ladies of Kiba."

Oh wow, yes. This could be good for me to meet the other women and maybe learn some things about having so many mates. I was going to ask Zara a lot of questions, that was for sure. I knew we really needed to sit down again as a family and work out how to help Ranger, but maybe we could do that tonight when I got back.

"Yes, that would be great. We'll be there." We were going to be late, so I pulled Ada to the car so we could leave.

As soon as we got in, she just looked at me, her eyes wide. "So I guess we're doing that tomorrow?" Then she put the car in drive and headed out of the Lovell property. Shit, I'd forgotten about her sister.

"Oh god, sorry, Ada. I forgot Destiny was here. You probably had plans tomorrow." She shrugged, then giggled.

"Actually, my parents have my aunt and uncle coming over with my cousins to see her, and I've seen them enough. I don't think they'll mind. Zara scares me, like a lot, but she's so nice too. I know she's inviting me because of Noah, but it would be interesting to really get a chance to speak to these ladies. I met so many of them already, but under bad circumstances," she said, and I nodded. I knew what she meant. Zara had been nothing but nice to me, but I hadn't met as many of the Kiba ladies as I had hoped. Then again, I didn't seem to have time for much these days. Something new happened every week.

I didn't know why, but I looked behind to see if they really weren't following us. All I saw was a large gray wolf standing on the side of the road, then another appeared beside him and let out a long howl. *Saint and Noah.*

I didn't know what to expect from Pack Rawlins. Their little town looked similar to Kiba. They didn't have the same court, but they did have a Rawlins Drive. It was long, and there were a lot of houses. They started off like the ones we had seen driving into Rawlins, but they got bigger and bigger as we made our way up to the large golden gates at the end. This was obviously the alpha's house, and there were two men dressed in cream colored short-sleeved shirts, the top button opened, and they weren't wearing ties. One was wearing what looked like blue and white boardshorts, and the other was in dark shorts. The thing that stood out about them was their hair. One had a wild, beautiful head of curls that was black with highlights of reddish brown mixed in. The other had a shorter head of curls, dark with a tattoo running up from under his shirt onto his neck. It was a black tribal pattern from what I could see.

Ada opened her window, and Mr. Boardshorts approached the car with a strut. I could see Ada shift in her seat. She was probably giving off a scent that she liked him. He smiled, his white teeth perfect as he rested his arm on the roof and looked into the car. Okay, he was hot, but he knew it. And shit...did thinking about them being hot make them know I thought that? I hadn't thought about this before I left. If word got out I was smelling all aroused, Ranger would lose his shit.

"Welcome, ladies. You must be Ada and Lexi." He used his thumb to gesture to the man behind him. "That's Maddox there, he will escort you to where the ceremony is taking place, and I can park your car for you. Later, just come looking for me or Maddox, and we'll grab it for you."

Ada didn't say anything. Oh boy, that wasn't good. She was very rarely lost for words.

"Not a problem, and your name is?" I asked, unclicking my belt and reaching for my little purse, which matched the shoes I was wearing. I was starting to feel like Galen's Barbie doll with all this shopping and dressing he did for me. But at the same time, I wouldn't have picked this or spent anywhere near as much as he did on it all. I didn't want to even know how much these shoes cost, but I suspected a lot.

"Oh sorry, Jaxson. Everyone calls me Jax." I opened the car door and stepped out. The sun was warm on my skin, and I walked around to meet Ada, who was still sitting in the car.

"Ada," I hissed under my breath. It snapped her out of her little moment, and she stumbled around, getting her belt off and grabbing her purse. She opened the door, and as she tried to get out, the car lurched forward.

"Woah," Jax called out, reaching in and putting the handbrake on.

"Oh sorry, I forgot to put it in park! I'm just so excited to be here, and do you know Huxley? He said he would be here, and I just wanted to know if he was here, now. Or will he be here soon?" Oh, there was the Ada I knew. Jax chuckled.

"Yeah, Hux is my cousin. He's here already. Maddox will be able to show you to him."

Ada stumbled towards me, her hand on her throat. "Oh, no.

That's okay. I'm here with my family, Destiny and my parents. We're supposed to sit together."

Maddox came over when Ada stumbled again and held out the crook of his arm, and Ada blushed as she took it. He turned to me and smiled.

"Your mate's markings are strong, warning me to stay away." I nodded. He was telling me why he wasn't offering his arm to me.

I was glad. I was going to avoid touching anyone here.

CHAPTER FORTY

LEXI

Graham and Michelle were seated next to another couple in this big, white open tent in the yard. Fairy lights hung from the roof, and the aisle was a white carpet through the middle. As we walked down, Ada still on Maddox's arm, I could see the place was full of families, and they were all so friendly—just like Kiba—as we walked down. Saying hello, some waving and smiling as we made our way down to the second row, where there were two seats behind her parents beside two other couples who smiled and said hello as we took our spots. They turned to us with big smiles. Her dad nodded at me and Ada, then turned around again to speak to the man beside him. Ada's mom was not happy.

"Where were you? You're late," she whispered so no one would hear us. Little did she know that she could shout that, and it would have the same impact here.

"I'm sorry, Galen was doing my hair..." I was going to say Zara did Ada's hair, but I didn't know if it would upset her mom or not that she didn't let her do it.

She looked to Ada, her hair, then to mine, and smiled.

"Oh wow, he's very talented. I could never do something like that. You both look so beautiful, and there are a lot of men around. You never know, one of you might catch someone's eyes." She winked at me, and Ada giggled nervously. I just smiled and held in the laugh that wanted to burst free. Ada poked me, and I held my hand over my mouth.

"Don't you dare," she warned me, her own smile huge.

"I wouldn't..." I told her. To her mom, I said, "Thank you, Michelle, but I already have four boyfriends. I don't think I could have anymore." I had told her the other night I was in a relationship like Kiara was, but not that I had double the men. Her mouth dropped open, and her eyes widened.

"Oh, oh wow. That's...um, wonderful, dear." I smiled and nodded. I guessed she would eventually know, so I might as well not lie.

A young guy with an acoustic guitar appeared at the front beside a large man. And when I said large, I mean huge, like Dwayne Johnson huge. Except this guy had the same wild curls as Maddox. I assumed he was either his father or uncle. This guy was the alpha. I'd seen him before, but his hair had been tamed and in a bun. I preferred this look.

"Thank you all for attending today. Will our grooms please come to the front?" We all turned and watched as two men made their way forward, almost bouncing down the aisle. Wearing big grins, they accepted handshakes and lots of excitement from everyone here. It was really nice. As they came down, one jumped in the air and did a three-sixty and landed on his knees, and everyone cheered and laughed. I loved it. This was so different to how I thought it would be.

"Oh, where is your sister?" I asked Ada. I'd assumed she would be sitting with her parents.

"Oh, sorry. I thought I told you she's a bridesmaid," Ada replied.

Michelle turned around and added, "She looked so nice, and I snuck in before and saw Kiara. Oh gosh, her mother is going to cry. Oh hell, I'll cry. I love weddings. This is a little different, since she's marrying two men, but oh, one day, I'll be the mother of the bride."

Ada's mom really wanted her girls to meet someone, and from the looks here, that wouldn't be a problem. I hadn't seen Huxley yet, although I could see Ada scanning the crowd for him.

I felt bad about what happened on Thursday with Ranger. I shouldn't have touched Huxley, I just didn't know it would set Ranger off like that.

The music started, and everyone stood. I followed them up and turned. This was just like the movies. I someone moving down the aisle, but I couldn't see, and Ada was having the same problem. We were seated in the middle of two other couples, and we were short compared to most shifters.

The people behind us turned to the aisle, and that's when I first saw her—Destiny. Wow, these girls were the spitting image of each other. How did I not even see that in their family pictures when I was at her house last week? I guessed I thought they were just of Ada.

She was wearing a baby pink dress to the knee, and her skin was a golden tan, whereas Ada was paler. She turned and smiled when she saw us, and I waved, then put my hand down. Oh that was embarrassing. There was a man walking behind her, and he was wearing the same outfit as Jax—boardshorts and a cream shirt.

Then another young woman was walking behind him. She smiled and mouthed 'hello' to Ada. Then Huxley—Wait.

Ada stiffened and turned to me, her eyes wide. He was part of the bridal party. He turned and looked to me, Ada still facing me, and he smiled and nodded. I couldn't help the huge grin I gave back, and Ada's eyebrows were in her hairline when she saw me. I chuckled, and she turned back just in time to see Huxley turn to look behind at her one more time.

Oh, my heart swooned. I felt like I was in a romance novel.

When Kiara came down the aisle, I understood what Michelle had said. Her dress was just spectacular. It was cream lace, fitted at the top and then flowed loosely around her waist to the floor into a small train behind her. A man I assumed her father had a big smile on his face as he walked her down. The song the guy on the guitar was playing was just perfect, and I realized it was "What a Wonderful World."

Everyone sat down, and I did too. Ada held my hand, and I squeezed back as we watched the alpha clear his throat.

"Everyone, we are gathered here today..."

CHAPTER FORTY-ONE

LEXI

Okay, if anyone says they don't cry at weddings, there was something wrong there. Oh my god, I was so glad I didn't do my usual smokey eye look. I would have been a panda by the end of the vows, and Michelle was amazing. She came prepared and handed us tissues. The guys, Elian and Dylan, wrote their own vows, and so did Kiara. That set me off with sniffles and a lone tear.

"We need to go do a makeup check, then I will go introduce you to Destiny and maybe...you know, find people." I held her hand as we ran across the green lawn to the huge mansion the Rawlins' alpha had. It was funny how similar the two packs lived, and I wondered if it was the same for Kenneally.

A group of older men were hovering around a table full of different dishes of food.

"Hello there, are you looking for the ladies' room?" one with graying hair asked. We both nodded, and he pointed down a hall. "It's the last door on your left." We walked as fast as we could, and once there, we locked ourselves in.

"Oh, this is so bad. Like, when I see him now, I can't even breathe." I looked at Ada through the mirror.

"What? Who?" Huxley? Her eyes flared, and she pointed in a circle.

"You know who! Oh god." She started pacing. What the hell was going on? She was all chatty Cathy earlier about him, and now she was hyperventilating in the bathroom.

"Sit down, breathe. What happened?" She sat down on the lid of the toilet, took a deep breath, and started to spill.

"He asked me to prom. Yesterday. When you were at Josh's adoption. And I didn't know what to say, so I freaked out and ran away. And I was all ready on the way here to tell him yes, but now I see him... What if he changed his mind, you know? Like, no one has ever asked me out, not like that. I haven't even been kissed."

I took a step to her, squatted, and held her hands. I didn't know that about her. I'd thought she had kissed guys before, but then she never said she had.

"Well, okay, I did kiss a boy at summer camp when I was twelve, but that wasn't a real kiss. And I didn't tell you, even though I was going to ask you what I should do. It's just...if he said no, I would've been so embarrassed to tell you. Like, here you are, this amazing, cool chick, and you have four perfect boyfriends. FOUR! And I can't even get one." She held up four fingers and flashed them at me twice.

I... Wow, I didn't know what to say. She thought I had four perfect boyfriends? I guessed I didn't tell her too much, since I kept a lot of the relationship stuff to myself.

"Hey, don't do that to yourself. You're always so positive, and he asked you, Ada Stephens. He didn't ask anyone else—"

She butted in, saying, "How do you know that?" I wanted to roll my eyes, but I wouldn't do that to her. She was just so clueless about how guys looked at her. Even that Jax guy had been checking her out.

"Ada, on Thursday after you went home, he came and asked me if you were all right." Her mouth dropped. "Yeah, he did. Said he tried to call you to see how you were, but you didn't answer. I told him to try you later, but first, I grabbed his arm. Ranger saw, and he seemed okay about it, like it was all good, but later, we were waiting for him, and Maverick knew where and what he was doing. He was fighting Huxley. Ranger challenged him, Ada. I don't have perfect boyfriends, there's no such thing. Everyone has flaws and secrets... Nobody is perfect, but we work on it, help each other. Do you know why he fought him?" She shook her head, her eyes wide with worry.

"Ranger was mad that he spoke to me, and he knew he liked you. He was worried if Huxley asked you out, that Noah would be pushed aside, and he loves him like a brother. I understand why he thought it was a good idea, sort of. I'm trying, at least. But what I'm trying to say is Huxley won't have asked anyone else. He'll be waiting for you to tell him yes."

I was starting to think I would be waiting forever for the guys to ask me, or maybe they just assumed I would go with them.

Ada got up, straightened out her dress, and hugged me. She didn't speak for a few minutes as she opened her purse and applied some makeup.

"Thank you. I guess I look at you and the guys and try to work out what's wrong with me. But you're right—I was just overthinking and thinking negatively when I'm usually more positive. I'm gonna go out there and tell him I will go to the prom with him." She turned to me, standing tall with a look of determination on her face.

"You go get him, tiger." She laughed as I tapped her ass on the way out. She chuckled, and we ran out past the food to where a huge party was happening. Music, dancing, food, and Huxley Moore looking right at Ada.

She turned to me and nodded, then surprised me when she took off, long strides to where he was standing. I saw him straighten up, his smile large and a little crooked from the scar. I had never seen him smile so much, and I thought that was because of Ada.

I watched as they talked. She swished her dress around a little nervously. He nodded and then laughed. They talked for a few more moments before she gave him a small wave and ran back to me. She was a little out of breath, but she didn't have to say anything, I already knew. He said yes.

"We're going to the prom," she squealed and wrapped her arms around me. I could see Huxley smiling still and watching us while talking to someone.

Destiny came up with two glasses of margaritas.

"Hello, I'm Destiny, Ada's sister. You must be Lexi, the amazing best friend who's dating Mr. Donovani. *Shut the front door.* That is unreal. Like, hell yeah, he was hot when I was at school, and you were the forbidden fruit he was waiting for." I looked to Ada, and she glanced away. I shook my head and laughed. Fuck it, everyone knew anyway.

"I'm the best friend, and you're the sister who had a leather jacket that fit me perfectly, like it was *destiny*." She snorted and laughed. Oh wow, how many drinks had she had already? It was only noon.

"Oh, that was funny when she told me." She sloshed a drink on her shoe and stared at it, blinking really slowly, then handed me one of the drinks. "Whoops! Here, I got you girls drinks. I can't believe you drove, Ada. I can get one of the guys to bring your car back tomorrow. Dad is the sober one tonight, so us Stephens ladies can get our drink on, but I might be staying here. I don't know... There are a lot of single guys here. Whoop whoop!" She fist-pumped the air, then stumbled a little, and I helped her, giving a worried looked to Ada. She held her other elbow to steady her.

"Okay, so I think I will stop drinking for a while. We had mimosas at breakfast...they go down so well. I'm not a big drinker, and the world is spinning a little."

I looked around and saw the older man from inside come over with a chair. I thanked him, and we helped her sit in it. She kicked off her heels and stretched back.

"Oh, this is so nice," she said, and I giggled. She was happy and a lot like Ada.

"Let's drink and party. We can get my dad to drive us home," Ada said as she tapped her glass with mine, and I looked down into it.

Fuck it. What was one drink?

CHAPTER FORTY-TWO

GALEN

I received a call at around four from Maddox Coleman, the alpha's eldest son and second-in-command. I got worried, but he told me that Lexi had had a few drinks, spent the afternoon dancing, was exhausted, and had asked if he could call me to come get her. She was going to get a lift with Ada's parents, but they weren't ready to leave yet and she was.

Ranger and Raff were out for a run, but Mav had stayed behind as I tried to work out how to fit a larger bed in the small bedroom of the cottage. Or maybe it would be better for us to all move out after graduation into a larger house in Kiba.

When I got to the golden gates of Rawlins, where the alpha, Erick, lived with his mate and two sons, they greeted me with a very happy Lexi. I jumped out to help her.

"Oh, love. What trouble have you got yourself into?" I asked with a laugh as she giggled.

"It was two, okay? That was all. But my feet hurt from too much dancing, which I didn't think could be a thing, since I heal so fast, but it is." I bent down and grabbed the back of her knees and hoisted her up to my chest.

"Thanks, guys, my knight has come. It was nice meeting you." She waved behind us as I walked back to the car. I got her in and seated, and she pulled me down before I could close the door and kissed me.

"Mmm...you taste yummy," she said, winking at me. Oh wow, two drinks was one too many for Lexi. I would get her home and sober her up.

I carried a sleeping Lexi inside, but she woke when Mav touched her.

"Hey, handsome," she said, and his brows rose as he chuckled.

"Oh, Lexi...you've had a fun time, I see," he said. I put her down on the sofa, and she reached for me, so I sat beside her.

"Just sleep some, love. You'll feel better soon." She nodded and was out in about twenty seconds. Mav came over and draped a blanket over her. I tried to move away, but she grabbed onto me. Well, I wasn't going to work out a bigger bed in that room anytime soon, so I turned on the TV and watched some old episodes of *Friends*.

Mav settled down into the armchair, and we watched in silence for three episodes before Lexi moaned and woke up. Her eyes meeting mine, she smiled and stretched.

"Love, feeling better?" I was wondering if it was more the lack of sleep and no breakfast that had her a little tipsy than anything else. She had lunch, I assumed, but she seemed better now.

"Oh, yep. I need to pee." She jumped up and ran to the bathroom, one that five of us share—another reason we should talk about a bigger place.

"Did you want me to leave?" Mav asked me out of nowhere, and I gave him a puzzled look. What gave him that idea? Lexi and I were taking things slow. If anything, I should be asking him that question. He deserved private time as well with her, even if it was to talk. I had already had that with her more than him, and I didn't want him to feel like he was being pushed aside. I had enjoyed our afternoon together, and he even kissed me. It was brief, but it was nice.

"Do you want me to leave?" I asked, and his brows now went up. When Lexi closed the bathroom door, he turned. His mouth dropped open, and I heard him make a strangled sound.

I turned to look behind me to see what she was doing, and my cock reacted immediately. She was standing there in the bra and thong I had bought for her, which was white with a small hint of this green that reminded me of Mav's eyes.

"I thought I would show you—both of you. I love this." She ran her hand down her side, and her whole body moved with it. I sat forward, speechless, and Mav growled low. He was affected just as much as me. My fangs itched, wanted her, wanting him…wanting to watch and join in. I didn't know what I wanted, but I wanted it all.

I had noticed then she had pulled her hairstyle out, and her hair flicked to the side as she exposed her neck. I couldn't stop my fangs from descending, and I was over to her in a spilt second.

"Love, you tease me. You awaken the dark in me." Her hand traced my jaw, her fingers on my lips. I darted my tongue out to taste her skin. God, I wanted to taste her blood, but I couldn't. I promised I wouldn't. I could end up mortal…or so we believed. But it was something I wanted. I wanted to grow old with Lexi, with Maverick, with Ranger and Rafferty. That was something I didn't think I could have, but I could possibly, with her blood.

She pressed her index finger against my fang, and I tasted her blood as she wiped it against my lips. I ran my tongue over them, licking it off and feeling that small bit of her.

"I want you, Galen." She pressed her lips to my jaw. My hands reached for her, pressing her against my hard body, showing her how much I wanted her. I just didn't want to rush her. I was in no rush. I would wait forever if it meant I could love her. When I didn't answer her, she stood on her toes and took my mouth with hers, her tongue darting out into my mouth, running over my fangs. I felt a shiver through my body at the feeling. God… Oh hell. I grabbed her throat and pressed my mouth hard to hers in a bruising kiss.

I could smell her, feel her, and she was so aroused, so needy that I hungered for her touch. Her touch was everything to me, and the way her hands roamed my body had my heart soaring.

"Mr. Donovani," she moaned against my lips, and that was my undoing.

CHAPTER FORTY-THREE

MAVERICK

I watched quietly as Galen devoured Lexi. She was beautiful, and he was handsome. She wore this little scrap of lace, and everything in me came alive. She was so sexy as she danced for us. I knew in her past, she did that for a living, but I didn't want to think about that. Only that she was mine—ours. My wolf wanted to take her, claim her and Galen then and there, but I didn't know how or if I wanted that. If they wanted that. Galen was mesmerizing as he took her, his jawline sharp, and his dark wavy curls made him look younger than his turned age of twenty-one.

He'd said he didn't like his body. I'd heard him at the football game, the way he compared himself to us. You couldn't compare yourself to a shifter. I wanted to tell him we were all built like this, bigger, stronger. I didn't have to do much to look this way. It was really unfair to humans who had to work out, do protein shakes, and everything. That was something I never had to do. I could eat pizza, chocolate, and ice cream every day and still look like this.

I preferred Galen's body to other shifters. He was smaller, yes, but he had wiry muscle under it all, a tapered waist, and long fingers.

He was like Lexi, delicate, but he was far more deadly than anyone I had ever been attracted to.

I'd wanted to kiss him earlier, but I wasn't sure if he wanted to, so I gave him a quick kiss... I guessed Galen makes me nervous, but not like Lexi did. With her, I knew where I stood. She came to me, kissed me, and let me set the pace. But tonight, that was all out the window. She had been with Ranger, and she'd liked how he was. I had more alpha in me, so I tended to get more heated. That was why I didn't be with anyone after Olivia. It scared me, but I knew that my mate would be able to handle me and my alpha size.

I watched as the two of them turned to me. I was so worked up, I didn't even realize they had stopped.

Lexi smiled at me, her mouth a little swollen, her pupils wide as she took me in. Yeah, I got comfy while I was watching. I had removed some clothing.

"Come, Mav," she said, reaching for me. She didn't usually call me Mav, she always used my full name, but I wasn't going to say no to her. I held her hand as she took Galen's and walked backwards to the bedroom. She licked her lips, and Galen flicked on the lamp. I moved to kiss her, but she shoved me and I fell onto the king-sized bed. I shuffled back and stretched out. I was only wearing my boxers, and even those were struggling to contain the hard-on I was sporting. I saw this little glint in Lexi's eyes as she climbed up on the bed and started to stalk up my body. I rested back on my elbows and watched her as my skin prickled at her light touch, her hair falling around her face, all curly and kinky from where Galen had done it for her. I loved it down, and as she got closer, I tugged on a few strands to pull her towards me.

Our lips met, but it wasn't sweet. No, this was full of pent-up sexual tension, love, and passion as I growled into her mouth, our tongues teasing each other. I bit her lip and pressed her small body to where I ached the most. Her legs parted around me, and she rubbed herself against my erection. I held her hips, pulling her back and forth as the friction built up. Fuck, I wasn't going to last like this. Her hands skated up my chest and into my hair.

"Mav..." she panted as I tilted her head to the side and kissed her throat, her neck, and up under the ear before taking her earlobe between my teeth and sucking.

"Oh fuck, yes," she gasped out. My wolf could smell her strong arousal, so thick in the air, but I could smell Galen's too. He was hovering in the corner, watching us. Why was he watching? He looked like he wanted to join in, and I wanted him to. We'd already had the talk, so he knew I wanted to kiss him, touch him. Just the thought of it had my cock leaking.

"Galen," I said, softly at first, and his eyes flashed to mine. They were dark but not completely. He was himself, but with that hint of dark in him, something I really didn't see from him. Something about it excited me. Lexi sat back on my lap, straddling me, and reached out to him with her hand.

"Galen," I commanded this time. I knew what he was doing to me when we had kissed. I could feel the way he wanted to dominate me, make me his, but I switched that up. He was mine and always would be. I wasn't sure how he would react, but both times, he'd given in to me, and it was the hottest thing I'd ever witnessed. I wanted him on his knees in front of me.

He joined us on the bed, his eyes flicking from me to Lexi. I didn't have the experience in the bedroom that I assumed he would, but it didn't mean I was going to let him lead. No, he was going to play by my rules tonight and do all the things I had dreamed of.

Lexi didn't hesitate. She tugged on Galen's hair and brought his mouth to hers. A primal sound escaped me, but I couldn't just watch. I cupped Lexi's breast through the lace. Her nipples were so hard, needing to be touched. I pulled the cups down, exposing her dusty pink nipples.

"Mine," I growled as my tongue darted out, taking one in my mouth as I palmed her other breast in my hand, my thumb bushing over the tight nipple. She moaned as I sucked and toyed with her nipples, but it wasn't enough. I'd waited so long for this moment with Lexi. I just never imagined Galen would be here too.

"Galen, take off your sweater, I want to see you," Lexi begged. I pulled back enough to see he was still nervous about his body. I had seen the scars already. He didn't need to hide them from us. He was beautiful, no matter what. I used my alpha blood again to command him.

"Take it off... All of it," I said, and his eyes widened. I didn't want to push him, but I was acting on pure instinct now. When I saw his eyes darken and the hint of fang, I knew he was struggling to control himself. He wanted this, he just needed a push and he wasn't expecting that from me.

He pulled up his sweater, exposing his pale chest. He had a dusting of dark hair that ran from his pecs and lead into his jeans. Lexi ran her hand down his chest, over the hills and valleys and to that V that aimed down to his hard cock straining against those jeans. I licked my lips and reached for the top button.

"Tell me no and I'll stop." I wouldn't take anything he wasn't willing to give. His hand came to mine, and he smiled.

"I never knew you would be so...alpha, Maverick. I like this side of you," he told me. I cocked my head as he let go of my hand and looked down as I popped the button off. Lexi held a hand on each of our chests. How far was I willing to go now that I had him here? I didn't know yet...but I was excited to find out as I lowered his zipper down.

CHAPTER FORTY-FOUR

LEXI

Maverick was so...bossy, alpha. I'd seen Ranger turn the alpha charm on, but it was nothing like this. Fuck, I was loving this dynamic between them with me in the bedroom. I watched as Galen removed his jeans... He was now completely naked. His erection, surrounded by dark curls, jutted out, and all I could think of was what it would look like with Maverick's mouth wrapped around it.

I was so wet. I rubbed my core against Maverick's cock. He was a big guy, and all I wanted was for someone to touch me. I wanted this. This was the perfect way to end the day. I wanted to do this every day for the rest of our lives.

I wanted it all, and I wanted it now.

I was wearing too many clothes, so I moved back and undid my bra, throwing it to the floor. I looked up and saw they both watched me, their eyes hungry with so much need, I felt free. I lifted myself off Mav and lowered my thong, exposing myself to them both.

Galen launched at me and pressed me deep into the bed. I chuckled at his reaction as his fangs scraped down along my throat and felt chills as another wave of desire hit me. The thrill for him to bite me was there, that he had to hold himself back from doing so. He'd told me how much he wanted my blood before everything.

I wanted him to take it, so I reached up and grabbed the back of his head, pressing his mouth tighter to my throat. I wanted to feel it. I trusted Galen, even if he didn't.

Hazel had told me how it heightened everything, and I wanted to feel that.

"Mav is here. He'll stop you if you go too far." Galen froze, his cold hands burning into my skin where he touched me, like little fireworks skating along my skin.

"I wasn't... I wasn't sure you were ready for me, Lexi. I can wait. I don't want to push you." I rolled my eyes, and Maverick moved in. He licked the side of my mouth, his hot breath mingling with mine as he peered into my eyes, then looked up to Galen.

"Bite her," Maverick said, speaking in that voice that made me so aware of him. The power there had me rubbing myself against Galen, wanting to find friction, but he didn't have his weight on me anymore. Needing it, I said, "Touch me, Mav."

I felt his large hand skirt across my waist and cup my bare mound, the heel of his palm pressing down to my clit, and I moaned at the sudden pleasure that rocked through my body at just that touch. He moved his palm again, and I gasped when I felt a piercing pain at my throat as Galen sank his fangs into my skin.

"Fuck yeah," Maverick said, encouraging him, and Galen palmed my breast as he drank from me. This feeling washed over me, my skin prickling at the air. Everything was heightened, and I could hear the deep breathing coming from both of them, my own chest rising and falling as I climbed closer to bliss.

I trembled as Maverick pressed his thumb to my clit, swirling around as he wet his fingers in my slick.

"God, you're so wet for us, Lexi," he murmured, and my hips rose to meet him. I wanted his fingers inside me, I was so close. So... Galen pulled away, licking his lips, his darker eyes following me. I felt a warm trickle down my throat and watched as his eyes darted to it. He bent and lapped it up, cleaning me, then I felt my body healing itself. It was as if I could control the speed, because when he looked back over at me, I realized I had completely healed.

"Lexi, I can feel you, love. You're so close. Come for me, come for Mav." And I did. I saw stars and fireworks behind my eyes as my nails dug into the sheets, holding on tight in case I drifted away to orgasm heaven.

Galen let out a deep groan, his hand fisting his cock as I watch him go over the edge. He came on my chest, spilling himself over and over, his body shaking from the intense orgasm he just felt through me with my blood.

"Oh fuck, I... Fuck," Galen hissed out as he dropped his head to my shoulder, and I felt him shudder a few more times.

"I guess I have two mates that get a bit over excited," I teased him, referring to when it took Ranger only a stroke before he came, and Galen chuckled.

"I really should have more stamina than him, but to be fair...it's been a while, and your orgasm was so intense, I didn't expect to feel that." Galen pulled back and cupped my cheek in his palm. "I love you... I love you both." He kissed me, and it was sweet. His chest was still rising and falling rapidly as he turned to Mav.

Mav took his fingers from my very sensitive heat and licked them, his lips glistening with my release. I stopped breathing as I watched Galen move in and lick Mav's mouth. I whimpered at the sight. I needed more... I reached down and stroked Mav through his boxers. Why was he still wearing clothes when we were all naked? I pulled them down and watched as the mushroom head of his cock popped out. I swiped my thumb across his leaking slit and spread it around his head. He moaned a low, wolfy growl, but it wasn't a warning to stop. It was a plea to not stop. Galen ran his hands down Mav's chest and hooked a finger in the elastic band, pressing his boxers down until Mav removed them and showed us his impressive cock.

Galen licked down Mav's neck and I watched his Adam's apple bob as he let out a small gasp, closing his eyes and titling his head back. He was on his knees in front of us both. I did the same as Galen, licking down the left side, swirling my tongue around Mav's nipple, over the dips and valleys of Maverick's impressive abs.

"Tell me to stop, and I will," Galen said as he inched closer and closer, his tongue darting out and licking the slit of Mav's cock. His body wavered as he reached out and cupped the back of my head. He did the same for Galen. I smiled as I moved over and licked where Galen just had.

"Oh, fuck…don't stop. Lick me, suck me. I am so close," Maverick groaned out hoarsely.

I dipped my head and licked him from base to tip, and Galen followed. We repeated this a few times before Mav's patience ran thin and he growled at us.

"Suck me," he growled out, and at first, I didn't know if he wanted me…or Galen. But he answered that as he tugged us both closer.

"Ladies first," Galen offered, and I let out a small throaty chuckle. So did Mav.

"Only if you want to," Mav said, and I felt him pull on my hair a little. I smiled up at him and licked my lips. He groaned and rolled his head back. His hand loosened on my hair, and I looked down to find Galen's lips wrapped around Maverick's cock. The sounds they were making had me reaching for myself, but Galen batted my hand away and replaced it with his, finding my clit. He almost had me bucking off the bed at his expert fingers.

He sucked Maverick deep into his throat, and I watched as he moved over and over along his length. Mav pulled my face to his in a bruising kiss as Galen slipped his finger into my needy heat, rubbing my clit with his thumb. I moaned on Mav's lips as Galen worked both of us, faster, harder, until we were both panting and holding each other up as I came undone, Maverick falling over the edge just after me. I watched as he held Galen's head, thrusting deeper as he grunted out his release. Letting go of our hair, he flopped down on the bed between us.

We were all panting, covered in sweat and other fluids. The room smelled like sex, and I just smiled to myself as I tried to catch my breath in a post-orgasmic haze. I kinda just had a threesome with my mates.

And I loved it.

CHAPTER FORTY-FIVE

LEXI

I felt amazing, so freaking good. I woke up to find us all crammed in the bed once again. It really wasn't big enough for five. Ranger's legs were dangling down onto the floor, which looked uncomfortable.

"Good morning," Raff said from beside me, sounded cheery. It was a good morning, and I smiled to myself. What happened last night was... There were no words.

Maverick was so different in the bedroom from how I pictured him. He was pretty headstrong, though, and always keeping Ranger in line. I guessed I never figured him to be so...dominating. That was a real eye opener.

But as much as I loved the sweet lovemaking with Rafferty and the alpha in Ranger getting fired up, I was going to be in for a wild ride with Maverick in charge again, especially with Galen involved. We didn't have sex last night, and I was kinda glad, but only because I wanted our first time to be a special one-on-one moment.

"A very good morning," I said as I stretched, pushing into bodies and hearing their groans as I moved around and yawned. The tee I was wearing rode up, and I wasn't wearing any underwear. The night before, I couldn't be bothered putting any back on.

I moved my hand over to Ranger's face. He was so relaxed, and he looked so happy like this. We would have to talk later, we all would. I hoped we could help him control his anger. I brushed some of his hair from his brow, and he sighed, his lips so plump and kissable. *Oh, Ranger, my big bad wolf.*

"What time do you leave? Did you want to have a shower with me?" Raff asked as he tickled my side, and I wiggled, causing Maverick to groan loudly when my foot hit his chest.

"My mate has icicles for feet," he growled out, and I laughed. My feet were a little cold.

"Well, if you didn't all hog the blankets, I wouldn't have cold feet." I pressed my foot against his chest again, and he flinched away. I tried again, and he grabbed my ankle in his large warm hand and pulled me down to him. Everyone was now awake, as Maverick rolled on top of me, pinning my arms above my head and pressing his body deep into mine. I wiggled, and he pressed my hands further into the mattress.

"Someone woke up happy," I teased as he growled.

"Well, it's pretty easy to wake up happy when you're in bed with me," he said, and a playful smirk played on his lips as he ground his erection into me. He was wearing boxers, they all were as always. Well...except Galen. He always covered his chest and arms. Not today. Today, he woke up looking like the other three. His hair looked extra fluffy, and I wondered if that was from all that hair pulling Maverick did last night. The memory replayed in my mind.

I felt the hot breath of Maverick on my neck before he licked the area Galen had bitten, although there was nothing left there now. I was amazed at how fast I healed now.

Maverick made a low growl as Raff moved closer. Oh, what the hell. Raff put his hands up, and I struggled under Maverick. He let go of my hands and sat back.

"Fuck, sorry, Raff. I didn't mean to." He looked so ashamed. Raff shook his head.

"Nah, it's all good. She just smells so tempting right now, she's working my wolf up, hard."

I sat up and untangled myself from Maverick and the rest of them. Galen was just sitting back and grinning. His hand lay on his bare chest, and I could really see it for the first time.

"Fuck, you're hot, Galen. But I need to go have a shower and get ready for ladies' day." I walked out of the room, swaying my hips and making sure they really got a good view. Raff jumped off the bed just as Ranger scrambled to his feet. They both tried to fit through the doorway, poking and jabbing each other and laughing. I just shook my head and walked to the bathroom, but before I closed the door, I called out, "The winner can wash my back."

There were growls and a loud crashing sound as I braced myself for who was running to me. I laughed when Raff closed the door behind him and locked it, his fingers brushing his hair out of his face.

"Just your back?" His head cocked to the side as his brows raised, his eyes trailing over my bare legs and up until they met my eyes. I lifted the hem of the tee and pulled it off over my head. When I glanced back at him, he was still looking me in the eye as he looped his thumbs into the elastic of his boxers and slid them down over his hard cock.

I stepped towards him, and my hand fell to his chest. His ink was amazing. I traced my fingers over my name and the roses, right down to where he didn't have ink... I fisted his cock in my palm, and he reached for me, his lips crashing to mine as I worked him in my hand.

"I don't hear the shower going," Ranger called from outside the door. We broke the kiss and started laughing.

"Sorry, just stroking my red wolf." Ranger growled and called out that he would wait, or if we took forever, he would go to the main house for a shower. Having one bathroom sucked.

Raff turned the water on, and when it was time to get in, he lifted me up and I wrapped my legs around his waist.

He walked in backwards, the water cascading over his hair and down his chest. He closed the door and moved in farther until I was under the water. I tilted my head back and felt the warm spray on my face, running down my hair and back.

My head tilted to his, and our foreheads rested against each other's, water trailing down our faces as we breathed the other in. I used my body to stroke his cock along my pussy, my clit humming at the wet friction between us, but my body wanted more. His fingers dug into my ass, trying to hold me as the water made it slippery between us. I wanted to fuck him here in the shower. It was what I'd wanted when I called out to them. I didn't care who it was, I just wanted their touch. I wanted to ride Raff's cock and to get lost in each other, but we didn't have any protection and I wasn't about to take chances.

"You didn't think this through when you won did you?"

His eyes darted to the side, and I watched as they flared at my meaning. He tilted his head to the roof and shouted, "Ranger. Can you get us a condom?"

I laughed and shook my head at him.

CHAPTER FORTY-SIX

RAFFERTY

When I asked Lexi if I could join her in the shower, this was exactly what I'd meant. She was so beautiful, and her hair, darker now that it was wet, was plastered to her back. I held her tight, not wanting to let her go. This was like the pool, just a little harder. The taps were behind me and it was a full glass shower, so there was one wall I could prop her against. But it was tiled and they were cold, so I wasn't sure exactly how this worked.

I could hear Ranger muttering about how next time I better play fair. I chuckled and Lexi's brow rose, wanting to know what was happening with the condom, I guess. Something I didn't think about when I slammed my elbow into Ranger's ribs and made the dash to the bathroom. I needed this time with her after everything on Friday. I wanted to be close to her, inside her.

Bang, bang. "Hey, fuckers. You locked the door."

"Shit," I hissed under my breath. I lower Lexi to the floor. When she was balanced, I let go and jumped out the shower, dripping water all over the floor and flicking the lock off. The door banged open, and Ranger's lips quirked into a smirk.

"Fuckers?" Lexi asked, and I could see her lathering herself up with body wash. Fuck. I was fucking this up. Wouldn't she wash herself after? I pressed my hand against Ranger's chest, my wolf not wanting to share right now, and I growled at him to stop from coming in farther. He ignored my warning and turned to Lexi, whistling at her perfectly naked form.

"You're right. I'm sorry, Lexi babe. There is no fucking going on. You needed one of these." He held the condom between his fingers, and I snatched it as he watched, distracted by Lexi.

"Hey," he protested, but he was too late. I jumped back in with Lexi, and she launched herself at me, wrapping her legs around my waist and pressing her wet breasts to my chest.

"Can I stay? I promise to be quiet." I was glad he was back to his more playful self. I was missing the old Ranger. I let out a sound that said I give up, I didn't care. It was up to Lexi.

"Are you going to play with yourself?" Lexi asked Ranger over my shoulder. He'd already closed the door and was leaning against the sink.

"Hell yeah," he replied, and she giggled. I loved when she giggled. It made me glad that she felt that free around us, so comfortable and so loved that she could giggle and be herself.

"You can stay, but no talking. Only your hand on your cock. Got it?" she said, and I chuckled at that as she pointed at him. It was just a funny thing to be told. Galen asked us to stop messing around and wasting water. She didn't hear him, but Ranger and I did.

I slapped her wet ass to get her attention back to me, and the sound rang through the room with *smack*. Her eyes flared and grew bright. Oh fuck, was she doing that thing again? Like she did on Friday, where everyone shared my emotions through her touch? I felt a huge wave of pleasure wash through me. I felt hot all over, and my balls tightened, ready to spill. My wolf hummed with desire. Her eyes widened.

"I don't know how I'm doing this, but I can feel you." She sounded worried, and she shouldn't have been. This was part of who she was. Ever since the blood moon, Lexi's powers had become stronger. Then just like that, it was gone. I felt like I had the most intense orgasm just from that connection alone. I didn't know it could feel like that for her.

I balanced her ass in one hand as I ripped the condom packet open with my teeth, then she took it from me.

I looked over to Ranger. He was fisting his cock hard as he watched us. Lexi leaned back against the tiles and peered down to my cock nestled between the lips of her pussy. She rolled the condom on, then wrapped her arms around me.

"While the big bad wolf watches, the red wolf gets to play," I growled out before my mouth crashed to her wet lips. It was slippery, the water spraying down on us as I tried to lift her. She reached down and centered me, then let out a long moan as she sank down on my cock. Her warm heat wrapped around me, squeezing me. I shuddered as a tingle ran up my spine. Fuck, I was so worked up.

"Slow, I need to go slow," I told her. I pulled her up, then lowered her down slowly, and she gasped as I slid in deep over and over, slowly making love, but I knew that wasn't what she needed. She needed it fast, hard.

"Think about me if you need to, but seriously, stop with the slow stuff. You need to fuck her. She wants to be fucked, needs to be. Look at her, she loves it, she craves it. Her clit slamming against you, you deep inside her, reaching all the places she needs." Lexi let out a moan as I felt her inner walls clench around me. She was getting off on Ranger's talking, but he was right, I knew that. I just wanted to make sure she got off before I came.

I reached back and grabbed her neck, my hand resting on the tiled wall, warm from her body heat. As I thrust harder, her legs quivered. "Yes," she whispered.

Over and over, I thrust deeper, her head thrown back hitting the wall at my every plunge. Her hands gripped deep into my shoulders, her fingertips biting into my skin. It didn't hurt, it just spurred me on.

There was a grunt from behind us, and I licked the water droplets from her throat up to her ear.

She was meeting me thrust for thrust now, and I was so close, my balls tingled with release. "Come for me, Lexi." I wasn't as good with words like Ranger was, but that was all she needed. Her arms wrapped around me, and I felt her heat clench me tight as her orgasm rolled over her. I braced my hand on the wall as I spilled into the condom, letting out a deep throaty growl as her legs shook. I could barely stand myself.

I pulled my softening cock from her and gently settled her on her feet. She swayed in my arms, and I held her close.

"I love you," I breathed out. She looked up to me, her eyes squinting from the water droplets. My chest rose and fell rapidly, then I pressed my mouth to hers and kissed her.

"I love you," she whispered before kissing me again.

CHAPTER FORTY-SEVEN

LEXI

Morning sex was amazing. Shower sex was even better than I thought it would be. I'd always wanted to try it, and now I got to have a first with Raff. Ranger watching was hot and I'd watched him for as long as I could, but the emotional thing where I could feel Raff and he could feel me... I didn't know how to control that. It was intense, since I could feel the way he loved me, how much he wanted me, and how aroused he was. It heightened my own arousal.

Ada had driven her dad's car over, and she wanted to ask if the guys and me would help her with getting her car back home. They all offered to help and took her keys for her dad's car and her car. They would do it while we were having ladies' day and drop her dad's car back for him and bring her car here. I knew they would say yes, but that was what I called service. No doubt, Noah or Saint would be involved in some way.

"Which one is Zara's?" I asked Ada. She was walking down Kiba court with me. We both held our bags, each containing a swimsuit and pajamas. Mine were the ones I got from Shelly, since they were the only ones I could find.

I couldn't remember where she lived. They kinda all looked the same. I hadn't been there, but I saw Noah going there that day they crashed our shopping trip, when he'd bought that fluffy pink pig and practically ran from the car from us.

Was it the second one on the right? Or the left? I looked at them both, but they looked the same—huge and white... Well, they were a little smaller than the Lovells'. One had a cottage in the back, but I didn't know if that was theirs. I pointed to the right, and Ada pointed to the left.

"Shit," she said and giggled. I stopped and looked around at the houses. I thought I was right, that it was that one. Ada spun in a circle and threw her hands up.

I started to laugh, and she did too. I threw my hands in the air too. I was sure it wouldn't take long for Puppy Dog Eyes—I mean Noah to find us and lead the way. But maybe it would be better if I asked the guys at the gate, who probably already knew we were lost from our conversation that they were listening into...as always.

I faced the Lovell mansion and saw one of them jogging towards me. Asher and Elijah were the gate keepers when we left, and I could see it was Elijah headed towards us. I was glad he would know where he lived. Asher, on the other hand, he rubbed me the wrong way. Maverick growled when he saw him this morning before kissing me goodbye, so that must have meant something. I would ask him when I got home later.

"Two lost ladies on their way to ladies' day, I am at your service." He bowed to us, and I laughed. He wasn't so bad. I had no idea why he was friends with Nash, though. He always seemed to be with him.

"Yeah, actually I don't know who lives at any of these houses at all. I guess I never go out." I didn't really have any reason to wander down here anyway.

"All right, so it goes by rank. Alpha is first at the end, and even though Nash is second in charge, there are betas who are also higher up and work with Alaric. So there," he pointed down near Lovells' to the left at the huge house there. "That is the Wood's, Saint lives there." He winked at Ada, and she blushed. I tried to hide the smile. Oh Ada. Wait until Saint heard about her prom date. He would do more than delete numbers from her phone. I was pretty sure he would crash the prom and demand all the dances, even though he wouldn't admit it.

"Next to them is Jones, my home and the location of ladies' day every month." So we were standing at the right house. It had this amazing garden, and Elijah walked forwards and opened a small garden gate. We followed him and walked through. He closed it behind us and waved.

"Have a great day, ladies." The way he said it had me a little nervous. What did he mean by that... What was ladies' day, really?

As soon as we knocked on the front door, we were greeted by three women with huge smiles staring at us. It was a little intimidating. The one with strawberry blonde hair broke free of the others and stepped to us, her hands reaching out and grabbing ours as she pulled us inside.

"Come in, girls! We've been waiting for you." She grinned as the door slammed shut behind us, and I jumped. Okay, that and what Elijah said had me on alert for something to happen. Like, I wasn't sure if there was an initiation or something that I hadn't been told about.

"Don't scare them," someone said, pushing them aside. "Sorry about that. Hallie was just excited to see you both. I'm Gemma." A younger woman with long dark hair, she was maybe thirty? It was really hard to tell, since they seemed to age so much slower around here. Like, look at Alaric. He didn't look like the father of five boys. But then, look at my own father, stuck in his early twenties like Galen.

"Hi, Gemma. I'm Ada." She held her hand out to shake, but Gemma just bypassed that and wrapped her in a hug.

"Oh, I know who you are. We met already, I just wasn't sure if you remembered our names." Okay, she was a hugger. I guessed I'd better introduce myself, not that they didn't already know who I was.

"I'm Lexi." They all laughed and nodded. Gemma held my hand and Ada's just like Hallie did and led us down into a huge lounge area, where four more women sat around a huge coffee table full of food, including Zara. The room had these lovely blue walls, and there was color everywhere, from photos on walls and colorful artwork. There were pillows and blankets scattered around the front of a huge cream couch that could fit at least ten comfortably.

"Come on in, the party has just started. I'll introduce you all to the ladies of Kiba." Gemma said, I looked around the room and noticed there weren't as many ladies as I thought there would be. "Everyone is invited to ladies' day, but not all come," Hallie added.

Everyone took a seat and gestured for us to sit together at the end.

"So we have Hallie, Gemma, Cassie, Stella, Peyton, and her little man Keanu. Yes, after the sexy actor." There was a little baby with red hair in her arms. That was the first baby I'd seen in Kiba. "And Tyra. Welcome to our ladies' day, where no males are to step foot on Jones land until the clock strikes midnight." My brows rose at that. I didn't realize it went so late.

"Oh, you don't have to leave at midnight, whenever you're ready," Peyton quickly explained. "My mates will come pick up Keanu soon, so I can stay late." She looked down to the little guy. He had chubby cheeks. He was adorable as he ate his little fists and cooed happily to himself.

"Oh wow, thank you for having us. So what do you all do on ladies' day?" Ada asked. She seemed really excited. I was still a little nervous, but mostly because I had never cared so much about what others thought until I came here and I cared what these women thought of me. I didn't want them to judge me in a bad light or anything.

"So, we do a lot of different things. We have a karaoke machine there and we all sing terribly, so don't worry. But after a few drinks, it's really fun. We chill out, watch romance movies. We like to stick with a theme for the day, so last month we did a tropical theme. We sang songs about the beach, ate fruit, and watched movies with the same themes. This month's theme is the nineties. So we have the playlist set up on the karaoke and today's movies are... Gemma?"

Oh wow. This was way different from what I'd expected. Honestly, I'd thought ladies' day would be sitting around a table and listening to gossip. This was way better. Ada was practically jumping off the seat beside me.

"I was a teen in the nineties so I got to pick the movies for today, but if you girls have a suggestion, you're welcome to add it. I found four great movies, *Dances with Wolves—*" Gemma held up her finger to Hallie, whose hand shot up. "It was nineteen-ninety, so don't tell me it's not, and its beautiful." The ladies chuckled.

"*Cruel Intentions*, hottie Ryan Phillippe. *Ten Things I Hate About You*. Heath Ledger, need I say more? And... *Legends of the Fall*." Gemma held her hands up, a huge smile on her face, and Hallie cheered loudly.

"Young Brad Pitt. You're the best." Everyone laughed, and I did too. I guessed she was a huge Brad Pitt fan.

"We also, eat, dance, chat. And there is a ten-person spa out the back, so that's why I said to bring your swimsuits. We sometimes like to get comfy in our pajamas to watch the movies. It's up to you what you want to do," Zara explained.

"It's just all great fun, laughs, and you can talk about your mates without fear they're listening in... Well inside. I can't be sure how well they listen to rules and linger on the sidelines to see if you're bitching about them, but the whole house here is completely sound-proof. We have a device in every room," Tyra added.

"Let's get the daiquiris flowing. You're welcome to drink, girls. No rules here...well, the only rule is to have fun." Zara smiled.

I wasn't so sure I wanted to drink after yesterday's two that left me a little tipsy. I didn't drink normally, and those had hit me fast. But today was special, and I was safe here like I was yesterday.

"Thanks, I think I'll try one." I stood up and followed Zara into her kitchen. It was colorful and so the opposite to the Lovell's house.

CHAPTER FORTY-EIGHT

LEXI

It was mid-afternoon, and I had listened to Ada sing three songs by the Backstreet Boys. It was so funny. She wasn't bad, but by song three, she was slurring the words and Peyton had to get up to help her finish.

"What song do you want to sing, Lexi?" I wasn't sure I was ready. I was a terrible singer. Compared to Ada slurring, "I Want It That Way," she was still ten times better than I would be.

"You're the last one, and you heard Hallie sing. Nothing could be worse than her voice."

Hallie turned to Tyra and called out, "Hey! Okay, that's fair. I'm terrible."

I got up and looked at the list to see what was left. Britney Spears. Yep, I knew that "Hit Me Baby One More Time" song.

I selected it and turned. I felt nervous butterflies in my stomach, so I closed my eyes as I started to sing. I opened them, and they were all watching me, so I nervously laughed and Zara smiled. By the time I finished, they all stood up and clapped their hands. My brows raised, and Ada gave me a huge hug. Oh wow, I thought the guys would have to drive her home. I didn't think her parents would be happy with Ada for being drunk on a school night.

"Wow, Lexi. You were amazing," Cassie said as she hugged me too. The others all started to say the same, that I had a beautiful singing voice and how I should sing more. I shook my head, confused. I always thought I was bad at singing. I guessed I was wrong.

"Okay, um… thanks. Movie time?"

Gemma jumped up and got the movie ready, and they all settled down into the couch. Ada needed to pee, Zara said she would show her, but Ada said she was fine so she pointed her where it was located and sat beside me.

"How are you, Lexi? How is life over in the cottage with the four of them?" I laughed. I'd been waiting for someone to ask me this, and Zara was who I thought might bring it up.

"Yeah, it's great. Maybe a little small with one bathroom. Why do guys leave the toilet seat up all the time? I almost fell in the other night." She chuckled and handed me a bowl of popcorn that was being passed around.

I took a handful and passed it down to Stella, who was lying on the pillows.

"Oh, they haven't lived with a female before, you need to train them. And yes, it would be a little small in there. I have four mates also, and this house sometimes feels small with all of them plus three grown boys." I nodded. I liked how she said three boys, not two, even though Callum wasn't here anymore. I didn't think I ever wouldn't feel a hint of guilt at that. I loved that she still included him, not like the rest of the pack, who seemed to have disowned him.

"So I need to train them?" It sounded funny coming from my mouth. She nodded.

"Yes, seat down, and don't pee on the floor is a good one to teach them too." I laughed. I didn't have that problem.

I turned to see Heath Ledger on the screen. I hadn't seen this movie before, but I knew who he was. And yeah, he was cute. I settled in beside Zara and started to watch the movie.

It had been about thirty minutes, and Ada wasn't back. Zara said she would go check on her, but I said I would. Shit, Ada. I hoped she wasn't sick from the daiquiris. She did have two. They were very easy to drink, but had a bit of a kick. Even I still felt a little warm from the one I'd had. I went to the restroom that Zara had shown her and the door was open.

"Ada?" I looked down the hallway. There were doors this way and a staircase at the other end. "Ada?" I hissed louder. Where the fuck was she?

I opened a door, but it was a laundry room. "Ada?" Did she go into the wrong room? Fuck, was she passed out somewhere? I didn't want anyone to know if she was. I didn't want them to regret letting her drink and not want to invite her again. I'd never seen her more in her element than she was here today.

She'd told me I was her first best friend, so I knew she didn't have many friends before I came here. She had made so many here today, because the women, they just accepted you into the group. No questions, you were Kiba. Family.

Fuck, did she go upstairs? I swear I was going to kill her if she did. I quickly ran up the stairs. "Ada?" I hissed louder this time. I listened, then I heard her.

"Lexi?" The way she said my name made her sound surprised I was up here, looking for her.

"Where are you?" I walked down the hall. Some doors were open, and I stopped at one room. It had dark blue walls and some posters of cars with women in bikinis. She was sitting on a king-sized bed, clutching something to her chest. Was that...?

"Fluffy pink pig?" She nodded and showed me. I laughed and rubbed my face as I took a deep breath. "Oh, Ada. What am I gonna do with you?"

She giggled and shrugged. I made sure to stand in the middle of the room so as not to leave my scent on anything.

"He has the pink pig. I don't think it was for his mom." I knew it wasn't for his mom, but I guessed she thought it was. Ranger was forever telling me how great Noah would be for Ada and to put in good words for him, which I just ignored, but from the look of this scene, Ada already thought some good things about him.

"Dude, remember when I told you not to stroke him when he was a wolf?" Her eyes widened. "You know how the guys mark me every day with their scent and mine rubs off on them?" She didn't blink. She looked around the room and then down to the pink pig.

"Oh shit. *Shit*, help me, Lexi. Get it off." She threw the pig at me, and I ducked to avoid touching it.

"Oh, hell no. I am not touching a thing. I already have a mate that's jealous, I can't have my scent touching Noah's things. How much did you touch?" She'd been gone a while. She bit her lip as she looked around the room again, then to a closet door that was slightly opened. I laughed, there was no helping her with this. I shook my head and broke out into giggles.

"He is going to know you were in here, I can't fix this." I pointed to the closet door and asked, "Did you touch his clothes?" She stood, swaying a little, and shook her head.

"Noooooo...maybe...yessss." She turned to the door, and I saw Zara standing there with her arms crossed against her chest. Oh no.

When her smile grew, she shook her head and laughed.

"Oh, Miss Ada. Have you been snooping in my son's room?" I thought Ada was going to faint or pass out the way she turned a beet red and swayed until her ass hit the bed, then she bounced back and rolled into sitting. I bit my bottom lip to stop myself from laughing. This wasn't a laughing matter... Well okay, it was a little, but Ada was my bestie so I wouldn't laugh at her. Only with her.

"I'm so sorry Z-Zara, I was just looking for the...ah. What?" I could see Zara wasn't mad, she looked happy.

"Lucky this is Noah's room. I think he would have been very upset to find you had snooped in the wrong brother's room. How did you know? Did you follow his scent?" I thought Zara forgot we couldn't smell like wolves do. Ada pointed to the discarded pig on the floor, and Zara laughed.

"He brought this home over a week ago and has been sleeping with it every night... Oh wait. Don't tell him I said that. I assumed it must have belonged to you."

Now that wasn't embarrassing for Noah... Ada stood up and stumbled over to it and picked it up.

"Let's get you some coffee, Ada. Did you want to bring the pig?"

She looked at it, and I saw her mouth twitch from side to side. She was trying to decide. I smiled when she hugged it and placed it on his bed.

"Let's go down. We're missing hottie Heath Ledger."

We laughed, and Ada held my hand as we walked out the room.

Noah was getting a big surprise when he got home.

CHAPTER FORTY-NINE

RANGER

It was nice to know I had this family that truly cared about me. As hard as it was to admit it, I had anger problems. There was just something in me. My wolf always thought I wanted to fight, hurt, destroy others, but it wasn't my wolf. It was just triggered by those feelings in me.

It was as engulfed in them as I was. I needed help with expressing myself better. I had done that this week. I had gone a whole week at school without shifting once. Lex, Raff, and Mav all made sure they were with me. Knowing they were there for me every step of the way helped a lot. I knew it wasn't going to be easy, and there were times when I wanted to shift and rip the throats out of people, but I didn't.

It was finally Saturday, and my reward this morning was a shower with Lex. Shower and sex with my mate...it was amazing. But today was a Lovell party. Some thought we should cancel, but we weren't going to let some assholes stop our tradition.

Plus, we had something huge planned, and Lexi had no idea. It was going to be a huge surprise. It was her birthday on Tuesday and we knew she wouldn't want a party or a big fuss, but she had mentioned the prom a few times during the week, hinting that she would like to go and how Ada had a date, which almost set me off. It shouldn't have, but Noah had told me how her scent was all over his room. She liked him, she just needed to admit it to him...to everyone.

"Do you have it all?" Galen asked me, and I raised my brows.

"Um, what do you think, old man? I have a great memory." He smacked the back of my head, and Mav chuckled.

"Ranger, you have a tendency to forget things, especially if you're distracted." I put my hands up and shook my head. Raff was going through the bags.

"No, I don't. I got everything you said—"

"Where are the balloons?" Raff asked, cutting me off. The what? *Fuck.*

"I thought, why have balloons, when we could have fireworks?" The three of them stopped what they were doing and stared at me, and I grinned. I was so excited to show them.

"I got fireworks. I know a place that if you ask the right people, they sell them to you, so I thought it would make the surprise better. You know, with fireworks."

They weren't smiling. Huh? I'd thought they would be more excited. It was better than the balloons idea.

"You can't set off fireworks, they're illegal, dumbass," Maverick said as he grabbed a bag off the floor and started looking through it. I'd bought the rest of the stuff they wanted.

"It's only illegal if you get caught by the cops...and guess what? Nash is a cop! We're all good, he'll be fine with it." I was sure he would be if Maverick told him. He wasn't my biggest supporter at times. Galen shook his head.

"No, take them back. Get balloons. How can you make a balloon archway without balloons?"

I mumbled to myself. Fuckers. I wasn't going to take them back. Maybe I could go and see if Jett wanted to play with them later.

I found Jett in the house preparing meat for the grill.

"Hey, so apparently, buying fireworks is something my packmates are against. You want to play with them later? We could set a few off?" He dropped a huge cut of meat onto the wooden chopping board and came down hard with the cleaver.

"You go down to Watson and get them?" he asked and I smiled. Yeah, he knew the guy.

"Sure did," I said, rocking on my feet. I was excited.

"You missed the meeting. Father was pissed. You didn't happen to bump into any panther shifters down there, did you?"

I shook my head. This was the first I was hearing about it. My wolf was interested. A panther shifter? Never met one before, and I wondered how good they were in a fight. I quickly cleared that thought.

"Yeah, they called up the packs in the area. One of them was visiting their mate's family here in Watson." He slammed the cleaver down hard again. "No idea who the mate was, but all the packs have been warned to stay away if you encounter him."

I gave him two thumbs up, then marched up to my bedroom to get ready for tonight. As much as I loved being with everyone in the cottage, there wasn't enough room for my clothes, and nothing compared to the huge shower here.

We needed a new place, and we were going to ask my father after Lex's birthday. Hopefully, we'd move out after graduation.

CHAPTER FIFTY

LEXI

I got ready at Ada's house. She thought it would be a good way for us to talk in private. The school week had been long, boring, and full of Olivia having hissy fits over no one speaking to her. I'd thought she would come and apologize, or at least say something nice to get me to turn it all back, but yesterday, she threw a half-eaten apple at me. So it might really take her a long time to realize you couldn't treat people like shit and get away with it.

"You're still dress shopping with me tomorrow, right?" Ada asked as she tried on another top. I swear she had tried that same one on earlier... She had tried on so much clothing in the last three hours that everything looked almost the same. It was gold and a little plain in style. I tilted my head from side to side, assessing it so she would know I was taking this seriously. I moved my finger in a circle, and she turned. It had three straps at the back holding it together.

"Oh wow, Ada. That looks amazing, and yes." Okay, that was hot. I got why it was plain at the front, as all of that skin was showing in the back.

"Is that a yes you're coming, or yes to the top? I bought it last week, but now I'm not sure. Is it too much?" I shook my head.

"No, I love it, and you look hot. And yes to both." I was going dress shopping, because ever since Ada said the guys got tickets, I had been hoping they would ask me to prom. Like, I'd hinted so much this past week, but nothing... I had come here mainly to sulk a little at not being asked. Like, did they just assume I would go with them? If I was going, I wanted them to ask me, not just assume.

"Okay, this is the top. I'm almost ready, then we'll go." I lay back on her bed, her room an explosion of clothes. Michelle popped her head in and took a look at the state of the room.

"Ada, you better clean all this up." She shook her head before turning to me. "You look lovely, Lexi. I hope you both have a lovely night." Then she closed the door as Ada called out she would pack it all up tomorrow.

"So glad I'm staying over, I think she would've made me clean it when I came home."

I laughed as she grabbed a few things, and then we left.

I was so happy to see Jett. I hadn't really talked to him much these last few weeks. I thought at first he was avoiding me, but he'd told me he was spending more time over at Mekhi's place, which was literally next door. I'd wiggled my brows at him, and he told me to stop thinking dirty thoughts about him, and if I wanted an upgrade, I should let him know.

"Hey, beautiful, looking for an upgrade?" he called to me. Ada laughed, and I smiled and shook my head at him. Ranger had been so good this week, I didn't want him set off over something like this.

"I told you, model two-point-ohhh is *so* much better than the first series." I stuck my tongue out at him, and Mekhi, Nash, and Saint laughed.

"Shot down again, brother," Nash said, slapping him on the back. He smiled at me before he walked off back to the house. Nash had been confusing me a lot lately, but I thought we had come to some understanding that I wasn't leaving, I was here for the long run, and I could live with that.

"So, see any girls you might like?" I'd made sure the guys extended their invitation to more of the students at school, not the same ones that apparently always got invited, but the ones who seemed to be overlooked. One of them might be someone's mate. Or get asked to prom. Ugh.

"Let's go find the guys." I held Ada's hand and took her away from Saint. He watched us, his face so impassive, it was hard to know what he was thinking.

"Thanks," Ada whispered, then put on a smile as one of the junior girls she knew from the library waved at us. We both waved back, and she turned and laughed at something and put her hand on the guy's arm.

"Ohh, matchmaking happening." It kinda made me feel good, like a cupid. He was a type of angel. *I think.* Fuck, I'd forgotten to call Tobias back. I'd do it tomorrow. Maybe he would want to come out on Tuesday for my birthday. Jack and Grayson had invited us all out to dinner to celebrate.

"Ada, did you want to come to my birthday dinner on Tuesday?" I asked, but she didn't answer me. It was like she didn't hear me she was so fixated on the girl from the library. When I looked back, she had her arm hooked in the crook of the tall guy's arm. Wait, oh shit. Tall guy turned around, and his eyes flared at Ada.

"Noah." My mouth dropped open. Ada had told me how much she liked him, but she liked Huxley and was going to prom with him. I didn't have any advice, really, except maybe that she should ask Noah if she wanted to. She hadn't decided, but she didn't seem happy. I watched as he released the girl from her grip and started towards us. Ada turned and ran.

I didn't know what to do as Noah came up to me. Ah...where were my mates? Like, how did I have four mates and none of them were out here? Fuck, fuck, fuc—

"Lexi, it wasn't what it looked like. She kept laughing and

touching me. Then she told me she felt dizzy, and I helped her not to fall."

Well, I was glad he wasn't the only clueless one in this...well, whatever this was between them. Oh, he was such a sweetie.

"I don't know. It looked like she was flirting with you, and I guess Ada saw that too." His hands went to his pockets, and he hunched forward. I wanted to hug him and tell him that one day this would all be over and he would have a mate, whether it was Ada or not. But he would be happy and all this *does she like me, does he like me* crap would all be over. But that was the fun of it all—the butterflies, the excitement that they chose you, that they wanted no one else but you.

I heard a loudspeaker make some static sound as the music disappeared, and then I heard the voice of one of my mates.

"Where is my beautiful Lex? You're wanted by the pool, babe."

Noah's face changed, and he was now smiling.

I shook my head. What the hell was Ranger doing?

CHAPTER FIFTY-ONE

LEXI

I walked over to the pool and froze when I saw red balloons made into an arch. Everyone was looking at me and smiling. Some of the girls pushed me forward, and I stumbled closer in shock.

What the hell was going on? Galen and Maverick stood to one side, Raff on the other, and Ranger right in the middle of the balloon arch, a microphone in his hand and what looked like a box of donuts. My brows raised as I nervously looked around. What the hell was happening?

"Everyone, can I have your attention, please? I would like to ask a question of my beautiful, bossy at times, but very understanding mate, Lexi Turner.

"Lex, babe. Would you be mine and go to prom with me?" My hands flew to my heated cheeks as he passed the microphone off to Raff, then he got down on one knee and opened the donut box. The donuts said 'Prom.' My heart was thundering, and I giggled nervously. Holy shit. I had wanted them to ask me to prom, but this... I didn't like being the center of attention, and now I was. But I also didn't care.

"Babe...come say yes. *Donut* make me." Ranger waved his hand for me to come over, but his eyes now looked worried, like this was a mistake and I would say no. A smirk appeared on my lips, and he shook his head and smiled.

"Come here," he growled playfully, and I laughed as I jogged over to him. He held the donuts high away from me as I wrapped my arms around his waist.

"You can't eat them until you say yes," he said. I held his shoulders and jumped up, wrapping my legs around him, and tried to reach for them. I could hear my mates laughing, and I turned to our audience. It was mostly Kiba boys, and a lot of them were laughing too, Jett one of them. His eyes lit up when I caught his eye.

"Can I have a donut, Lexi?" he called out. My mouth dropped open, and I quickly turned to Ranger, but he kept smiling. It made my heart sore that he didn't rise to his brother's bait.

"Yes, I will go to prom with you...if you give me my donuts." I kissed him before he could say anything, and everyone cheered.

"And will you be mine?" His brow raised, and I giggled.

"Always," I replied, and my lips met his again in a blinding kiss.

"Okay, move along, next..." someone shouted. I started to laugh as I peeled my lips from Ranger. He had a huge grin as he slapped my ass playfully and dropped me down.

"I'll feed you donuts after, babe." He winked, leaving me under the arch. He walked away, and Raff appeared in front of me. His shy smile was doing things to me as he shuffled his feet and froze when he saw the small crowd now quietly watching us. I reached out and took his hand. His eyes focused back to me, and he loosened up slightly.

He put the microphone to his mouth and closed his eyes.

"Lexi, the first time you held my hand, I felt the world stop. Now, you make my world turn."

My mouth went dry, my knees a little weak, and I let out a shaky breath. I was going to be in tears at the end of this, and I realized this was more than just a promposal. I understood what Jett had said now.

This was them claiming me as their mate in front of their pack, their peers.

I cupped his cheek, and he opened his eyes. Those amazing eyes, like sunshine on a clear blue lake, they bore into me. He was my soulmate—one of four.

"When you cared for me, healed my wounds, I knew you had a big heart, one that could love someone...someone like me." My heart was breaking.

"Raff," I said, my throat thick and my voice full of emotion.

"When I knew I could be the one to chase away the nightmares, when you trusted me to keep you safe. I knew then, what love was. I love you, Lexi Turner."

"I love you, Rafferty King." The microphone dropped and let out a horrible thud and distorted squeal through the speakers. He took my face in his hands and kissed me gently, and when he pulled back, I licked my lips. They tasted a little salty, and I realized he'd shed a few tears. *Oh, Rafferty.* I wiped them from his cheek with my thumb.

"Will you go to prom with me? And can I claim you as mine?" I nodded, and his watery smile gave me butterflies.

"Yes, yes, a million times yes."

I needed a few moments before Maverick was next. He could see I needed to compose myself. This was important to them. It was something I had heard talked about over and over from the first moment I walked into the high school and Parker Tolson challenged Raff over his claim to me. Jett had told me he and Mekhi didn't claim Clare, that it was like a marriage proposal and they didn't want to bind her to them until she was ready.

I knew I was ready, even though it hadn't been long. I knew in my heart that I wouldn't want to be with anyone else, or be anywhere but here. Kiba was my home, and it would be forever.

"Lexi, when you first came to Kiba, we got off on the wrong foot,"

Maverick started, and I chuckled. "But you were stubborn and wild. You didn't care about rules or authority. You live your life according to you. It scared me, because I knew in my heart you were made for me." My hand went to my chest. "So when you kissed me, even though I totally cheated with spin the bottle—don't tell my brother..." Ranger called out hey, and I laughed. He'd cheated? "You helped open me up, made me feel whole. You are the star in my night sky, Lexi, guiding me home."

Tears fell, and I couldn't help it. I knew what he was saying about me...and Galen.

"Will you be mine?" I nodded, and everyone cheered. I jumped up into his arms before he was ready and took him off guard.

"Yes, always yes."

CHAPTER FIFTY-TWO

GALEN

Before Lexi, I didn't let myself get too close, even with the pack. I tried not to get close, because you never know who will fail you or leave you. Ranger didn't get that memo though and drove me crazy for the last five years, more so in the past year. And every time he called me an old man...well, it made me happy.

He wasn't doing it to upset me or in teasing. He did it because that was just another way in which Ranger showed you that he liked you, and he must have liked me plenty. He took my history class, after all.

"Hurry up, old man," he grumbled. Maverick was still having his moment with Lexi, but I knew it was my turn. I'd asked to go last. Ranger had wanted to be first. Although after Raff's and Mav's speech, I knew he was rethinking his. It wasn't the same as the other two, but it was Ranger. Fuck, I didn't even know if I wanted to go after Raff and Mav. Those were very hard to follow.

Technically, I didn't have to claim Lexi since I wasn't a shifter, but Alaric had said it was good for unity, to see me claim her openly would solidify my position in the pack. And I wanted to keep my position. I was now working with the council, and Shelly had said she thought she'd found a replacement vamp for the high school. She was just making sure it was final. I was glad this meant I could fully cut ties with the school, so I could take Lexi to prom. If there were issues, I would compel all the teachers. Easy. I rolled my eyes. No, it wouldn't be. I was just banking on them turning a blind eye, now that I wasn't a teacher there anymore.

"Maverick, I'll take it from here." I stepped forward and held my hand out to Lexi. She placed her warm hands in my cold ones. I didn't drink today, and I hadn't wanted to. She'd told me she didn't mind the cold, and the others hadn't complained when they touched me either, so I hadn't been drinking to warm myself.

"Galen, here," Mav said, and I dropped one of her hands as he handed me the microphone. There were things I couldn't say in front of the humans, but I would tell them to her privately.

She wiped a few happy tears away. Her eye makeup was smudged, but she looked beautiful, no doubt about it.

"Lexi Turner," I said into the microphone, and everyone quieted down.

She smiled and murmured, "Mr. Donovani." Fuck... Why did that always go straight to my cock when she said that? She gave me a teasing smile, and I cleared my throat.

"When I first...saw you." *Smelled you.* Fuck, this was hard, but she understood my meaning by the way she nodded. "I had never seen someone so sure of herself. You had me entranced and intrigued by this mystery that is you, love" She always gave off this sweeter smell when I called her love, so I did it at every chance I got.

"When I took you for breakfast and you asked if I sparkled, I knew then that I would go to the end of the earth for you, even if it was so you could tell me you didn't like my type again. But I knew deep down, you wouldn't have stayed if you did." The huge grin on her face made me chuckle at the memory.

"I didn't want to waste a really good breakfast," she said, and some of the shifters chuckled at that. My heart was racing, but I already knew she would say yes to prom and to my claiming her.

"You see me as a man who has worth, my past long forgotten and a future written with yours. Would you do me the honor of being my date for the prom and spending forever with me?"

She rushed at me and bumped the microphone. I threw it towards Jett, who was standing to the side now. Her warm hands pulled at my neck to lower my face to hers. We were so close in height, but she was smaller than all four of us. I loved that about her. She was tiny but tough.

When she pressed her forehead to mine, this huge grin on her face and her eyes tearing up again, I could feel her inside. I felt what she was thinking, how happy she was, the love she had for me so powerful. I let out a shuddering breath. I never knew someone could love me that strongly and without fault.

"Forever always, Mr. Donovani," she murmured. I could feel my fangs itching to descend, so I kissed her, hard and fast, in the hopes they wouldn't. We got lost in each other, the cheering fading to the background.

I pulled away and saw her dazed eyes and swollen lips, and she smiled up at me like I hung the moon and the stars. But she was the one who had hung them all for me. I could hear the confusion from some of the females, about how Lexi had four guys and it wasn't fair. One called her a name that no woman ever should be called. It was wrong, and luckily, Nash was onto it fast. He took her and led her to the gate. Lexi wouldn't know any different.

This was the way of life here with the packs. If human girls didn't like it, they wouldn't ever fit in. So best to remove any negativity they had at sharing mates.

"Okay, that's all the entertainment for promposals and love declaring. Now, let's get this party started! My brother Ranger has found some fireworks—" I turned and eyed Ranger, but he shrugged and held his hands up. I glared at him and he gave me a challenging look. "—so we're really gonna have some fun tonight. Stick around for the show."

Everyone cheered, and I just shook my head and smiled as Lexi laughed.

"Oh, you don't approve?" she said, poking me. "Old man." She bit her lower lip, teasing me. *Cheeky girl.* Her cheeks pinked as she opened her mouth to say more, but before she had a chance, I kissed her until she was speechless and moaning against my lips.

I wanted to take her to bed and kiss her lower, much lower. After that night with Mav, I couldn't stop thinking about it, but I had told myself I wasn't going to go further. Not yet. I was waiting until her birthday. It just felt...wrong. My age, her youth. I wouldn't take her a day earlier than her eighteenth birthday, and I think she knew that. She hadn't pushed me, not that she would.

But on Tuesday, I had a surprise for her, and I hoped it didn't change anything when I gave it to her. I knew she didn't like me buying her things, but this was a little different. It was her birthday.

And she deserved the world.

CHAPTER FIFTY-THREE

LEXI

I found Ada standing by herself in the corner of the kitchen, and when she saw me, she smiled.

"Oh my gosh, that was better than I imagined. Congratulations!" *Huh?* Better than she imagined? Did she know?

"You knew?" And she kept it a secret! I swear Galen better not have compelled her.

She giggled and wrapped me in a hug.

"Well, duh. In what world does it make sense to get ready at my place, all afternoon, when there is a party at your house? And seriously, I tried on so many tops, I thought you were going to die of boredom. If it wasn't for the fact that I drove you, I for sure thought you would have run away screaming." I laughed and hugged her tighter.

"You knew the whole time, and I spent most that time complaining about them not asking me." It was funny how something I didn't want to do turned into something I wanted. The prom wasn't important to me, but when I was presented with the chance, I wanted to go. It was like a normal thing for a teenager—prom, graduate...then go to college.

Which was something I was going to ask Alaric about. If we

could go to Port Angeles to shop when it was okay with the bear shifters, maybe we could go to the college there. I could join Ada, and I didn't even care if I joined the same classes as her, as long as I got to go.

That was the most important thing to me. Coming here, I'd had two goals—I wanted to pass high school and go to college. I wanted to succeed at life. I didn't want to be...like my mother. I wanted to have an education that could set me up with a career. Now, with everything that I was and my healing powers, I knew there was some good I could do in the world. Even if it was only for the shifters of Kiba... and Rawlins and Kenneally. I wanted to help.

I rested against the counter and looked over to Ada. I knew she was upset with that girl touching Noah, but she needed to figure it out. Saint seemed to have backed off, though. I didn't know if that made Ada happy or not. She hadn't really said much about it.

The door opened and closed, and I saw Ada stiffen. *Oh, Noah.* I turned, expecting it to be him, but it wasn't.

"Yeah, you bitch. Thought you won? You might have the Kiba boys at school wrapped around your finger, but not all of them." The fuck? Olivia? I looked at Ada. She had hurt her, and now someone had invited her here to hurt Ada and me?

"You don't have the power here, I do. I was here first. I fucked Ranger first, and I took Maverick's virginity. I was here before you, and I will be here after you. You're just a fun toy to play with before they're both mine."

Who in their right mind would have invited Olivia? The door opened, and in rushed Maverick and Saint. Good, they could get rid of her, because she was destroying what was supposed to be my night. I just... I looked up and tried to calm my anger. This girl had no clue, none. She had no self-respect, and I didn't think anything I said or did would ever change her mind.

"What the fuck are you doing here? You are not welcome here, Olivia," Maverick said. She smiled sweetly and sauntered over to him, like that would change his mind. Jealously reared up in me, and I felt my skin prickle. She'd better not touch him. He was mine.

"Saint invited me. He asked me to prom, and I accepted. I know how close you two are. I was hoping the three of us could go together."

Maverick turned to Saint, but his face was impassive as he stared right past me to Ada. I heard her make a small sound before she ran off up the stairs. He watched her as Maverick yelled at him.

"You're a fucking prick," was all I said to him as I took off after Ada. I couldn't believe he did that, especially after what she did to Ada.

"Ada?" I looked in my room, but I couldn't see her. Shit. "Ada?" I heard a door open, and I turned to see Lyell looking out from his room. He waved at me and pointed inside his room. I rushed over to see Ada curled up on his bed, sobbing. He smiled sadly at me.

"I think she accidently came in here thinking it was your room," he said, and I nodded. It was right next to my room. If you weren't thinking straight, it was easy to miss.

"Welcome to the family, Lexi. I'm glad my brothers claimed you. You're good for them." I thought that was the most words he'd ever spoken to me before, but I guessed after the whole Galen compelling shifters and him being the guinea pig—well, the wolf chasing his tail—he had sort of avoided me.

"Thank you."

He left, and I lay down beside her and wrapped her in a big hug. Saint was her first crush, and even though he left her more confused every time he saw her, this was too far. After what Olivia did to her, that was a low blow, even from him. Maverick had said he had handled it, that Saint really liked her.

Well, if this was how he showed someone he liked them, imagine him being in love. She was better off without him. To have her heart broken now was better than in the long run if he was just going to play games.

"It's okay, don't worry about him. You have Huxley. He is taking you to prom, and I have seen the way he looks at you and the way you look at him."

She turned to me, her eyes bloodshot, her makeup ruined. She sniffled a few times, and I leaned over and grabbed a box of tissues sitting on the nightstand. Oh...there was a lot of used tissues on the floor. "Eeeeww," I said as I dropped the box next to her. I didn't know if I wanted to touch it. She looked at it like I was crazy.

"I think this is Lyell's happy tissue box. Shifters don't get sick." Her eyes flared as she looked at the floor and screwed up her face, then we both cracked up laughing. I had a feeling Lyell would be avoiding me even longer.

The door opened, and it was Jett. "Hey, beautiful ladies, I heard the news that you found Lyell's tissue collection. All those wasted tissues... Trees have been cut down so he can wipe his jizz on them. I've told him to jerk off in the shower like everyone else does. I save the planet twice a day, and I feel like a hero every time I come."

My mouth dropped open, and Ada just blinked. "Jett, that was a total overshare. We didn't want to know that."

He chuckled. "All guys jerk off, even your mates. You just don't know. Ask them, I dare you." I slapped him away as he lay down next to Ada and I.

"I know they do, I just didn't want to know that about you." I wasn't stupid. Hell, I took care of myself a couple of times in the shower, and I knew they heard me. They all wore funny grins on their faces when I got out and fought about who was taking the next shower.

He winked at Ada, and she blushed. I knew he was trying to cheer her up, but I couldn't help it, I rolled my eyes at him and shook my head.

"Ada, you wanna dance with me?" I could hear the music downstairs, and I guessed we were getting fireworks soon.

"Ah...okay. I just need to fix my makeup." She pushed off the bed and straightened her top, then went into Lyell's bathroom. I hoped there were no used tissues in there.

"Oh, just a heads-up... Your fathers are here and want to see you."

I sat up straighter. Fathers?

"Jack and Grayson?" I asked, a smile on my lips. They were here? Was Josh here too?

"Yeah, and Tobias. They were hiding inside and listening with my father. He invited them after the guys said they were going to claim you. Traditionally, the whole pack is here, but they didn't want it like that. They thought it would be better for you with a smaller group. They've been planning this for about two weeks. We all knew but you. I loved it. And I know Lyell already said it, but I will too. Welcome to the family...sister."

He gave me a hug, then sat back and looked over to the bathroom.

He patted my leg and said, "You go to them, and I'll take care of Ada. Don't worry. Mekhi is kicking Saint's ass as we speak."

That made me laugh. Jett and Mekhi were awesome. I hoped they would one day be able to move on...with someone nice. Maybe someone who could handle Jett, because he was a handful, just like Ranger.

CHAPTER FIFTY-FOUR

LEXI

It was strange seeing Tobias in the same room as Jack and Grayson, but they were all laughing and talking like they were old friends.

"Here is the special lady. Congratulations." Grayson was the first to hug me, then Jack. I pulled away and saw Tobias.

"Congrats, my dear. They will all make fine mates for you, I know." He tapped his head, and I froze. I didn't like that he could hear their thoughts. That was...well, it was weird and an invasion of privacy. You don't just go around listening to people's thoughts.

"I only want what is best for you. I had to make sure myself. I don't wish to hear others' thoughts, and I cannot control what I hear or don't hear, but I will do my best not to listen in from now on."

I let out a deep breath and nodded. I guessed I was hearing Galen's thoughts sometimes when he didn't mean for me too. So it must be hard not to listen in.

"Thank you." I gave him an awkward hug. We weren't there yet, and things were still a little new. Alaric was next, and I had never hugged him either. But there he was with his arms open and a huge grin. I stepped forward and hugged him. It was...nice.

"Alexis Turner, if I knew months ago that two of my boys would have a strong, independent, and intelligent mate, I would have bought a lottery ticket. It takes a special person to love my twin boys. They have been through so much, and you brought them together. You showed Maverick it was okay to love openly. Ranger has become more grounded and well..." he chuckled, "less trouble for me."

I laughed at that. Yeah, he was my trouble now.

"Well, we won't keep you. Your mates are looking for you. Have a great night, and we will see you on Tuesday for dinner." Jack said.

It felt so good to be accepted like that. All these men were father figures to me, and they accepted my mates.

I ran out and looked for my mates. I wanted to see the fireworks with them, but when I found Ranger, he looked upset.

"Babe? What's wrong?" I loved the way he reacted to my pet name for him. He called me babe, so I started to call him it in return. It was our thing. I was worried he was upset about Olivia and Saint, but when he turned to me, he stuck out his bottom lip.

"Lex babe, my father took all my fireworks away." I laughed, and he pouted even more, so I hugged him.

"I know a way I can cheer you up." He looked down at me. His bottom lip was now between his teeth, and he growled.

The next morning, I woke up and smiled to myself. I couldn't believe the night I'd had. I ignored the bad part—Olivia—and only focused on the good. I was going to prom, and I'd been claimed by my mates. Today was dress shopping. Ada had said we should've shopped weeks ago and that all the good dresses would be gone, but I'd wanted to be sure I was going. Now that I was, I was a little giddy this morning.

"I get to take you dress shopping, Lex. But please, please don't kill me with any girl talk. I have no idea why Saint did what he did, and Noah is at home crying in his room," Ranger said. Noah was what? My mouth fell open. "Yeah, like full-on crying. Zara had to tell him it was normal and shit. But yeah, I left. The boy had no idea that girl was flirting with him, and I wasn't sticking around to explain that to him."

Aww, I felt bad for Noah. Shit, I really hoped Ada didn't ask Ranger any questions about him. I didn't think she would do well knowing he was crying. She would be upset with herself, and I wanted her to have a nice day. But I wasn't going to tell him there would be no girl talk. That was what we did.

"Dress shopping and lunch?" he asked, holding up Galen's credit card.

Dress shopping was so much better with a credit card with no limit. Galen had told us both to use it. So all the good dresses were still here, just no one from Port Willow High could afford them. I was feeling better today about spending money on a nice dress. Galen had explained that it was important for him to provide for me, and after being around for over three hundred years, he had raked up a decent portfolio. Basically, my mate was a multi-millionaire with no need for it.

"There's a cute little place in Watson that serves burgers and fries. Let's go eat there. Then you can just drop me off after," Ada suggested. So we hopped in the Jeep, and Ranger drove us there as we discussed our dresses, in code of course, because Ranger wasn't going to see it until prom night like the others.

The burger place was busy, but we got seats outside. Ranger started telling us how he was going to find his fireworks and steal them back from his father. I really hoped that Alaric was smart enough to have gotten rid of them. I knew Ranger could heal super-fast, I just didn't know if he blew a finger off how that would work and I didn't want to find out.

"Oh, what?" Ranger muttered as he turned and started waving to a girl with long black hair. She wore a yellow dress that made her golden skin almost glow, and she was with a guy who had a shaved head and this scruffy short facial hair. The way he carried himself was what I would say looked just like Ranger swagger. He was attractive, and Ada had noticed too.

"Oh my god, Clare," she called out, waving to her. Clare...Jett and Mekhi's Clare? Oh shit, she had moved on. I felt bad for them, but I really didn't understand their break-up.

Ranger growled low and shifted in his seat. The guy Clare was with, his eyes flashed as he did the same. I felt like I was in a movie and this was a standoff. I didn't know what to do. Did she know she was dating a shifter? Like, did she just trade up now that she had left?

"Hey, Ada, how have you been?" She dragged the guy over to our table. She didn't seem to notice the way he was acting, so I guessed she didn't know he was a shifter.

Ranger jumped up, and I thought he was going to hit the guy. But instead, he wrapped his arms around Clare. I didn't feel jealous, not at all. The fact that she looked really uncomfortable with Ranger made me feel bad for him. He had looked up to this girl, and now she was acting like he was a stranger.

"Oh, hi." She patted his back, and he pulled away. "Ah...you're Jett's brother, right?" Her brows raised, and even Ada dropped her fry.

"What?" Ranger looked taken aback. "Am I Jett's brother?" He cracked up laughing, but she didn't. If anything, she just looked puzzled.

"Well, it was, ah...nice seeing you. Ada, we should catch up. I'm here for the week. My parents are having their twenty-fifth wedding anniversary, so we flew in. This is my boyfriend, Frankie." The guy nodded to us. His eyes stayed trained on Ranger, though, and he sensed this. He was getting worked up, so I needed this to end quickly so I could take him home.

"Hi, I'm Lexi. It's nice meeting you, I think it's time we were going." I got up and took Ranger's arm, and Ada followed, calling out to Clare that she would call her.

When we got to the car, Ada stopped and said, "Holy shit... Galen compelled her."

Ranger and I turned, and Ada nodded.

"It makes perfect sense. She had no idea who you were, Ranger. She was going to skip college and stay here, with Jett and Mekhi. Then they broke up with her…and she was upset, but for only a few days. Then she was super happy, like crazy happy. I always thought it was strange. And now…" She pointed to where they just were.

"Why the hell would Galen do that?" Ranger asked.

"So she would be happy…and so she would leave," I said. That was my guess, and Ada nodded.

I guessed the only way to find out was by asking the people who would know the truth.

CHAPTER FIFTY-FIVE

LEXI

I was nervous, and I didn't want to open my eyes. I'd heard the guys get up early, but I pretended that I was sleeping. They tried to be quiet, but Maverick fell onto the floor, which had made me wake up. I would've gone back to sleep if it wasn't for all their hissing and whispers about being quiet that had me alert. It had to be the crack of dawn when they got up. I just wanted to get ready. I'd never celebrated my birthday before, because I couldn't afford that luxury or the foster parents forgot or couldn't spare money for a cake.

I had told them not to make a big deal, and they'd promised. I guessed that was why they did the big prom and claiming speeches on Saturday night when I wasn't expecting it, because if I'd known... well, I would've overblown it in my mind and hidden somewhere.

"I know you're awake, I can tell by your breathing and your heart rate. I just didn't tell the boys, love." I stretched and yawned, and Galen chuckled. A smile crept over my face as I cracked open an eye and saw him standing in the doorway, a mug in his hand and a bowl in the other.

"Happy birthday." He was wearing blue jeans and a white tee. Like, he was actually wearing a short-sleeved top. I was taken aback, and I blinked a few times to see if I was really awake. He smirked and cocked his head. He hadn't shown off his arms before, and I had never seen him wear a T-shirt. It was fitted, molded tight to his body... Oh, he looked so fine, like Ryan Gosling from *The Notebook*. I loved the knitted sweater Galen, he was hot in his own right, but this Galen...

"You're thinking naughty thoughts, aren't you?" I laughed and nodded as he crossed the room and bent down, his lips brushing lightly over mine.

"Here's breakfast in bed for a very special birthday girl." He handed me a warm mug of tea and bowl of cereal... That was new. I looked inside.

"Lucky Charms?" He shrugged as his eyes darted to the door. I could hear the others, but I was glad they weren't all busting down the door to see me. I was still taking in the fact someone had wished me a happy birthday.

"I saw them a few times when I was shopping. They seemed like a birthday type cereal, and I didn't want you to have the same breakfast you have every day. But I can make bacon and eggs for you if you prefer. The boys ate the rest of it. *Pigs*."

"Wolves!" Ranger yelled from the kitchen, and I laughed. I had never had Lucky Charms before. I smiled.

"Thank you, Galen." He nodded and left the room, and I rested the bowl on my lap as I drank the hot tea. He knew how to make great tea, must be the English in him. No one else came in for a while, and I settled back and relaxed. There was no point in school today. I went yesterday but it was so boring, and Galen said he would fix the whole passing thing for me and Ada, who was even more bored than me. She was used to doing so much, but he seemed to be busy most days and didn't have time.

He was just stalling me, and now there really was no point. After this week, there wasn't much left I could do to change my grades, anyway.

It didn't take long before I could hear their harsh whispers about who was going in next. Raff and Ranger were arguing that they wanted to be next, and Galen was trying to get them to stop. I shook my head and chuckled when Maverick appeared at the door. He put his finger to his lips as his dimples appeared with his huge grin. I held in a snort of laughter as he quickly closed the door behind him and the guys yelled out.

I said, "That was sneaky, but I'm glad you're next." And I was. He seemed to always go last for things, and I didn't know if he thought it was because he deserved last or just who he was, but I wanted him to feel equal. that was the most important thing to me. I put the mug and bowl on the side table and reached out to him.

"Happy birthday, Lexi." He pressed me into a huge weighted hug, and I breathed him in. He was always so fresh, pine and all man. I'd better get wolves today. It was my birthday, and I wanted a puppy pile. He pulled back, and I kissed him.

"I got you a gift. I actually bought it a while ago and I was going to give it to you so many times, but so much happened that I just pushed it to the side for the right time." He handed me a small wrapped package that was hidden in a drawer. It felt like a book, and I laughed.

"A book? You know me too well." I loved the Kindle he'd bought, but nothing was better than the smell of a real book. I peeled off the red paper and saw it was a black leather hardback, the gold detail very familiar as I stroked the lines. I flipped it over, and my heart hammered. It was the one I had seen in his room when I first moved here to the Lovells'. Well, when I thought it was Lyell's room and borrowed his sweats. I'd forgotten about all that. Now... Oh, the emotions. *Hold it together, Lexi.*

Maverick cleared his throat, and in the most terrible English accent I had ever heard, said, "It is a truth universally acknowledged, that four single men in possession of good looks and skills, must be in want of a mate...and that is true." I laughed at how he knew the words...well, he ad-libbed most of them so it suited us.

"I love it, thank you, Maverick." I felt teary. He'd bought me a beautiful copy of *Pride and Prejudice*, even before he was mine.

He bowed and tipped an imaginary hat. "You are welcome, my dear." I shook my head. Oh boy. Yep, that was the worst accent I had ever heard.

Raff and Ranger came in together, and I laughed as they jumped onto the bed and wrapped me up like a burrito. Ranger peppered kisses all over my face as I tried to squirm away, and Raff tickled me through the blankets.

"Happy, happy birthday." They were singing it over and over, out of tune and on top of one another, until they finally let up with huge smiles and looked down at me.

"I have a gift for you, Lex, but I can't give mine until Galen gives his big gift. I can't wait… You're gonna be so excited." I looked to Raff, and he chuckled.

"Don't look so worried, it's not like he bought you a horse," he said, and Ranger cracked up laughing. What did that mean? Ranger winked at me, then jumped off the bed.

"I'll leave you lovebirds for a moment, then you better get your ass up so Galen and I can give you our gifts." He closed the door behind him, and I pulled the blankets off. I was wearing shorts and a tank. I had found out that even though I loved to wear their T-shirts, they were big and when I tried to roll over, I'd get tangled or someone was lying on it and I'd have to pull it. I was waking up more than I should've been, so the tighter the clothes, the better.

"Lexi, I thought long and hard about what I wanted to get you. If I could give you everything in the world, I would. But I knew even then, that wasn't enough." I reached out to hold his hand. Our fingers interlaced, and he let out a slow breath. I didn't want the world. I just wanted him.

"When I was little, my mom had a special bracelet made. It's a memory that I remember really well. She took me to the store every week until she paid it off. Then she had it engraved. She wore it every day until my uncles got mad and took it from her.

"They locked me in my room a lot for breaking their rules. She would always come to me and repeat, 'Be wild, be free. Rafferty's rules.' I was young, too young to fully understand what that meant. It wasn't until we went back there that it came back to me, the way she would chant it through the bedroom door.

"Galen heard me chanting to it to myself last week. He asked if I knew what 'Rafferty's rules' meant. I just thought it was my rules that my uncles had given me, that my mom had meant for me to be wild and free but to listen to the rules." My heart thumped wildly, and a tear rolled down my cheek. His thumb gently wiped the tear away, and he gave me a small smile.

"He said it meant 'no rules at all.'" He laughed. "It was some old saying. I had stolen the bracelet back from them that same week. I found where they had hidden it, and I took it. I broke the rules and gave it back to my mom. She told me to keep it hidden until the day we could run away, and then she would wear it again to let me know I was safe."

My throat was thick. I was so choked up from his story about his mom.

"Don't cry, Lexi. I didn't want to make you cry on your birthday. I just wanted to tell you, so when I gave you this, you would understand." He pulled out a little gold chain with a small gold plate, then turned my hand over and gently placed it my palm. It was so delicate and beautiful, and there was the name Rafferty engraved with a rose beside it.

My hand went to my throat. I couldn't accept this. It was too much.

"I want you to have it, Lexi, for you to wear it." His voice wavered a little. I closed my hand on it, and when I looked up, his eyes were glassy. More tears fell, but they weren't full of sadness, just hope and love. I would wear it every day and let him know he was safe.

"Thank you for sharing that story. The meaning of this gift is one I will treasure for the rest of my life."

Our kiss was slow and sweet. He then placed it on my wrist, and we held each other for a while. I felt closer to Raff. I understood him more and what he had been through, the pain, the love for his mom, the young rulebreaker that he was.

How fate had set us on a course that would lead us to this very moment.

CHAPTER FIFTY-SIX

LEXI

Ranger couldn't wait for me to get dressed, so he came and smuggled me away from Raff. I giggled when he jumped around and said, "I just want to give you mine now. But you were taking *sooooo* long. So close your eyes."

I did, and he wrapped his hand across them. "Galen," he shouted out, and I could hear them moving around.

"Okay, we have to walk outside." Ranger started to move me. My hands went up to his arm that was holding my eyes as I stumbled over a few things.

"Don't break her," Maverick teased, and I laughed when I bumped into something again.

"Shit. Sorry, I was distracted... You know I can see right down your—Hey." I was jolted slightly, then Ranger grumbled, "Asshole."

"That's no way to talk to your mate, let me do this." I laughed at Maverick. My hero took over from Ranger, but instead of leading me, he wrapped me in his arms and pulled me to his chest.

"Close your eyes... Are you ready for a big surprise?"

Ranger snorted, and I couldn't help the giggles at what he'd said.

"Maverick is now rhyming about Galen's *big* surprise. How big is his...*surprise?*" I shook my head as Maverick growled at Ranger. I didn't think he meant it in that way, but Ranger...well, he was being Ranger. I loved that about him.

When we got outside, I felt the warm sun kiss my skin, and it felt amazing. Yesterday had rained, but I loved the sun. So I was glad it was here for my birthday.

"I'm going to put you on your feet, but keep your eyes closed."

I nodded and said, "Promise." I giggled. "I promise, eyes closed." I felt giddy and nervous. What the hell did Galen buy that was so big it couldn't come in the cottage? It wasn't a horse...that was what Raff had said.

"Okay, love. Open your eyes." I slowly opened my eyes, squinting at first, and when I saw the sparkly white and big red bow, I opened them wide and stood straighter.

"You...you bought me a car? I can't even drive!" I exclaimed, my hand on my chest. He bought me a car, a big car. It was huge. I looked over to Galen. His brows were furrowed but he had such a hopeful smile that I wasn't about to kill him. I was going to kill him, but not for this. He promised me nothing expensive, and that looked brand new.

"It's an Audi Q7. It has seven seats, so we can all be comfortable and fit two more people if we need. And the driving part... Well, here." He handed me a freaking driver's license with my photo and all my details.

"What the hell, Galen? I haven't driven a car in my life, and I told you I didn't want you to cheat with this."

Ranger stepped forward and wrapped me up in his arms.

"Lex, I told him to, because your birthday gift from me is driving lessons. I'll teach you everything you need to know." My mouth dropped open. "Hey, you'll catch flies like that." He pushed my chin until my mouth closed. "The license was my idea. I wanted to coordinate with him, and especially after Saturday night, I wanted to make sure my gift worked." I turned in his arms and gave him my best *don't you start now* look.

He had been upset that he didn't give some amazing speech like the others did. He thought it was just a, "will you go to prom and can I claim you." I had told him so many times since then that I got the best Ranger public speech and that I would take all the dirty talk he could give me in private. That had seemed to keep him happy. He was happy last night when he went down on me, using his tongue for more than just dirty words.

I turned to Galen. His smile didn't reach his eyes.

"I love it. It's big, but you're right—we can all fit in. And we can take Ada or Josh with us to places over the summer. Like...our trip to Forks?" I may have mentioned I wanted to go there, even though Galen told me he really didn't know any vamps who actually lived there. It was now a no vamp zone, because so many people went there, hoping to meet one. I didn't need to...I already had one.

"I love you." I kissed Galen, running my fingers through his soft curls. "Thank you, I'm sorry, it's just bigger than I expected."

He chuckled, and the other three did too. "Well..." Galen started. I turned and looked at them all. "Raff saw an R8 while we were there..." My mouth dropped. He'd bought two cars. "They gave us a discount, if that makes it better. Plus, I thought it would be a nice date night car."

I couldn't believe them, and I was pretty sure no matter what I said or did, they would always want to spoil me like I wanted to spoil them. I hugged them all, then I heard the screeching voice of Jett.

"Cupcake!" He was running with a pink box in his hand and a huge grin. He was also only wearing some basketball shorts.

We had come home Sunday and told him we bumped into Clare and her shifter boyfriend. Yeah, he was a panther shifter. It was exciting, but also, I felt terrible for Jett and Mekhi. But I was mad too, because Ada was right. They kept shaking their heads, and Ranger was upset. He knew they were lying. It was Mekhi who broke down and said they begged Galen to compel her to forget about them. They wanted her to fulfil her dream of college and to become a veterinarian. They told her they would wait for her while she was in

Colorado, but she didn't want to leave. She wanted to stay here with them both.

I felt terrible for her. They really should have let her grieve properly. It was her choice, and they took that from her. I understood they wanted her to go to college, and I loved that about them both. They knew how important that was for her. But taking memories from her, years of them, that wasn't the way to do it. I told Galen he could never do that again.

To anyone, ever.

CHAPTER FIFTY-SEVEN

MAVERICK

We spent the afternoon doing Lexi's favorite thing—her puppy pile. I was grateful really. I felt like it had been forever since my wolf was stroked by her, and nothing felt better than my mate, my claimed mate, running her fingers through my fur, scratching behind my ears, and making those sweet sighs of happiness.

She read my book, the hardback. She refused to at first, said it was too fancy and her old one would suffice. I told her it wasn't fancy, that it was cheap, not much more than her own paperback, but she said it didn't matter, she still wanted to treat it properly.

"It's a book, if you don't read it, then you're not treating it properly," I told her. She finally agreed and took it with us to spend the day in the sun. There was a cool ocean breeze as the day wore on, but she just snuggled in closer to us. I was nervous about dinner. She had invited my father as well, and I wasn't overly happy about that.

We had all mentioned to him many times these last few weeks about moving out to a larger house. He was very fixed on us being here, that we could move into the main house with him, that Galen could take a spare room up there. That a vampire would soon be working again at the school and Galen would need to relocate, anyway.

Galen didn't want to be in the main house, and I certainly didn't want to be either. It worked for some pack families, but I wanted privacy. He had such a huge problem before about hearing us, which was why we were all living on top of each other at Galen's cottage.

I had asked why one of the other packs couldn't have the vampire, at least until we could talk him around. The pack owned most of the houses in Kiba, we couldn't just move into one, we had to get permission from the alpha, and he wasn't very understanding about our needs.

He went on for thirty minutes about how it was a pleasure and privilege to have the vampire stay here. I started to believe it was a power thing more—he had the last one, give Rawlins the next one.

My wolf wasn't the only one on edge, I could see Ranger was too. There had been no fighting, he had been very restrained in that area, but he was a ticking timebomb. I really thought he should go let it out before it became a huge issue and he exploded and did more than just hurt someone.

Maybe a run before dinner would clear my head. I got up, and Lexi knew what I needed. I shook my fur out, and she held her hands up to block her face.

"Seriously, I'm getting a dog brush. You are molting, Maverick." I let out a whuff as I laughed at her. Ranger nuzzled into her throat, and she stroked his chin. Raff pushed him aside and tried to curl in a ball on her lap. She was laughing and cussing at us all. He was smaller than us, but there was no way he could fit on her lap like he was a puppy.

"Go, all three of you, and meet back at the house to get ready. We need a shower now." Galen was wiping fur from his dark jeans. I used his distraction to pounce on him and lick his face.

"Bad boy," he hissed low. His eyes darkened, and I knew I'd woken his monster. I like it, I liked it a lot.

We drove the Audi Q7 over to Port Angeles to the restaurant. It looked over the water, and it was magical. Tobias had made the reservations. It was a great location and a perfect evening, even if it was a little colder than Lexi preferred. She would need to wear something later if we decided to go for a walk down along the water.

She wore a green silk dress, and it flowed down her body to the floor with a large slit up one side, hugging her body in all the right places. It had an open back, and she wasn't wearing a bra. The cold air had made her nipples hard, and it was difficult to stop my cock from reacting. I was glad I wasn't the only one affected by it. She was even giving off the faint scent of arousal. I wanted to reach under the table and run my hand up the slit and into her panties.

"They have two forks." Josh held the forks up to show us. I wanted to tell him I don't get it either, but Tobias cleared his throat.

"I wanted to give you a gift that made up for the last eighteen missed birthdays, Lexi. I wasn't sure what to get. So I spoke with Alaric, and we agreed that we would give you all a home of your own that is larger than where you are now."

Lexi's mouth dropped open in an audible gulp. Galen turned so fast, it almost set off my wolf. Raff sat back puzzled as he rubbed his brows, and Ranger did exactly the same as me. "What?" We looked to my father. *He what?*

My father gave a big belly laugh, and I didn't know how to take it.

"Oh, you should look at your faces. I've had to keep this secret for weeks. That was harder than you will ever know. Every time you asked and I had to turn you down, I felt like a terrible father. I wanted to give you that. As much as I love you all, I don't want you to move back into the house.

"This is an important time for you, as new mates, to learn, grow, and be together without distractions. Let's face it, the boys and I don't want to hear what you get up to."

I laughed, and Lexi's face heated to a nice shade of pink. Ranger slapped the table.

"Hell yeah, Lexi and I get up to a lot." I couldn't believe Ranger just said that...in front of her father, Jack, and Grayson.

"Do you watch *Teen Titans Go?*" Josh asked all innocently. Raff growled at Ranger before I could. Fucker, destroying this poor innocent child. I wanted to smack him, but he was quick to recover.

"No, I'm not allowed. I've been told the only person she can watch that with is her brother, and that's you, buddy. She makes me watch love movies... Eeewww."

Josh giggled and shook his head. "Eewww, kissing movies are gross." We all laughed, because when you find the perfect girl to kiss, you can't think of anything else you would ever want to do.

I loved that I could share kisses with Lexi, and Galen too. I wasn't sure how this would all work, how it would play out, but Galen had asked if tonight we went for a run when we came back. That he wanted to spend alone time with Lexi. We all agreed, since it was important to have the balance. But that meant after tonight, I was the last one to make love to her. I had gone down on her twice, and she'd dry-humped me on Sunday, but I hadn't gone all the way with her.

I would ask for private time on Saturday, after prom, like they do in all those cheesy teen movies. Sex on prom night was usually what happened, but I would make it better than that. My wolf hummed within me. He wanted to fully claim her. I couldn't and I wouldn't, but she would be mine, and that made him settle.

CHAPTER FIFTY-EIGHT

LEXI

We got back to the cottage, and my three wolves started stripping and chucking their clothes back into the car.

"What are you doing?" I asked. Maverick winked and kissed my cheek before he turned into a wolf. Raff blushed before he was on four paws, and Ranger turned and showed me his ass and slapped it before shifting and letting out an ear-piercing howl.

"They're giving us time alone, Lexi. I hope that's okay?"

Oh, *oh*. I nodded. Yes, oh hell yes, this was more than okay.

We walked inside, and Galen took his suit jacket from my shoulders. I'd needed it. The dress was gorgeous. He had picked it out for me, saying that he loved the color green on me, that it suited my golden brown hair. I felt like I was a princess wearing it, and I kept having to tell myself that this was real. As much as I wanted Galen to stop buying me things, it made him happy. As he kept telling me, it was an old custom, and he wanted to buy me nice things. So long as it wasn't all the time.

I already had my graduation dress. And this dress... Well, I didn't know if I would ever wear it again, and I hated that. It was beautiful and needed to be seen.

"Love?" I turned into him. His white button-up shirt looked hot on him, but no shirt would look even better. He brushed his knuckles over my lips, and his eyes grew darker. I opened my mouth, and one of his fingers found its way inside. I swirled my tongue around it, and he groaned loudly, stepping forward. He grabbed my ass and pulled me against his body. He had been drinking at dinner, so he felt warm. I wondered if it was for my benefit, or if it was to look like he was human on a liquid diet.

"Lexi." He pressed his erection against my core, and I shivered into his body. He pulled my bottom lip down before grabbing my chin and licking my lower lip, a small nibble, and I could feel his fangs before his tongue swept into my mouth. Our lips crashed together in a heated wave of built-up sexual tension.

I wanted to show him how much I loved him, how badly I needed his body in mine. To feel him in me, to be one with each other. This was something we both needed, and now was the perfect time.

"Tell me you want this, that you need me as much as I need you, Lexi. For a girl of many words, you seem to be lost for them now." I let out a small laugh. He was right—I was lost for words because what I wanted right now didn't involve words.

"I want you. I want you inside me in all ways." I tilted my neck to the side. I wanted to hear him and feel him. I felt his tongue tracing the column of my throat, and his hand found the slit of my dress, tracing my inner thigh, creeping higher and higher to where I was soaked. I needed his touch more than anything, craved it as his fingers finally found the wet fabric of my thong. He hissed and ripped them off.

The fabric fell to the floor, and one finger found my clit. My knees buckled at the sudden pleasure as I moaned for more. When he finally found my opening, he pressed in two fingers, finding that magic spot inside, and my toes curled as he worked me.

"Bite me, please, Galen." I wanted it. I wanted the vampire, the man, I wanted my Galen. "Please," I begged again, and I felt his fangs pierce my skin and the flow of blood as he drank from me. My toes curled off the floor as wave after wave of pleasure rocked through me until he was left holding me up, my legs like jelly. He licked my throat, the bite healing fast.

"Let's lay you down before you drop." He carried me to the sofa, and before he laid me down, he pulled the little strap off one shoulder, then the other. The whole dress fell, pooling at my hips, then one little shimmy and I was naked before him. It wasn't the first time he had seen me naked, but the way he devoured me with his eyes felt like he was seeing me for the first time.

He reached for the buttons on his shirt, and one by one, slowly undid them. I wanted it all, and I didn't want to wait for him. I reached for his belt and undid it. With his shirt off, he watched as my hands found the button and the fly to his slacks. I dropped them and found him naked underneath.

"The guys are wearing off on me." He cocked his brow. They didn't often wear underwear, mostly just for sleeping. I laughed, but those eyes darkened again, and hard, warm hands rolled down my body.

My legs fell open when he crawled up the sofa between my legs, but instead of coming to kiss me, he stopped and hooked my knee over his shoulder, biting gently on my inner thigh, not breaking the skin, as he kissed his way up to my aching core.

"Fuck, Galen." His tongue dragged along my slit before he sucked my clit into his mouth. I bucked and grabbed handfuls of his hair as I rode out another climax on his mouth, my thighs shaking at the intensity of it. I was panting and grinding myself against his talented mouth until I was gasping for air, and he pulled back, watching what he had done to me, and a smile crept across his face. "You are so beautiful, so amazing. I love you, Lexi." I kissed his mouth. He tasted like me, and I didn't care. It was hot.

"I love you, Galen."

His erection was hard against my core, rubbing through my release.

"I can use a condom, but I can't get you pregnant and I'm a

vampire, so I don't have diseases." That was something I'd never even thought of. I wanted this—no barriers, just each other.

"No condom, I want to feel you inside." He pressed his mouth to mine, biting my lip, and we breathed each other in as he entered me. I arched my back as he hit that spot inside that felt so good. I opened my eyes to see him staring down at me. A small kiss, and he started to thrust gently inside, but it didn't take long before we swapped positions.

He was now seated on the sofa, and I rode him, my nipples peaking as I felt another orgasm rip through me. This time, I took him with me as he held my waist and pumped into me, over and over, spilling himself inside me until my heart slowed and I collapsed onto his chest. Sweat covered our bodies. We didn't say anything as he hugged me tight and pulled himself from my body, his chest rising and falling like mine. He said something I didn't understand as I closed my eyes and fell into a deep, happy sleep.

CHAPTER FIFTY-NINE

LEXI

It was Saturday, prom day. I had my dress, and I was sitting in the cottage while the guys all got dressed elsewhere. I was frustrated. Galen was supposed to be back hours ago, but he said he was running late. How could you be late on prom day?

I took a deep breath. Okay, it would be fine. He could meet us there. I just...I had worked up in my head how I wanted it to go, and this wasn't it.

There was a knock on the door. I was supposed to come out and show them my dress, the one that I had picked with Ada, but I guessed Galen had better things to do. I was a little grumpy, and okay, something had come up, but this was important too. Just as important as finding out more about my blood and if it could heal him of his vampirism. The prom was maybe just a little higher on importance because he could do that science stuff with Pack Bardoul any other day... Hell, he'd been there most of the week.

I stood up and brushed my dress down. It was dark purple, with little white diamonds...not real ones, fake ones. But they reminded me of Maverick's painting when I saw it, and I knew it was meant to be. I opened the door, expecting to see three of my mates, but Grayson stood there with Jack and Joshy.

"Lexi, you look stunning." My hand went to my throat, and I let out a sob. This was better, Galen could be late, but seeing them here, huge smiles and a camera in hand...

"We wouldn't miss seeing you go to prom," Jack said, hugging me as Josh hugged my legs.

"Galen was stalling. He knew we wanted to be here, and we were running late." I looked over and saw all four of them in tuxedos, and they each wore a black mask.

I could tell them apart, but they all looked so handsome together like that.

I heard a camera, and Grayson smiled when I caught him taking photos of me, Jack, and Josh, then they swapped and took turns in taking my photo. The guys waited patiently by the Audi.

Eventually, I was free to go to them, the camera clicking behind me as I made my way over. Rafferty was first. He held his hand out to mine, and I reached for him. He bent down and kissed it.

"You look like a queen," he said, and I blushed and giggled a little. I could feel the feather in my mask as it tickled my neck.

"My love, you look spectacular." Galen took my hand and kissed my knuckles. I took a step to Maverick. He might've been built like Ranger, but I could tell the difference between them.

"Mine..." he growled, and my body swayed to his. Oh, boy.

Ranger snatched my hand from Maverick and got to one knee, produced a white rose corsage, and placed it on my wrist. I noticed then they all had matching white rose boutineers.

After what felt like an hour to take photos, we were on our way. I was so excited. This was it. I was going to prom.

Ada found me almost instantly and dragged me out to the dance floor. "That dress is killer. I should say thank you to Galen for mine."

She ran her hands down the red satin, V-neck dress. It had matching red lace. She looked amazing.

"You look killer too, and don't thank Galen. I kinda didn't tell him." Her mouth dropped open. "Where's Huxley?"

She pointed to a table with a group of guys. "He's there with the Rawlins crew." I shook my head. Why would he want to be with them, when he could be dancing with Ada?

She shrugged.

"May I have this dance?" Maverick asked, holding his hand out to me, and Ada nodded as she danced over to the Rawlins table. I placed my hand in his, and he spun me in a circle.

"Wow, you can dance?" He held me to him and started to sway me. He gave me a wicked smile.

"I sure can, you just have never asked me to. My mother made us all learn. She said, 'Someday, you'll find a girl and she will want to dance. Be the man who dances with her, not the one who watches as she dances with others,' and so that's why all the Lovells know how to dance."

I wished I could have met his mother. Every time I heard something about her, she just sounded more and more amazing.

We danced for so long that my feet were hurting. I swapped between each of them, and when it was Maverick's turn again, he swung me in his arms and carried me off the dance floor.

I was having so much fun, and Ada was dancing. Then they announced prom king and queen.

Of course, Olivia got prom queen, but I was surprised that Ranger didn't get prom king, since she wanted him so much. It was a boy I hadn't even heard of before. Apparently, he didn't think he would win either, so the poor thing looked so nervous as he went up and got his crown.

"Let's go home." Mav said, I nodded and yawned. Maybe I was more tired than I thought.

When we got out to the car, I saw the blue one…the one we didn't drive here. That Audi R8 that Raff wanted was sitting there beside the Q7.

Maverick opened the door for me, but I stopped and looked at the other three.

"We'll see you at home, love." Then they waved before getting in and driving off. Maverick took his mask off, and I did the same.

"I was hoping you would go for a drive with me?"

I nodded and got in. It was low to the ground. I hadn't been in it yet, since we all just seemed to take the other cars.

We didn't drive far, just to a lookout. It was dark, but the moonlight sparkled against his beautiful face. He took my hand in his and kissed it softly. "Would you like to dance?" He turned the music on and opened his door, then he came around to open mine. I smiled and felt butterflies. He was handsome, and so sweet, until alpha Maverick came out to play. Then he was wicked...dirty and hot.

We danced on the grass barefoot. It was cool and soft under my toes. He dipped me, then twirled me in his arms.

"Lexi, I love you." I kissed him as he spun us in a circle.

"I love you, Maverick."

CHAPTER SIXTY

LEXI

Ten weeks later

They gave us a full-sized house in Kiba. I couldn't believe it when Alaric and Tobias said they were giving one to us. I couldn't breathe. I was so happy, but now that we had moved in and our lives were slowly getting into a routine, I would just stop and look around and think...

Ours!

There were four large bedrooms, and the master bedroom was for a pack family, so it was insane, and we had three king-sized beds in there, so we could all sleep together and be comfortable. We also had a double shower, which was something I didn't think was important until we moved in, and now I had morning sex in there every day.

My favorite thing was the painting in the hallway. It was Maverick's from art class. Every day, I would look at it and be reminded that we all were stars in this universe, and how lucky I was to have found myself floating beside them in our own universe.

"I'm not going to be late on my first day. This is important, for us and the pack. So get your asses moving," I called out.

I had slowly worn Alaric down about going to a community college in Port Angeles. He finally had a sit-down meeting with the bear shifters and their sleuth and a treaty was made that we could attend here. They apparently were surprised that none of the packs has asked before, and they didn't mind as long as everyone kept the peace.

They were happier knowing that if things got out of hand and if there were any issues where humans saw, that Galen would step in and fix the problem. They had asked for his help on a few matters already, and he was happy to help if it meant I could go to college.

"Don't forget, I'm picking up Ada on my way there." I had learned to drive. I wasn't amazing, but I felt better when one of them was with me. Ranger was coming to college with me. His classes were later than mine, but I didn't care. If he didn't come now, I was leaving without him.

"Did you eat breakfast?" Galen asked as he handed me an orange juice, and I nodded. Ever since my birthday, I had been eating Lucky Charms every day.

"Here's your bag, your schedule, and a planner." Maverick handed me the backpack that I started off in Kiba with, and I smiled as I swung it over my shoulder and thought of the journey it had taken.

"If you need anything, just text me and I'll grab it for you. You're going to have the best first day." Raff kissed my lips, then pulled away and licked his. "Mmm. That's some good OJ."

I felt nervous and excited all at the same time.

"Let's go, babe, you can't be late on your first day." I rolled my eyes and shoved Ranger. He was the only one of my mates that was taking classes at the college. Maverick was doing some online business class, one he had enrolled in before I even arrived here in Kiba. He was going to help the pack and all their businesses.

Rafferty didn't know what he wanted to do yet, so Alaric had said he could join security. That was what most the pack did, and he could do it until he figured it out or if he wanted to do it full time.

I was marked by all my mates before I left, *twice*. I had told them not to worry, but I was slightly worried about Ranger around bear shifters. But he had started his own fight club for shifters who wanted to learn to protect themselves. At first, I thought it was a bad idea, but it helped, really helped him, and he had a class of fresh shifters. Most were thirteen, and he was training them to be able to defend themselves. It made me so proud.

We arrived to the college, and the butterflies in my stomach made me feel like I was going to throw up.

"Are you okay?" Ada asked. Her eyes were wide, and she looked just as nervous as me. I nodded and swallowed. Yeah, I was okay...not really. I'd thought long and hard on what I wanted to do and finally convinced myself I would try nursing. They offered it here, and Ada had decided that nursing was the path she wanted to take.

Galen got us both enrolled, and I just hoped that didn't backfire on us when we started classes. If I could add my healing touch to the skills I would learn to be a nurse, I could save lives.

All three of us got out and made our way over to the main campus building, and Ada froze. I turned back, and she scowled at me.

"Why didn't you tell me?" she hissed under her breath. Tell her what?

I looked over just as Saint was walking towards us. Ranger put his hands up in a *don't shoot me* way. Ugh...really? Saint had been fucking with Ada all summer. I wasn't going to let him ruin the first day. I tugged on her hand and led us to the double doors.

"Hi there, I'm James and you are?"

I looked over and saw a big muscular guy smiling at Ada. I saw her shift a little as she responded with, "Hi."

There were growls behind us. We both turned to see what the hell was going on. Saint and Ranger both had their teeth bared. Fuck...

"Bear," Saint growled lowly.

"Wolf," the big guy, James, growled in return.

I looped my arm through Ada's. I wasn't going to let some dumb territorial males ruin our first day. I had gone from being homeless and working at a strip club to having a family, a little brother, and mates who would die for me, and finding out I was part angel. Life had thrown a lot of things my way, but nothing got in the way of my goals. I smirked as I had more bounce in my step. *College.*

I did it. I made it.

The end.

ALSO BY BELLE HARPER

Click here to get it FREE

It's Christmas at Pack Kiba. Join Lexi, Galen, Maverick, Rafferty and Ranger for their first Christmas. **Group scenes, and MM Themes/scenes**

Get Midnight Prince Here

Hazel

Nothing like a break up, a few bottles of wine and an impulse buy.

That's right, I bought a house. An old house that was in need of some love in this cute little town in Washington.

What else was in need of love was me... when a sexy tall dark stranger walked into the local bar I was drawn to him.

Yet, weeks later and he is no where to be found and the wolves outside are getting closer to my door.

Benedict

When I saw her, that red dress. I wanted—for the first time in a century— to know her. Be with her.

I don't get close to humans, I haven't in a long time. How do you when you will outlive them. *Never growing old.*

Yet the Russet shifter pack have been getting closer to her during the night, trying to take her.

I have done everything in my power to protect her. She just doesn't know it.

But with one bite... Will that be the end?

~MF Vampire and Human, Novella of 16k words. HEA~

BELLE HARPER

FALLEN WOLF
FULL MOON SERIES

Pre Order Now

My whole life, all I wished for was a best friend and a boyfriend who treated me like a princess.

Well for me, living in a small community where everyone knows everyone. And everyone knew me as the "annoying" girl, it was hard for me to get even one of those wishes.

But when new girl Lexi Turner strolled into English class and sat next to me. My wish finally came true.

For the first time, in eighteen years. Me. Ada Stephens, had a best friend.

Lexi wasn't a regular new girl who blended into the background. No, she was turning every male head in the high school, especially the Kiba boys. Ugh... they were so hot and knew it.

But they didn't hold a flame to Saint Wood. He graduated last year and I never stopped crushing... how could you.

He was Saint-freaking-Wood.

Now I had the bestie, I was just missing the one other thing I wished for.

Only... I think I wished a little too hard.

But not everything is what it seems. The Kiba boys held secrets... ones I shouldn't have known.

ACKNOWLEDGMENTS

Thank you Readers for taking another chance on me especially after having to push back Rising Sun by a month. This year has been hectic, but it has been such an amazing, yet challenging journey to write this story for you all. Also if you find any spelling mistakes please email me, I'm an Aussie and different spelling/words/phrases sometimes slip through and I try my best.

This is the end of the story for Lexi and the guys. I am so grateful that you have love them too and gone on this journey with me. It was sad to write this ending, but they had been through so much, and grown so much together that they deserved a slightly normal-ish life and a HFN/HEA. But we will get to see them all in Ada's Books, and Jett and Mekhi. Did any of you see that twist with Clare coming?? I did.

Here is the pre order for Shadow Wolf, Jett, Clare, Mekhi and Frankie's story. This is a standalone. Click here to Pre Order Shadow Wolf **Release date Mid 2021**

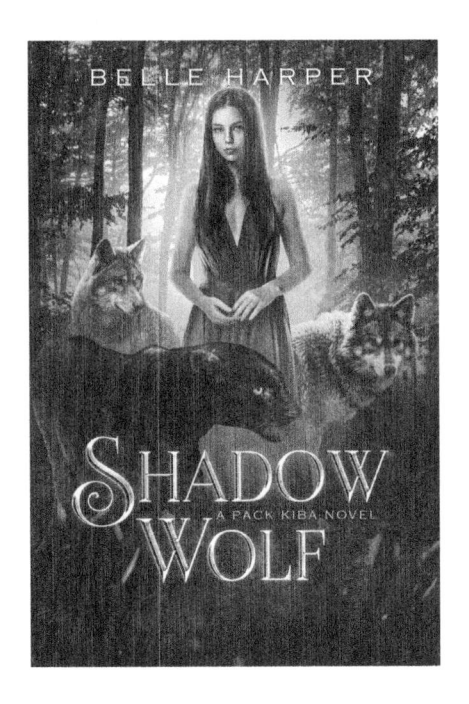

Before I wrote Twice bitten, I had started on a series. About an Angel... Her name is Cate and she is half angel and half...? You will have to find out. I don't have an estimated release date, but 2021 is all I can say. To find out, join my mailing list **This is not YA but NA and will contain a lot more adult scenes, it is RH**

If you have a chance, would you please consider leaving a review? All reviews, good and bad help other readers find their next book. And I am very grateful to all the reviews I have received.

I want to thank my amazing PA Andi Jeffree, Sam Hall, and all my amazing Awkward Noodle Authors. xx

I want to thank my editors, Meghan and Amanda, you have both been amazing. And all the stress I had been under with lockdowns in my state and homeschooling my kids full time and dealing with me sending chunks of book to you. Haha, you have seriously been a champion. I am so glad to have you both on my team.

Thank you all so much,
Belle xx

BELLE'S BOOKS

SEEKING EDEN SERIES

Dystopian/ Post Apocalyptic RH
Finding Nova
Protecting Nova
Rescuing Harlow
Claiming Harlow

BRIDES OF THE AASHI SERIES

Luna Touched
Brooklyn's Baggage
Quinn Inspired ~March 2021
Jessica's Mates ~April 2021
Elle Embraced ~ May 2021
Hadley's Heroes ~ June 2021

NEW MOON SERIES

Twice Bitten
Blood Moon
Rising Sun

FULL MOON SERIES

Fallen Wolf ~ April 2021

#2 TBA ~ 2021

#3 TBA ~ 2021

OTHER BOOKS IN THE PARANORMAL WORLD

Shadow Wolf ~ Jett & Mehki

Midnight Prince

STANDALONES

Naughty and Nice ~ Christmas Novella

Alien Embrace ~ Anthology

ABOUT THE AUTHOR

Belle is an Artist, Author, Wife and Mother.

She has an addiction to reading, notebooks, coloured pens and mint chocolate. She lives in the beautiful Australian bush, surrounded by wildlife and the smell of eucalyptus trees.

She also has a strong love for all 60's music, believes she was born in the wrong era and should have been at Woodstock.

If you would like to find out more about Belle, please come like and follow her:

Click Here to Like Belle's Facebook Page

Join Belle in her Facebook Group

www.authorbelleharper.com

Sign up to my Newsletter to keep up to date with my new Releases, Free Books and Giveaways.

SUBSCRIBE TO MY NEWSLETTER

Printed in Great Britain
by Amazon